SIMON DIEPPE

In the Doldrums

First edition

This book was professionally typeset on Reedsy.
Find out more at reedsy.com

Acknowledgement

As always with my writing projects, a big thank you to my wife Claire who unbegrudgingly allows me the time to disappear into another world. Thank you also to Grace for her intelligent feedback, encouragement and unfaltering enthusiasm.

1

The End: September 13th, 20##

When it happened, I remember, I didn't feel fear, or sorrow or despair; strangely, I felt a pulse of excitement. Then, when the enormity of what had happened washed over me like the thermal flash and fireball that accounted for so many millions that day, I felt guilt. Guilt over misplaced emotions; the inappropriateness of my own thoughts.

When we watched it unfold from the side of the ship, I was most struck by its beauty. The horizons awash with colour. I thought first of Edvard Munch's paintings: The Scream. Not, you might think, because of the haunting figure of anguish in the foreground, but because of the kaleidoscope of colour in the background. Munch, I recall, had painted from life in the years following the eruption of Krakatoa in 1883; the glowing scarlets, the fulgent oranges, the blues and greens as light bounced off particles of ash and soot in the stratosphere. History repeating itself, but this time not by the hand of Mother Nature but the foolery of Man. We were the lucky ones, to be silent observers protected by a thousand miles of ocean.

We had followed the build-up for the days and weeks before. We'd been hunkered down with our phones or laptops in private moments or huddled around the single TV in the Officers' Lounge. The first deaths from the mystery disease in Britain, then its spread like wildfire around Europe, the Americas, Southern Asia. The frightening mortality rates, the confusion, the panic, the recriminations. Then the accusations, questions as to why this new plague was leaving China and Russia untouched. Then, as the bodies were stacking up and Western civilisation buckling, the evidence; proof that this was not just a biological accident, but a strategic weapon, a Biblical pandemic by design. How to respond? Methodical, rational diplomacy? A tit-for-tat spilling of deadly microbes? Even up until this point it had all seemed unreal, that like previous trips to the precipice, it would all, eventually, be defused. It could never really happen. That no-one would ever unleash this thing, not even the Tweet-toting imbecile in the White House.

The first missiles were launched at key Russian and Chinese cities and military targets. Before they had even hit, Europe was reciprocally targeted, then North America, Korea, Japan, Australia. India and Pakistan grabbed the coat tails of the grown-up nuclear powers and inexplicably took the opportunity to obliterate each other. From our vantage point, at approximately 4 degrees north of the Equator in the middle of the Atlantic Ocean, our experience of Doomsday was the polychromatic light show on every horizon. Then the silence as the world we had left just weeks before changed into something else. Then we went below; hoping to put as many layers of steel as possible between us and what would come next.

2

Sea dogs

Let me tell you about radiation. The evil genius of nuclear weaponry; the bomb that just keeps on giving. If there is a Devil, he must have had a hand in it; surreptitiously guiding Oppenheimer and his team through their research, rubbing his hands in gleeful anticipation. You see, if you can survive the initial explosion and dodge the fireball that is hotter than the Sun's 15-million-degree core, avoid the thermal flash and the blast wave that flattens buildings and throws glass and debris at you at hundreds of miles-per-hour. If you can hide from the firestorm that sucks in the oxygen from hungry lungs. If you can recover from thermal flash burns or get medical help for impact injuries in a world now devoid of medicines. If you can find food and water in a world with no farming, no infrastructure, no fuel. If you can keep yourself and your loved-ones safe from your fellow survivors who are hungry and desperate. If you can survive this fast-track decline back into the dark ages, then you can call yourself a nuclear holocaust survivor. Congratulations. But then, just as you are patting yourself on the back for a job well done, along comes Mr. Fallout.

For the first few days to weeks the most lethal contamination occurs within the direct vicinity of the explosion, and by 'direct' I mean within a hundred miles radius depending on the prevailing winds. That might have been it if the Devil had left it there with Oppenheimer's initial fusion bombs, but He whispered and cajoled other great minds into developing thermonuclear bombs that create the phenomenon of global fallout. These monsters force radioactive clouds high up into the stratosphere where it spreads like a blanket, releasing deadly radiation for years, if not decades. Nowhere with exposure to the skies is safe. The water cycle becomes poisoned. Burns, cancers, reduced immunity, birth deformities; a slow strangulation of what might be left of humanity.

How do I know all this? It's a good question. It's not like there have been documentaries to watch, or 24-7 news channels, or even the Internet since. The ship's library is restricted to a tatty collection of crime novels and travel guides to places we will never go. The fact is that in my early teens I'd obsessed over dystopian fiction and gorged on post-apocalyptic movies. I'd read survival guides on the Internet, and academic studies on the science of nuclear weapons and what a post-nuclear world might be like. I don't know what drew me to it; I think it was the grotesqueness of it all, the notion that Mankind had found a way to destroy itself so efficiently. Like a snake swallowing its own tail. Then, in just the same way that I had grown out of dinosaurs and sharks as a child, I moved on to modern literature, to high-school and university examinations, to cars, to girls. But I'd remembered it all, locked away in a recess.

So, on that fateful day, protected by so much ocean, we had avoided the cataclysmic phases of the bombs. We saw nothing of the destruction and death; left only to imagine what we knew of such things. I tried not to share my heightened knowledge unless it gave solace and comfort. That perhaps death had been quick and painless. Of course, everyone on board had loved ones. We all mourned. There was despair conjoined to hope; hope that there were survivors. But merchant ships, I have learnt, are places of pragmatism. They are ruled by routine, governed by hierarchies, driven by practicalities. What we all knew in those initial days was that we had been gifted a chance of survival. By some trick of providence, we had been in one of the few places on Earth to be untouched, protected in the rolling folds of the ocean. There were others – we've seen them since; floating nubs of humanity, micro-societies drifting the seas like dandelion seeds; waiting, hoping for fertile soil. But our task then, at the beginning, was to prolong our gift.

I've come to realise since that I owe my survival not so much to the hand of fate that left me here, on this ship, at a specific space in time, but to the resourcefulness and utilitarianism of the people with me. Merchant seaman are a special breed. When there was global trade, they went about their business in the shadows, quietly navigating storms, groundings, engine failures, fatigue and loneliness to facilitate the exchange of goods from one corner of the globe to the other. They were the termites to the termite mound of capitalistic globalism. As we scoured supermarket shelves searching for Chilean wines or the latest shiny smartphone, few of us gave a second thought to the Herculaneum efforts of those tasked with putting them there. Nor did we contemplate how relatively few people guided each Leviathan container ship from one port to the next. *The Thalassa*, our own ark, had a crew of just twenty-one people. Yet, her deck is 367 metres from bow to stern – the length of three-and-a-half football pitches. She weighs, unloaded, 20,000 tons, can carry a dead weight of 130,000 tons and she can hold up to 16,000 twenty-foot-long containers. A comparably sized cruise ship would have had upwards of five-hundred crew members. *The Thalassa* was by no-means unusual in the frugality of her manpower. Just twenty-one crew members; five officers, three engineers, one bosun, one chief steward, three galley staff, two electricians, two oilers, three able bodied seamen and one deck cadet...and me, but I don't count as crew. A little like Noah's menagerie. This is my apocalypse family.

I'm sure that if I had been holed up somewhere else, in a deep bunker perhaps with the proverbial tinker, tailor and candlestick maker we would have torn ourselves apart long ago. Despair, disorder, lack of routine, boredom would have seen to us by now. Seamen, however, are used to solitude, to an absence of words, to the plotting of time. After the initial shock and horror, the disbelief, the lamentation over loved ones, the crew of *The Thalassa* collectively focused itself on survival in much the same way that they would prepare for a storm. The officers, led stoically by Captain Thomsen, identified the key threats, and ordered them by importance and necessity.

At the time I was still an outsider, but I listened and watched from the periphery as these five sea dogs reasoned, calculated and strategised their way through a plan. A plan to stay out at sea indefinitely, to avoid land at all costs.

3

September 13th - One year later

Anniversaries are tough. To be fair, every single day promised to drag you into over-thinking, to the darkest of thoughts, but the anniversary of the actual day it happened just helped to focus the mind that little bit more.

As we approached the twelve-month milestone, the seas were as still as a mill pond. This wasn´t unexpected as we had deliberately sailed into the Doldrums, a belt around the Earth extending approximately five degrees north and south of the Equator. Here, the prevailing trade winds of the northern hemisphere blow to the southwest and collide with the southern hemisphere's driving northwest trade winds. The result: no wind, less need to use fuel. We were able to effectively tread water. Without the distraction of inclement weather, Captain Thomsen had come up with a master plan, that being that we´d paint the upper decks. 'Busy minds are quiet minds' he said. He claimed it was a Danish idiom.

Maintenance is a constant aboard ship, but even more so since we had decided to abandon land. The Captain was fanatical about it, and it went unquestioned. We all knew that the ship had to stay seaworthy, but also that our grip on sanity was dependent on having a never-ending list of tasks to keep us occupied. We had seen what could happen if you allowed yourself to succumb to idleness; to become unmoored from the daily routines, drifting into the swirling currents of self-reflection.

We'd used up the stock of company regulated blue and red paints more than six months ago but had been fortunate enough to stumble upon a container full of paint. These had been every colour under the rainbow so we were now slowly creating a patchwork canvas of yellows, purples, oranges and greens that was gradually usurping the old corporate colours. The whole ship was beginning to blend in with multi-coloured wall of containers.

We had all been grouped into pairs for the day's task; I was with Dmitriy, our Second Officer. Dmitriy was a mountainous ex-Russian, towering over me at six foot six. When I had first met him in the first few weeks of our voyage, he had honestly terrified me. Broad shouldered, broad chinned, broad everything; he was the epitome of a hardened mariner, right down to the tattoos, gold earring and eye-patch. I had been surprised to discover that he still possessed two fully functioning legs. He always maintained that he lost the sight in his eye after a particularly gruelling vodka marathon but confessed to me later that he'd run into a branch during a picnic with his family. I came to realise that he used his appearance to build an aura of inapproachability, to mimic hostility to unwanted sociability. Obviously, at the start when I was a mere passenger – albeit with a mission – and he was busy doing his job, we had had little to do with each other aside from one uncomfortable, relatively unproductive interview. Subsequently, we had become firm friends.

We had been allocated the deck of the forecastle. I was armed with a fetching Buckingham Green, whilst Dmitriy was spreading sunshine with a Cornfield Yellow. Our plan was to create an effigy of summer fields. A long lull in conversation was broken by Dmitriy, who had evidently decided to address the elephant in the room.

'So, what is it you miss the most?' We both knew that this was not about people, about family, lovers, friends. Such things were better hidden, buried.

'You mean *everything* I miss the most?'

'Let us just say three things. I let you think, I go first.' Despite years of speaking practically no Russian, his accent was still strong, and his complete disregard for future forms criminal. I almost think he did it on purpose. 'I miss trees. I miss their size, their shape. I miss the way they change from season to season. I miss the texture of their bark. I miss the way that light filters through their leaves.'

'That surprises me. That someone so obviously cast from a sailor-mould could possibly be so emotionally attached to trees.'

'Why so? It is not long ago that all ships were made from trees. Besides, I was not born on a ship. I grew up amongst forests. As child, I hunt with my father. He worked for a forestry company.' This was a rare insight from Dmitriy, he rarely ventured into talk of his childhood.

'I'd always assumed you were the son of a seaman, who was the son of a seaman, who was the son of a seaman...going back to Ulysses.'

'No, I chose the sea, it wasn't chosen for me.' A moment's

reflection, which I chose to break.

'...And do you, out of your hankering for trees, have a favourite. A tree above all trees?'

'That is tricky one. There are *many* fine trees, but I think Copper Beech - F*agus sylvatica purpurea.* As mature tree, it is huge, majestic. It is the king of trees. Purple is the colour of kings, right?'

'I believe it was. I never had you down as a Latin scholar either. You never cease to amaze me Dmitriy.'

'I am man of much depth. Many talents. Now, it is your go. Tell me something you miss.'

'Do you know, and you are going to think I'm crazy, but I miss deadlines. I always saw them as a negative before, the ticking clock as I tried to perfect an article. I used to feel that being hounded by my editor was some-kind of punishment, an anathema to creative perfection. But now, now that deadlines don't exist – not external ones anyway, the ones that matter, I really miss them. I miss the pumping adrenaline, the need for caffeine, the sense of achievement mixed with regret that it wasn't *quite* good enough even as I hit the send button at the eleventh hour.'

'You are right my friend. You are crazy. The lack of deadlines is one of the *good* things.'

'Go on then, give me your second.'

'Steak.'

'Steak?'

'Yes, a big fat succulent steak, with the juices running. A fillet. Maybe a tomahawk. Cooked rare to medium...so there is pink, but not too much pink.' He sat back, his paintbrush cradled in both massive hands, staring into the middle distance. 'Do you think there are still cows?' he said.

'Who knows. If there are, maybe they'll evolve into the dominant species. They can't do much worse than we did. Maybe they'll crave Man-meat. With a blue cheese sauce and a glass of Chianti.'

'...and your second?'

'I miss waking up in the morning and not knowing what the day will bring. You know, those days when you'd walk out of your apartment, thinking you were going to go to one place, and you'd bump into someone unexpected, someone you hadn't seen for years, and you'd end up going somewhere completely different. Then you'd meet new people who'd tell you stories about themselves, things you couldn't ever have imagined. I guess I miss the deliciousness of unpredictability.'

'Not my thing. Predictability is why I choose to work on ships. Everything is set out. Everything has procedure. Even the weather is predictable, at least what you do to ride it. Everything you miss, I hate.'

'No, wait, I have one more. Silence. I miss silence. There is never a moment when something on this rig isn't clanking or rolling or creaking. Even at night, when you're in your bunk, there's noise. The sound of water against the hull. Wind. Metal on metal. What I'd give for the kind of silence you'd get if you climbed a mountain; at the top, looking down.'

'There you go. We have found something in common that we miss. I miss mountains too!'

'And you...your last?'

'It is easy. I trump everything. Women.'

4

Running away to sea

I'd reached an impasse; one of those junctions in life where you can clearly see diverging paths. At the age of 32, the road behind me was a litany of near successes and missed opportunities. The bombast of my twenties, those years when you thought you were invincible and destined for greatness in equal measure, had withered and spluttered, to be replaced by a fear that time was running out. Not *running out*, *running out* – nothing as morbid as that, but that the time to leave my mark, to do something significant was slowing ebbing away.

One path was obvious. The one that required getting a 'proper' job, as my mother put it, with a regular salary, settling down with an-as-yet unspecified Mrs. Donal O'Brien, two-point-four children, a labrador, a nice shiny car to polish on Sundays. The whole notion of it terrified me, which is probably why I'd split with Beth. Of course, I'd kid myself that it was something else, that she wasn't 'the one', that I was holding *her* back, that *she* deserved better. All those clichés. But if I was honest with myself, she was as close to the *one* I had ever met or was probably ever likely to meet...and that's what scared me.

I'd been living in New York (another Irish cliché) for just over a year. We'd met at a literary prize event that I'd gate-crashed; it was a prize I'd entered and not even made it onto the long-list. I was keen to see what these people – these short-listers – looked like. Were there visible characteristics that separated them from me (aside from the fact that they were all women?) Was there some kind of charisma exuded that I lacked? On a practical level, by speaking to them, could I absorb some of their star dust, or trick them into sharing the secret to their success and my failure? The answer on all counts was 'no'. The eight women short-listed for the prize were only extra-ordinary in their ordinariness. The eventual winner, named on the night, was a forty-seven-year-old librarian from Maine. Her novel, a debut, was about a librarian (original) during the rise of the Nazis in Germany – it was a missive on censorship. She received her prize (a cheque for $10,000 and a publishing deal) with shy smiles and a disbelieving owlish look greatly magnified by her oversized librarian glasses. I expected her to ask the assembled throng to 'shhh' at any minute. So, I didn't discover anything like the elixir of success but I did meet Beth, who had organised the event.

Our first interaction that evening had centred around my lack of ticket. I'd employed 'charming Irish rogue' mode and was explaining to the lady on the front desk that I'd lost said ticket, and that I couldn't imagine why I wasn't on the invitation list, when Beth entered the fray. She'd admitted later that she had known from the start that I was a fraud but had let me in *'because I had a cute arse.'* Such objectification. After the winner's presentation, when both interest and the supply of fizzy wine had ebbed, I had bumped into her again. We'd chatted about her career in event management, her love of art, her passion for Japanese food, my career in journalism, a bit about the Irish Potato Famine...and three hours later ended up sleeping with each other. All hail the Irish Rogue Charm.

Six months later, we exchanged both of our tiny, rented apartments for one single, marginally less tiny apartment in Greenwich Town and began our life as a couple. Don't get me wrong, I'd 'moved in' before, usually for no longer than six months, before I'd unceremoniously 'moved out', but this was the first time that I'd gone out and found a place with someone else. We'd agreed on most things, in that I had agreed to all of Beth's preferences; the fact being that I didn't feel strongly enough about the location, decor or furnishings to disagree. We painted walls shades of duck-egg blue and shopped together for kitchen utensils and cushions. Beth continued to build her events management empire, and I wrote pithy articles for trendy magazines and slaved over my latest unpublished novel. We lived manifestly different lives, orbiting around a small orb of shared interests. It was nice. We had fun. It was uncomplicated. I met both of Beth's parents (acrimoniously divorced) and got on just fine with each. We did family Christmas', Thanksgiving, and became permanently ensconced on the 'friends' wedding conveyor belt. It was just like the early years of anyone else's pre-marriage relationship. Which is what scared me witless.

Then, three years in, during a romantic night out at our favourite Lebanese restaurant, just as we had finished our Kousa Mehshe and were building up to a light dessert, the conversation suddenly and unexpectedly turned to children.

Not the children of friends or family members, but *our* future children. It just slipped in so sleekly, like a fox into a chicken coop. Outwardly, I kept my shit together. I smiled when required, I rattled off a list of favourite names, I tried to look doughy eyed at the right moments, but inside, I was locked in a soundless scream. Here was the sign warning me of a major crossroads ahead.

I had managed to convince myself that this cosy stasis could go on for ever, that I could live with this beautiful woman, enjoy all the benefits of co-habitation, yet still live in my own selfish little world of literary dream hunting and the quest to become an acknowledged, acclaimed, accredited writer. I'd seen enough of my friends slip into parenthood, watched as their own ambitions had been flushed away with the baby's bath water to know that this one decision would change everything. So, I did what every scared male does: I blocked it out and hoped it would go away. I closed my eyes and crossed my fingers that it was just the musty Lebanese wine talking, and that the next day everything would go back to normal; that we'd laugh at how silly the whole conversation had been. It didn't. After a sleepless night staring at the ceiling, I was roused from the little sleep I had snatched by Beth, holding a tray of lovingly cooked breakfast, coffee and fresh orange juice. She kissed me deeply and said she loved me, before telling me that I had to keep my strength up for 'Maeve and Lorcan's' sake; we had, of course, chosen Irish names. And so it went on for the next three weeks; Beth talking babies at every given opportunity, and me pretending to be as into it as she was. I'd tried to deflect, by suggesting that Maeve and Lorcan would be equally great names for cats, or that perhaps we should save up for one last epic, adventurous trip...for old-times-sake, but

Beth was having none of it. She had become a thing possessed.

One night, I'd found myself drowning my perceived sorrows in a particularly grotty Irish bar in the old docks area near the Hudson Bridge. I'd opted for solitary inebriation, but somehow got chatting to two guys at the bar. Both were Polish and were on a twenty-four-hour shore leave from a merchant ship. This was a world that I knew nothing about, and the more I heard about it – the strange group of oddballs that were attracted to work in it, the battles with Mother-Nature, the blatant exploitation by multinational shipping companies, the sheer scale of both the ships and the industry – the more I wanted to find out. By midnight, like countless men before me, I had been seduced by stories of the sea. I now knew how my greatness would come, and it would need just one, last throw of the dice before I gave it all up for diapers and kid's birthday parties.

In retrospect, I should have reflected on it first; given the idea a few days to germinate and formulate what I was actually asking Beth to do. As it happened, I blurted it all out at 2 a.m. in a whiskey-fuelled jumble of half-baked plans and barely intelligible insecurities. I think I'd intended to ask Beth for a reprieve, for a sabbatical, but by the end of what become an emotional shouting match, I somehow washed up on the shores of an irrevocably wrecked relationship. In the space of thirty minutes, it had become clear to Beth that we both wanted very different things; that she wanted children, financial security, commitment, and that I didn't. More specifically, I wanted to sail off around the world gathering stories about other men who were also running away from similar things. I thought she'd give me the time to flush this out of my system, but time was one thing that Beth was unprepared to give. She said that she'd already invested three years into us. She mentioned ticking body clocks. She said she couldn't waste any more time on a commitment-phobe man-child. She had a point.

So, the next day, I called a shipping agent and I bought a six-month round-the-world voyage on board a flotilla of different merchant ships. I was going to do what I'd never done before; immerse myself not only in writing, but in the subject. This was going to be my moment of greatness. Two weeks later, I left. Four weeks later, New York had been returned to its primeval state of primordial swamp, with mounds of concrete and skeletal steel girders the only suggestion that it had ever been anything else.

5

Water, water everywhere

Cargo ships are designed to spend weeks, if not months at sea. I remember Alon, one of our Oilers, telling me that after the 2008 financial crash some shipping companies mothballed whole segments of their fleets as demand for stowage evaporated. He found himself imprisoned on a container ship a hundred miles off the coast of Manila for eight months awaiting the reignition of the global economy. If you can cocoon twenty people for eight months, he explained, why not eighteen? Why not forever?

If you want to sit out the end of the world, it turns out that a container ship is one of the best possible places to do it. You'd think, long-term, that water would be an issue, but it isn't. To start with, *The Thalassa* had over a thousand tons of freshwater stored from port. If stored correctly, cleaned and rationed, this would be able to keep us going for months, if not years. Failing that, we had our very own desalination systems, both steam powered and flash evaporators, that would allow us to create

40 tons of freshwater per day. As long as we stayed in deep ocean where the radiation would be diluted to less harmful levels, we could have a bottomless supply of safe, fresh water.

Food was marginally more of an issue. We had the supplies in the galley which were stocked to last the duration of the planned voyage, plus a bit more, but that was twelve months maximum. What we also had was approximately 14,623 containers on board, many of which would yield something edible. It might be difficult to believe, but the crew of the ships themselves aren't given a list of what they are carrying, aside from refrigerated and hazardous goods that need to be monitored, and live cargo...which needs to be kept alive. Angelo, our Steward and previously a citizen of the Philippines, had once told me of a consignment of live lobsters that his ship had carried across the Atlantic. He had had to check on the salinity and temperature of the water every two hours. He joked that he had put more love and care into the wellbeing of those crustaceans than he had his own kids. Everything else in the containers was a mystery, the theory being that not knowing staved off the temptation to steal. I'd been quite outraged by this unwritten rule, that the shipping companies had such little faith in their crews, but my shipmates were unfazed by it. They failed to see the injustice, the implied insult. They focused on the practical, as ever. 'I'd rather not know,' Dmitriy had said, 'What good could it do knowing what was in each container. I'd rather just see them as big metal box that I need to get from one place to another.'

Of the 14,623 containers on *The Thalassa*, we knew that 42 were refrigerated goods: pork that had been destined for the Chinese market; shellfish from Vietnam that were heading for the West Coast of the USA; Australian cheese; frozen chicken. Eight were deemed hazardous, mostly chemicals and fertilizers. The remaining 14,210 were a veritable lucky dip, although of these only around 11,000 were fully accessible owing to the way they were stacked, with some doors being obscured by other containers or the fabric of the ship. That was still 11,000 containers to be explored, their contents recorded and their usefulness assessed. This was a gargantuan task, but for the first six months it was a huge factor in keeping up our morale; not only did it keep us all occupied, but it gave us the sense of being hunter-gatherers.

All of us were assigned container duties on a weekly rota. It quickly became the highlight of the week and we all looked forward to our shifts, not only because it wasn't cleaning, or painting, or greasing, or emptying the bilge tanks, but because it gave us the opportunity to return to the mess in triumph. Like primeval Man returning to his cave with a hunk of mammoth, we could return to our clan with a tasty or nutritious addition to the menu, or with something that would make our lives infinitely more interesting or comfortable.

It wasn't just food either. The containers surrendered a cornucopia of goods that were cardinal in sustaining our bodies, minds and souls: clothes, medicines, books, batteries, boardgames, trainers, basketballs, plastic plants. There were also those containers that had yielded treasures that we had yet to find a use, like the ton of women's fashion wigs and consignment of lawnmowers.

Occasionally, we happened across something which was truly life-changing, or even life giving. It had been early on in our foraging, perhaps even as early as the first two weeks when Polina (Chief Steward and one-time Ukrainian) and Crisanto (Steward's Assistant and ex-Filipino) had returned to the mess having found a container of various drugs and medicines. They had spent the majority of the day cataloguing the contents. In the evening, I had given the list a cursory glance over dinner and something quite miraculous leapt off the page. My mother, like the majority of Irish women of that generation, possessed a litany of old-wives' tales and idiomatic sayings. One such, that was recited on far too many occasions during my journey to adulthood, was *'You have to earn your luck!'* This always seemed contradictory to me – surely luck was the one thing, by its very nature, that you didn't have to earn, but my mother was resolute. If this *was* the case, then someone on our ship had worked very hard that day, for amongst the aspirin and haemorrhoid creams were seventy crates of Thyrosafe Tablets; I'd read about them, or at least their main ingredient, during my adolescent nuclear apocalypse obsession. Potassium iodide is a chemical compound, medication and supplement. As a medication, it's used to treat hyperthyroidism and to protect the thyroid gland during types of cancer radiation treatments. It also happens to be on every 'how to survive the nuclear holocaust' wish list. In a nutshell, it floods the thyroid with a safe amount of iodine to prevent the body from absorbing any more from other sources. This is crucial, as radioactive iodine is a major component of nuclear fallout. One tablet would provide each of us with protection for a 24-hour period...and we had thousands upon thousands of tablets.

I've never believed in a God. That's not true, as a good Irish Catholic child I believed and feared. But when I could wield my own judgement and theologise, I turned my back on religion and its deities. I don't favour concepts of predestination, or notions of 'reaping what you sow'. There isn't a divine entity dolling out the good and the bad to the deserving and undeserving. I'm a believer in the doctrine that 'shit just happens.' It happened that day, and almost, almost made me rethink my theophobia. What were the chances of that one specific drug being cargo on this particular hunk of floating metal? What were the chances of us finding it, in all those thousands of containers? What were the chances of us finding it when we did, within the first few weeks, when it could still be of critical use to us? Why wasn't it in one of the inaccessible containers? What if I hadn't taken that quick glance at Polina and Crisanto's list? I don't want to exaggerate, because we made various decisions in the early weeks and months which greatly reduced our exposure to the radioactive fallout, but this one single slice of good fortune probably saved us all.

There were other moments when the ship gifted us beyond reasonable expectations. One time, in our sixth month as flotsam, I had been on container duty with Henning, the Chief Engineer. He was rarely afforded the opportunity to scour the cargo, with most of his allotted shifts being allocated to maintaining the lucidity of our engines and generators. It was a rare excursion that he embraced with a child-like enthusiasm, which seemed incongruous to his fifty-three years and greying temples. He, like the Captain, was of Danish ancestry and blessed with the same practical stoicism. It had been our fourth container of that day when we came across our treasure, our only success thus far being a stash of tinned sardines.

'I hope this one offers something that will give us hero status,' he had said, as we cut the ties and forced the latches on our next container. 'Tinned fish is nice, but hardly the spoils of a true Viking raid.'

'What are you hoping for, a box full of Anglo-Saxon maidens?'

'I was thinking more of gold and silver, or the equivalent, but your idea has merit.' We switched on our torches and scanned the crates at the very front of the container.

'What do we have here?' said Henning, as much to himself as to me. He read the branding on the packaging, 'Esosteric Hydroponics...this could be very interesting, very interesting indeed.'

'Why, what is it?'

'You don't know what hydroponics is?'

'Something to do with water? We've got enough of that haven't we?'

'Hydroponics is the growing of plants without soil, using nutrients in water. Soil is something we don't have, but as you say, we have plenty of water. Help me get one of these crates out so we can open it up and see what's inside.' They were large and heavy, and it took us some time to manhandle it into a space where we could remove the plastic protective wrapping and gain access. They contained a huge number of metal rods, plastic piping and small, black plastic trays the size of ice-cream tubs. It was a kit for something. Henning found a booklet encased in cellophane, and ripped it open hungrily. I watched as he scanned the contents. 'This is an all-in-one hydroponics tower. Each wall of the heptagonal unit can house fifty individual plants. That's...three-hundred and fifty in total.' He stuck his head back into the container. 'There must be at least fifty, maybe sixty of these boxes in there.' As we rummaged further into the depths of the container, we found more boxes, containing water pumps, wicking material to line the growing trays, sulpha plasma lighting systems, soluble nutrient packs and a whole casement of seeds. Scanning down the inventory, these included lettuces, tomatoes, spinach, peppers, spring onions, basil, coriander and even strawberries. Henning was almost delirious with excitement. 'You see what we have discovered here Donal, what riches we have uncovered?'

'A whole bunch of gardening stuff!'

'We have found a way to feed ourselves with fresh food... indefinitely. An endless supply, on a ship, in the ocean without an ounce of soil.'

And that is how Henning Moritzen, master of pistons, gear drives, oil sumps and turbo chargers became our Chief Horticulturist, and how I, manipulator of words and master of imagery, became his assistant.

6

Thalassians

Every merchant ship in the ocean is a rainbow of nations. There are the shipping companies, such as Maersk (Danish), COSCO (Chinese) and Hapag-Lloyd (German) that are affiliated to a particular nation, but all this shows is into which national balance sheet the profits eventually flow. In reality, these behemoth corporates are the flagstone of the global economy, or at least they were.

The vessels' names don't follow nationalistic lines either, but are a mixture of past histories, mythology and fanciful personification. Take the *Maersk Gower* for example. A Danish ship named after a stretch of Welsh coastline. Our own ship, *The Thalassa*, was named after the Greek primordial goddess of the sea. Then you get ships christened *The Invincible*, *The Endeavour*, *Serenity*. There is almost as much logic in the naming of racehorses. The flags under which the ships sail have less to do with its point of origin or ultimate ownership than with the laxity of the flag bearer's marine regulations.

The proliferation of ships being registered under the Panama flag, for instance, began in 1920s USA when shipowners wished to sidestep prohibition and to serve alcohol to passengers.

The same nationalistic ambiguity can also be found amongst maritime crews. On any given container ship, you might have as many as ten different nationalities. Officers can be from anywhere, with a tendency to be dominated by nationals of the parent company – hence the disproportionate number of Scandinavians, Dutch and Germans. The deck crew, engineering and stewarding functions however tend to be dominated by Filipinos, then Ukrainians, Russians, the Chinese, Poles, Indonesians, Bulgarians, Romanians and Turks. It's a proverbial pea soup of ethnicity.

There are nine nations represented amongst the crew of *The Thalassa*. Ten, if you include me. In the initial weeks following the war that finally ended all wars, this provided a potentially conflagratory backdrop, especially with a Russian and two Chinese on board.

Recriminations didn't really rear their ugly head until the second or third week, when the initial shock had dissipated, the sense of loss had sunk in and the practicalities of our own situation had been addressed. It was only then, against the distant reality of nation states tearing each other apart, that the crew started to remember that they too had a national identity. That's when the sideways glances started, the huddled whispers, the deliberate avoidances.

It had been, perhaps not surprisingly, Dmitriy who had first addressed the issue. Early on, the officers had decreed that all crew members should convene together once a day - something that was previously unheard of, what with the hierarchical division between officers and the rest of the crew; it was not unknown for a captain to barely speak to a deckhand during a six-month voyage. One such meeting was to be a movie night, and on that particular evening someone had chosen, retrospectively quite unwisely, the testosterone-heavy Rocky IV. This is the one where American hero, Rocky Balboa takes on the indestructible Soviet, Ivan Drago, to avenge the death of his long time-sparring partner and fellow American hero, Apollo Creed. Not my genre at all, but it's a good film, as long as you can ignore the blatant jingoism and propagandistic xenophobia. Dmitriy couldn't. To be fair, he had made it as far as the final fight scene, with the Soviet crowd cheering on the rookie Rocky.

'What is this shit?' he had said. 'Russians are always portrayed as evil bastards or idiots. There have been many power-crazy, stupid Americans. Some of them have been president. Also, why is the crowd cheering the American? It makes no sense. Plus, you can't be punched like that and still get up. I know, because I've been punched like that, and I didn't get up.'

'Maybe the Russians are portrayed like that because it's true. Look at your long line of leaders, and how they have pulled the wool over their people's eyes – Lenin, Stalin, Putin, Kovalev. All megalomaniac, expansionist, empire builders leading a comatose population. And it was Kovalev that started all this.' The words of Ton Vanderloo, the Dutch First Officer. Despite the film building to its noisy climax, there was a crackling silence in the room. A collective intake of breath.

'For start, Stalin was a Georgian, not a Russian. Second, I was no fan of Putin or Kovelev – why do you think I chose career in merchant navy, and that I have always avoided Russian ships? Third, Kovalev didn't start this. It was the Americans and

Europeans who went nuclear!'

'After the Russians and Chinese had tried to change the world order by releasing a new plague. A reasonable provocation, don't you think?' This from Arjun, our Indian Second Engineer. There was an unusual edge to his voice for someone normally so passive. Somebody paused the film. Rocky was mid swipe to a cowering Drago.

'That is what Western media tell us. But what do we know. It was a theory. There was only two days before the theory emerged and the West pressed the button. Hardly time to verify.'

'Come on, Dmitriy! Kovalev's own deputy broke ranks and admitted it in return for sanctuary. He said that the Russian authorities had been building up immunity through the water supply for years. You can't get stronger validity than that.'

'Maybe he had axe to grind. Maybe he was on the way out and needed good story to tempt the Americans to help him.'

'So why were no Russians or Chinese dying of this disease then? Was it just luck? In my country, it was spreading like wildfire, with a 60% death rate, but across the border, nothing!' Now Jerzy, our Polish Chief Cook had entered the fray.

'Maybe it just hadn't reached us yet! Anyway, even if it was Kovalev and the Russian government to blame...'

'And the Chinese!' interjected Tanmay.

'...and the Chinese government, that doesn't make the Russian and Chinese people culpable. It doesn't justify full-scale annihilation.' Our two Chinese crew members, Chen and Li, both oilers and less than confident with their English, tried to melt into the background, despite both being closest to the TV.

'But are you saying that murdering great swathes of the

world's population through a biological weapon *is* justifiable? That the West should have just turned the other cheek?'

'That isn't what I said. All I say is that we are all guilty of stereotyping. The Russians want to take over the World. Americans are self-righteous. The Chinese are crafty. The Danish are dull...'

'Hey, wait one second!' said Henning.

'No, Henning, it is true, the Danish are dull,' corrected the Captain, in an attempt, I thought, to lighten the mood. 'The fact is gentlemen, that terrible and unspeakable things have been done by men and women of every nation. Terror and destruction is not just the domain of one country or state. What was done, was done by people well beyond our, and most people's, sphere of influence. Dmitriy is right, we cannot allow ourselves to associate what has happened with any one of us by virtue of a man's nationality. At sea, in the merchant navy, we have always been stateless. I therefore propose that from now on, we do away with such conceits. I for one, renounce being Danish. I am a Thalassian. This is our new nation. Let us not carry the mistakes of Mankind that led us here into the future.' His words were followed by a tense silence.

'I've always liked being Irish, but I'll give being Thalassian a crack,' I said, hoping to follow the Captain's lead in sprinkling a little levity on what felt like a watershed moment.

'If I can break my association with clogs, cheese and bicycles, I'll take being Thalassian over being Dutch any day,' added Ton Vanderloo, the First Officer.

'What does 'Indonesian' mean anyway?' said Banya. 'My country is made up of 17,000 islands, and three hundred different ethnic groups. Being Thalassian is way simpler.' There were smiles and nods of agreement around the room.

We all knew what this meant. It wasn't the amputation of our heritage, or a snub to our past, but a framework for our future.

Dmitriy stood, unfolding like a crane. Just as suddenly as the atmosphere had lightened, the tension returned. His face was expressionless, and his huge bulk dominated the room. 'If I am no-longer Russian, but Thalassian, as you say, then I will need a drink to celebrate such a repatriation,' he said slowly. There was, officially, no alcohol aboard *The Thalassa*; it was company policy. He spoke to the room but directed his words to the Captain.

'I am sure I can find something,' he said. 'We cannot inaugurate a new nation without whetting the heads of its new citizens.'

With that, the nomadic, floating state of Thalassa, population twenty-two, was born.

7

Hello, is anybody there?

Aside from the initial explosion, the thermal flash, the blast wave, firestorm and fallout, nuclear weapons have one other gift to give. Exploded at high altitude, they cause a massive electromagnetic pulse, where intense gamma rays knock electrons out of atoms in the surrounding air. These electrons generate an intense pulse of radio waves that frazzle computers, communication devices and satellites. Although we were far enough from the detonations to avoid the rest of it, radio waves can travel thousands of miles.

Naturally, after witnessing the kaleidoscopic light show that day, our first instinct was to try and contact family and friends, as well as trying to find out what had happened and exactly how bad it was. We might as well have been on another planet. If our phones switched on, which most didn't, then there was nothing left to connect too. The Internet had disappeared in the blink of an eye, cellular networks consigned to history. Satellite communications, which had become almost essential to modern shipping as smartphones were to teenagers, had become pie in the sky. We were unable to use *The Thalassa's* instruments to navigate, to communicate or to even pilot the ship. We were shipwrecked above water, floating in a borderless echo-chamber.

We, in this modern world, have become so used to seamless communications and the instantaneous spread of words and pictures. Once upon a time, in the not-too-distant past, the spreading of news from one continent to another had been wholly dependent on ships. It might take days if not weeks for a newspaper in London to discover word of a rebellion within the empire; it had taken over two weeks for the British Government to learn news of the Boston Tea Party. Within two-hundred years and the invention of the telegraph, the relationship between shipping and communications had been tipped on its head. Now, shipping was completely dependent on technology – to navigate, to track other vessels, to monitor weather and currents, to keep ahead of political and economic developments that might affect a ship's course.

For the tens of thousands of men, and miniscule number of women who work in the merchant navy, modern communications had made the pain of prolonged separation bearable. They had made it possible to be months at sea and still have daily contact with family and loved ones back on shore. Unlike the mariners of yesteryear, ship crews now had 24/7 access to world news. Stepping off a ship after a two-year voyage of discovery in the 16th and 17th centuries, a seaman wouldn't know if his family were alive or dead, let alone who was on throne.

The only saving grace to our new – or was it old - situation was that we were all in the same boat; metaphorically now, as well as literally. None of us could contact home, and all, as a result, were able to harbour hope. With that solidarity of predicament, came solidarity of spirit. Imagine if some of us had been able to make contact, if some of us had, beyond all expectation, spoken to our parents, wives or children to find them safe. Those lucky ones might have basked in their own relief, leaving the remainder to imagine the worst, that the reason they couldn't make contact was because.... The worry, the jealousy directed at those not having to worry, would have festered and wept like an open sore, breeding resentment and discourse.

It had been for this reason that the Captain had decreed an amnesty of all our mobile phones. As a group, he explained, we couldn't run the risk that one might miraculously rise from the dead, cursing the owner with the power to shatter our fragile community. Instead, he and the First Officer would twice a day, every day, monitor the airwaves for news, and scan the horizon for drifting voices. There was reluctance from some, especially the younger members of the crew, but a combination of the Captain's calm, reasoned explanation, and the adherence to rank, resulted in obedience. What we didn't realise then, was the absolute power this control over communication would heap upon those bestowed with it.

Strangely, whereas the ship's main two-way radio had been rendered useless, the Captain's own portable radio, with which he used to listen to long-wave performances of his favourite operas and the BBC World Service, appeared still to be mechanically sound. Despite that, the swirling maelstrom of radio waves caused by the bombs rendered it only capable of delivering a concerto of static. Over time, he was able to report back to us on the occasional clatter of words, that at least, he said, showed that there was maybe some life still out there.

I was still very much an outsider in those early days. Merchant ships often carry civilian passengers; most container ships are equipped to carry up to twelve, but rarely did. Latterly, merchant ship travel had been the domain of the adventurous traveller with both money and time to burn, or the eco-hippy hitching a lift to reduce their carbon footprint by piggybacking on someone else's. Usually, passengers were well catered for by a lowly steward, but kept at a respectful distance from the rest of the crew, who were, after all, there to primarily deliver a far more lucrative cargo. I was different in that I was there *specifically* to speak as much as I could to the crew. Once I'd explained that I planned to write a series of syndicated articles and, ultimately, a book - an exposé if you will - of the shadowy world of merchant shipping, focusing on the real lives of real seamen, I'd been met by a mixture of responses. Some had gone out of their way to avoid me – Dmitriy being a prime example – whilst others had relished the opportunity to open their souls. Then there was the middle ground, those who were guarded, yet intrigued enough to feed me snippets of their story. Paresh was one of these.

I'd interviewed him once, before It happened. In the old normal. We'd agreed to meet up in the crew mess after one of his shifts. As a third engineer, Paresh worked long hours, carrying out watch-keeping duties, undertaking planned and preventative maintenance to ensure uninterrupted service on the engine room plant, and as a trouble-shooter. He was twenty-four years of age, and this was his third year as crew, and the second on-board *The Thalassa*. He had, he said, his career plan mapped out – and to prove it he had produced a multi-coloured spreadsheet detailing important milestones.

Those that he had achieved were already blocked out in red. In a further two years, he aimed to become a Second Engineer. By the age of 32, he would be a Chief Engineer. He had even included his salary expectation at each stage, and between as he sidestepped between shipping companies to maximise remuneration. I was impressed.

'Where did you grow up Paresh?' I asked.

'I grew up in New Delhi, sir. My father was a minor civil servant, and my mother a teacher.' He spoke with a lilting, sing-song accent that swung high and low like the waves of the sea. He peppered his speech with polite terms of deference, as was a habit of many Indians I had known.

'So, when did you decide that you wanted to join the merchant navy? Why engineering?'

'I was always good with numbers sir, even at a very young age. At school, I loved science, especially physics. It was a teacher who suggested engineering. I did well in my exams and secured a place at New Delphi University to read Mechanical Engineering.'

'It's unusual for a third engineer to have a degree isn't it, it's normally seen as a vocational route?'

'That is true sir. University was hugely expensive. My parents sacrificed many things to allow me to go, but then my father got sick and was unable to work. On just the one salary, it was no longer possible to finance my studies.'

'So, you looked around at other options?'

'Yes, I still wanted to do engineering. A friend told me about her brother who worked on a cargo ship. She said he sent good money back each month. She managed to get me a contact. I called them, and they were impressed with my background and the fact that I had gone to university, if only for a short time.'

'How did your parents feel about you running away to sea?' He smiled at the imagery.

'We were a tight-knit family, me, my mother, father and brother. They were sad that I would be leaving for long periods of time, but they were happy that I had found a way to continue my love of engineering.'

'You said....,' I flicked back through my notes. '...that your friend had mentioned that her brother sent 'good money back each month.' Looking at your career plan, you have very detailed salary expectations. It that important to you...the money?'

'Of course, sir, isn't it important to everyone?'

'Why is it so important to you?'

'My mother and father are getting older. My father still cannot work. My brother, he is now sixteen, is much brighter than me. He is practically a genius, sir. He deserves to go to university. The money I send home will allow him to go.'

'Is that why you have such an ambitious plan to become a second engineer in just two years?

'Yes, a salary of $40,000 then will coincide with Charun's first year at university.'

We'd carried on talking for some time, about what Paresh liked and disliked about the shipping lifestyle, about his thoughts on shipping companies and how they treated their employees, his fellow crew members, places he had been. What had struck me afterwards, as I had consolidated my notes, was how different this shy, slim young man was to the children I'd grown up with back home, those who had shared my education and first forages into the workplace. We, in the West, had always been in it for ourselves. It had all been about building reputations, spending and saving money for our own individual benefit. When we left home, it was a one-way cutting of the strings, with zero reflection on what happened to our parents next, as long as they could perform a bank transfer to ease us out of a tight spot. Siblings became photographs, and a hastily written birthday card if we remembered.

It was so different for Paresh. As he mapped out his adult life, it was always with a look over his shoulder to ensure that those dearest to him were provided for, that they were comfortable, safe, and could follow their dreams. There was no resentment or bitterness. Just an overwhelming desire to ensure that his brother could be afforded the opportunities denied to him.

And so it came, that I happened to be watching Paresh as we queued that day to handover our phones. We were all shell-shocked by recent events, but Paresh wore an expression of complete and utter devastation. I had noticed that he had barely spoken to a soul in days, preferring his own company. He had done everything asked of him, but he seemed like a shell, an automaton passing the hours. As he stood, waiting, he stared absentmindedly at the phone in his hands, a small and old-fashioned Nokia, his fingers brushing against the worn keypad. As we moved towards the front of the queue, and the Captain, I couldn't help noticing a phone-shaped bulge in Paresh's back pocket. This was bigger and sleeker than the one he was holding. I waited to see what he would do. Would he relinquish both devices? Then the moment came and went. Avoiding the Captain's eye contact, he dropped the Nokia into the bag and passed by, his back self-consciously to the wall.

I had seen it. A blatant disregard for the rules. A pre-planned rouse to fane compliance. Paresh was a rule taker, not a rule breaker. What was he doing, and why? I weighed up the

Captain's words, the importance of a collegiate approach, and the obvious pain and suffering of this young man. Where did my allegiance lie? I said nothing.

I didn't know it then, but it was the worst thing I could have done.

8

In the Doldrums

When we left the Port of Recife on the 25th of August 20##, fifteen days before the bombs fell, we'd just taken on 3.2 million gallons of fuel. I know. It sounds crazy. 3.2 million. Your average car takes about sixteen. At the optimum cruising speed of 24 knots, the *Thalassa* uses approximately 48,000 gallons of fuel in a twenty-four-hour period. Between leaving port and the 13th of September, we'd used approximately 720,000 gallons. That left us with around 2.3 million gallons to last us for the rest of eternity.

It sounds like a lot. If you cruise at a lower speed of between 12 and 15 knots, you can reduce fuel consumption to a third of that needed to run at 24 knots; that takes you down to around 16,000 gallons a day. With no deadlines, customers or employers to worry about, we could afford to idle. Technically, that meant that we could chug around the World's oceans for 144 days before we'd finally run out of fuel. This wasn't part of the plan though. The plan was to conserve as much fuel as possible, to run the engines sparingly whilst keeping them ticking over. We had to maintain the power of propulsion however – without fuel or working engines we would be at the mercy of the sea and its currents.

Of course, the best way to conserve fuel was to up-anchor in shallower waters, but this came with inherent risks. Shallow generally meant nearer to shore, which meant heightened risk: more exposure to fall-out; more vulnerability to attack by desperate survivors who might view us as a floating supermarket; increased susceptibility to contact with the disease. It was these reasons that kept us out at sea. It had not, initially, been a unanimous decision. Ton and Rieko, the First and Third Officers, had argued that there were plenty of remote island archipelagos that might give us both privacy and sanctuary. From our position in the Atlantic, there were the Azores, Ascension, St.Helena, Tristan da Cunha, as well as Trindade & Martim Vaz and the Saint Peter & Saint Paul Archipelago off the North-East coast of Brazil. These ranged from having scant populations to being completely uninhabited. Ton argued that because of their position in the middle of the ocean, even those that were populated were just larger, static versions of ourselves; they were likely unblemished by the nuclear conflict, but completely cut-off from the modern world. He reasoned that these tiny islands might give us the opportunity to set anchor, conserve fuel and possibly provide us with fresh food and water. The Captain and Henning saw it differently. They reasoned that any contact with land, at least initially, was to flirt with unnecessary risk. They argued for a cautious approach, where we would stay at sea and monitor the situation. Their view was that we were a citadel, a floating fortress that could isolate itself almost indefinitely against the unknown.

It was the Captain's idea to set sail for the Doldrums; this, he said, was the best of both worlds. We could conserve fuel by taking advantage of the calmer waters, floating with the currents until we needed to re-adjust our position – that would give us the opportunity to keep the engines in good working order. He estimated that it would take five days to pilot the ship at a slow speed to a mid-way point in the Doldrums. This might cost us 80,000 to 100,000 gallons of fuel, leaving us approximately 2.2 million gallons for prosperity. He then calculated that with daily positional corrections, we might use as little as 3000 gallons a day – which would be enough to keep us going for a minimum of two full years. His concession to Ton and Rieko was that we would re-assess the strategy monthly, taking into account any further intelligence gleaned from any contact with fellow survivors, our observations of changes in climate and our own ability to remain self-sufficient.

We had stayed in the Doldrums, perhaps metaphorically as well as literally, ever since. As the Captain had calculated, we had used minimal fuel and, with the exception of countering the odd storm, which required full engine capacity, we had kept consumption down to well below the 3000 gallons a day predicted. However, we all knew that at some point in the future, perhaps not that far off, we would need to reassess our strategy.

It was a constant topic of discussion amongst the crew, but usually out of earshot of the Captain or Henning, both of whom seemed reluctant to broach the subject. The Filipino contingent were strong advocates for scoping out the western coastline of Africa or the eastern seaboard of South America, which we again assumed would have been spared the worst of the nuclear destruction. Ton and Rieko still argued for the half-way house approach of scouting out the Atlantic islands in the first instance – to gage what had happened to smaller communities that were already used to being partially cut-off from mainstream civilisation.

For an indigenous native of one of the largest Atlantic islands, I found myself to be surprisingly ignorant of Ireland's cousins. I mean, I'd heard of some of them – I could even picture the little head statues on one of them, until Ton pointed out that Easter Island was in fact in the Pacific. One evening, I asked Ton and Rieko's to tell me more about them, and which they thought were the most suitable if we were ever to change tack.

'The Holy Trinity are Ascension, Saint Helena and Tristen da Cunha; they follow the Mid-Atlantic Ridge that snakes down the middle of the Atlantic,' began Ton.

'The furthest north is Ascension, which sits at 7 degrees north of the equator, 1000 miles from the coast of Eastern Africa and 1400 miles east of South America.' Rieko had picked up the narrative and had helpfully opened a battered atlas that was usually used to prop open the mess door. 'Go about 800 miles south and you'll hit Saint Helena...another 1500 miles south-southwest and you'll hit Tristan da Cunha.' I followed Rieko's finger down the spine of the Atlantic.

'Then you've got the Azores up here, 600 miles west of Portugal. It's by far the most populated of the islands, but way too close to Europe for us to contemplate,' added Ton, 'Way too close to the action.'

'What about the other two you mentioned...Saint Paul and Martin Vaz, or whatever you said? Sounds more like a rap collaboration than an archipelago!'

'You mean Saint Peter and Saint Paul, and Trindade and

Martim Vaz. Both small, rocky archipelagos around 600 miles east of the Brazilian coastline. To be honest, I only added them to the list because I was trying to look clever. I think the largest of the islands is only about four miles square...they are pretty much inhabited rocks in the middle of the ocean. I'm not even sure if they have big enough bays for us to anchor off.

'So, that leaves us with the Holy Trinity then?'

'Well, we think two of them might be viable,' said Rieko.

'Tristan da Cunha is too far south. Probably too small. It does have a permanent population of around 250 though, mostly farmers I think. We'd use up too much fuel getting there though,' interjected Ton.

'Leaving us with Ascension and Saint Helena!'

'Ascension is the closest to our current position, but the smallest of the two islands at thirty-four square miles. It has... or had a transient population of around eight hundred people who worked for the various organisations based on the island – mostly communications companies, an RAF base and an outpost of the European Space Agency. Along with the other two islands, it is a British Overseas Territory – so you'd mostly find Brits, St. Helenians and a few Americans there. It was used as a victualling station for the British Navy for years on account of its natural spring water, then as a strategic naval communications hub during the Battle of the Atlantic.'

'It's also got an onshore petroleum supply depot, which used to be topped up by a chartered tanker called the *Maersk Rapier* every two months, which could obviously be very useful to us,' added Ton.

'There's a deep enough bay for us to sit in just off the capital, Georgetown...that's also where the fuel depot is.'

'And Saint Helena?' I asked.

'Bigger, although not by much at forty-seven square miles, but with a population of nearly four-and-a-half thousand. It's more of a community, with its own government, commercial airport and economy.'

'It was the place to be before the Suez Canal was opened in 1869. Before then, over a thousand ships a year would set anchor there on their way around the Cape of Good Hope. By the mid-1870s, they would be lucky to get two hundred.'

'It's been used as a place to exile megalomaniac national leaders...'

'Napoleon, in case you didn't know,' interrupted Ton.

'...as a staging post for the liberation of thousands of African slaves after the abolition of the Trans-Atlantic Slave Trade in the 1840s, and as a water-bound concentration camp during the Boer War,' continued Rieko, throwing an annoyed side glance at Ton.

'More recently, and with the opening of an airport in 2017, it has begun to court tourists. Jamestown, its capital, even looks like a real town!'

'So, which of the two do you think would be the better bet?' I asked.

'Well, Ascension's fuel depot is hugely attractive...,' started Rieko.

'...but Saint Helena is a proper colony,' continued Ton, as Rieko paused. 'I reckon that the best option would be to try Ascension first, see if there's any fuel left and then move on to Saint Helena. Who knows, we might be able to take anybody who wanted or needed to move on with us.'

'However, as I was going to say, the problem with both is that neither island is self-sufficient. Without supplies from the mainland, who knows what kind of primeval breakdown of civilisation might take place. The longer we leave it, the crazier it might get.'

'So, you'd go sooner rather than later?' They both nodded in unison, the first time they'd been in sync all evening. 'Yes, but the Captain and Henning feel very differently. We've tried... many times, but they won't budge. They think we've safer here, and who knows, they might be right.'

'Couldn't we just vote...as a crew that is, and go with the majority view?'

'That's mutiny Mr. Christian, mutiny! You can't go talking like that aboard a ship, Donal; the Captain will make you walk the plank,' scoffed Ton. I think he was joking, but I wasn't sure.

'In all seriousness though,' said Rieko, 'That's not how we do it. We just have to wait until circumstances demand a rethink. We're Okay out here now, we're doing pretty good, but when we get down to our last half-a-million gallons of fuel, we'll have to start thinking more long term. We'll have to either go on a hunt for more fuel, or find a new, permanent home where we can either moor-up or join what's left of civilisation.

9

Chilling out

We'd all grown up with the threat of climate change hovering over us like the sword of Damocles. Owing to our inexhaustible appetite for fossil fuels, methane spewing cattle and oil-based plastics, we'd be faced with an ever-hotter climate. What was once pasture would become desert. Sea levels would rise, enveloping whole swathes of humanity under the waves. The weather would become more extreme, with bigger, stronger, longer storms. By the time I'd reached my mid-twenties, we'd supposedly reached the tipping point where global temperatures had exceeded the 'safe' 2.5 degrees above pre-industrial levels. We were doomed, but a strangling, slow-motion car crash type of doom, which still allowed for some denial. So, irony of ironies, who would have thought that Mankind's final act of self-destruction would actually result in a cooling of the climate. If only I had known, I wouldn't have felt as guilty about leaving the lights on.

The atmospheric scientist, Richard P. Turco was the first

to coin the phase 'Nuclear Winter' back in 1983. The theory was that any major nuclear conflict would pump vast amounts of soot into the stratosphere, thereby reducing natural solar radiation to the Earth's surface. Modelling produced a cooling effect of up to 20 degrees Celsius in core agricultural regions of the US, Europe and China, and up to 35 degrees Celsius in Russia. These rapid reductions in temperature were speculated to last from months to years and were expected to devastate agricultural production...assuming there was anyone left to still grow food. The sea, however, was expected to take decades if not centuries to recover.

The impact of a nuclear apocalypse on the oceans was just beginning to be studied as my doomsday fixation waned. My knowledge of the subject, much to my sea-bound colleagues' disgust, was patchy. The theory was that such massive and sudden changes in temperature could trigger a mini-ice age in the Northern Hemisphere. As a result, salinity and currents would be affected, along with phytoplankton production. The latter, in particular, would have major ramifications for marine ecosystems.

Much of the theorizing on the impact on climate and oceans had been little more than scientific conjecture, sprinkled with small amounts of actual data from nuclear tests, Hiroshima and Nagasaki, volcanic eruptions and even the smoke plumes over Iraq as the oil wells burned after the 1991 Gulf War. Unlike those scientists, we were able to make first-hand observations.

In the days and weeks following the detonations, the skies darkened. Initially, a grey haze stripped away the blue azure, which itself transformed the ocean into an impenetrable slab of slate. Where the day became devoid of colour, the sunrises and sunsets were flooded, as if the rising and setting of the sun used up every-last drop of spectral light. Then, after the first few weeks, the cloud began to build, and with it the wind and rain.

We knew that the worst of the devastation had been wrought upon the Northern Hemisphere. My snippet of half-knowledge about the possibility of expanding ice sheets in the north, along with the fear of higher levels of radiation quickly led the Captain to decide to move us further south towards Ascension, mid-way between the Brazil Basin and Southern Mid-Atlantic Ridge.

As time went on, dark clouds became a permanent feature and the temperature dropped steadily. Luckily, the sunlight was still strong enough to fuel our solar panels, which catered for most of our energy needs. It wasn't until March, nearly seven months after Doomsday, that we first started to observe changes in the ocean's flora and fauna.

I was out on deck, doing my daily jog around the perimeter of the ship with Jerzy, the Chef, when I spotted what looked initially like a small, capsized boat fifty or so metres off starboard. I stopped mid-stride, leaning on the guardrails whilst I both caught my breath and tried to make sense of what I was seeing. Jerzy stopped a few paces ahead, turned and jogged back.

'You are so unfit. You can't even make it around one lap?' he jibed.

'It's not that...well, it is, but I also saw something, over there, look!' As I was pointing, I noticed another similar object another twenty or thirty metres behind the first, then another. They were oval in shape, with what looked like one tapered end. They were approximately ten metres in length, and four or five wide. The surface of each was shiny and white, somehow bloated in a strangely organic way. They bobbed around in the gentle swell. As we watched, we saw huge dark shadows sweeping past under the surface of the water.

'They're whales,' said Jerzy. 'Young ones judging by their size. Dead.' Just as he spoke, one of the dark shapes broke the surface of the water next to the infant whale closest to us. A gigantic black barnacled beak rose into the air, gently nudging the young whale's carcass, before silently receding back beneath the inky waves. 'Adult whales mourn their young, they can stay with them for days, sometimes weeks. I've never seen it before in real life, only in documentaries.'

'Is it unusual for three to die at the same time?'

'I don't know. I guess so. We don't usually see pods of this size as far out, normally only nearer the coast, in shallower waters. Maybe they've been driven deeper into the ocean, like us.'

'Why are only the young ones dying?'

'Who knows! Maybe they are more susceptible to changes in the water, or something has happened to the mother's milk. It said in the documentaries that the young always feel the brunt of contamination first. Let's face it, we've gone way beyond simple pollution this time. Maybe we've poisoned the seas for good.'

We both stared at the scene before us in quiet contemplation as the carcasses bobbed languidly in the still waters, the shadows sweeping beneath. This was the first death that we had actually observed; the first visible results of our species' self-destruction. It made all the other loss suddenly more real. When Jerzy turned, I could see that there were tears streaming down his face. Instinctively, I put my hand on his shoulder, only to quickly question the appropriateness of such a tactile gesture on our island of masculinity. I slapped him twice on the back, in what I hoped was both a reassuring and more manly gesture and removed my hand back to the rail. My awkwardness evaporated as he grabbed the back of my elbow and squeezed gently. It was an acknowledgment of shared thoughts, of shared loss. 'Let's not bring this to the attention of anyone else,' he said. 'If they happen to see, then so be it, but let's not point it out. There is no need.' I agreed. We were cocooned on the *Thalassa*, sheltered from the realities of the carnage beyond the horizon. The longer we could maintain the illusion, hold on to hope, the better. We continued our jog in silence. No one else mentioned the whales that day.

We only shared what we had seen long after the event, when other signs of the ocean's sickness became apparent. The Captain was insistent that we record everything we experienced and saw. He said it would be of great benefit to those in the future, to those whose job it would be to re-build. It was reassuring to hear someone talk of such a future, of any future.

So, over time, we recorded vast shoals of fish, floating, lifeless on the surface of the water. We watched as dolphins and porpoises repeatedly swam into the hull of the ship until they were bloodied and battered. We saw many more pods of whales and dolphins with dead or dying young, and huge swathes of dark green algae that covered the sea around us for days at a time like thick, viscous oil. Countless birds reached the sanctuary of our floating sanctuary, only to die hours or days later.

As time went on, we also saw more and more debris drifting in makeshift rafts across the ocean's surface, collecting in our wake. This bric-a-brac of human existence had been scattered into the seas by the force of the explosions and cast by the currents far-and-wide. Bits of furniture, plastic toys, cans, clothing, food packaging with faded branding still visible. As best we could, we tried to ignore such things. These simple items, these vestiges of our lost civilisation, were like sirens, tempting us into dark, lonely memories. They dragged us from the here and now of ship maintenance, of cleaning, of salvaging, of growing and preparing food, to thoughts of everything that we thought we had lost. A salt-bleached, patterned scrap of fabric might raise memories of a mother, a wife, a lover. A saturated, rotting teddy bear might be a child's love. A limp, deflated lilo the embodiment of past family holidays. After a time, we stopped looking, fixing our gaze into the middle distance; beyond to the mottled grey horizons, away from the flotsam-and-jetsam ghosts.

10

Ping Pong

Maritime history is littered with stories of shipwreck and survival. Alexander Selkirk, a Scottish privateer and Royal Navy Officer, was one such castaway. Famed for being Daniel Defoe's inspiration for Robinson Crusoe, Selkirk had actually requested to be put ashore on the uninhabited Juan Fernandez islands, west of Chile, in 1704 when he judged that his ship, the *Cinque Ports*, was unseaworthy. His Captain, Thomas Straddling, took him up on the offer and landed him on the island with just a musket, a hatchet, a knife, a cooking pot, a Bible, bedding and clothing. Although Selkirk got cold feet and tried to reverse his decision, Straddling declined to allow him back aboard. One can only assume that he must have been monumentally insufferable to have both been ejected in the first place, and then refused the opportunity to change his mind. There began Selkirk's four-year stint of solitude, which might have been made marginally less mortifying if he'd known that the *Cinque Ports* had limped, leaking like a colander, as far as the coast of Columbia before sinking. Those crewmembers that survived were hoovered up by the Spanish and imprisoned in Lima until a ransom was paid.

Selkirk, meanwhile, gorged on spiny lobsters and waited on the beaches for rescue until he was forced inland by a raft of boisterous sea lions who had descended on the island to mate. Once in the interior, he discovered a population of feral goats which provided him with meat and milk, a plentiful crop of wild turnips and a myriad of fruits and spices. He built his own huts, made his own clothes and generally lived more healthily than he would have had on-board or back home in his native Scotland. When he was rescued four years and four months after being marooned, it was noted that he was almost '*incoherent with joy*'. The Captain of the rescuing ship, Woodes Rogers, was impressed with Selkirk's physical condition, and observed of him '*one may see that solitude and retirement from the world is not such an insufferable state of life as most men imagine...*' Despite this, Selkirk later wrote in his memoires that it had been the loneliness and boredom that had proved the greatest challenges.

The *Thalassa* was our very own desert island. Like Selkirk's, it provided for almost our every need. There, you might argue, the similarities ceased. Selkirk was alone. We were marooned with twenty-one other people. We, unlike him, had an endless list of chores to perform to prevent our island from rotting and disappearing under the waves. Nevertheless, despite these two very salient points, our lives *were* wracked with both loneliness and boredom. The hours where we were busy, industrially and socially, were fine. All of the characteristics of a ship's crew that were evident in the old world – comradery, tolerance, cooperation – were, to a degree, enhanced in our new, endless voyage. This didn't mean that we didn't fall out with each other, that there weren't confrontations, avoidances – but on the whole, for sixteen hours a day, life was more than bearable. Then you went to your cabin. Then it changed. That's where Selkirk's loneliness kicked in, with an embellishment of insomnia and a sprinkling of claustrophobia. I know for a fact, although no one acknowledges it, that a number of us have taken to sharing rooms, and even beds. Angelo and Crisanto have, along with Chen and Li. I suspected that Ton and Rieko were occasional sharers. I'm not going to speculate whether it is anything sexual – who knows what happens behind closed doors – but I can wholly understand the need for the closeness of a fellow human at night, the rhythmic sound of another's breathing in the darkness. Don't get me wrong, I've fallen asleep in other people's cabins – during or after films, following late-night card games – that kind of thing – but I prefer the sanctity of my own space where I can wrestle my own demons in private. Each to their own.

Boredom is a far trickier beast. You can be busy and bored. You can be socially engaged and bored. Being around the same twenty-one people, day in day out, is boring. Watching the same films, reading the same books, is boring. Staring at the same flat, grey stretch of sea is infinitely boring. Jogging around the same two-hundred square meters of deck is boring. Eating pretty much the same food every single day is boring. The monotony of our existence makes *us* boring. We try to draw on our previous lives to make us less boring. We navigate our way around stories and anecdotes that might interest or amuse, yet which don't reach into those darker places where our families, friends and lovers reside; where scratching the surface might cause a rupture that won't be contained. But these stories are not infinite. As time passes, the stories dry up. Like a cardboard carton of wine, your stories gush out of the little tap, spreading warmth and goodwill until there's nothing left but a stale, empty bag with no hope of replenishment. You start repeating yourself. You hear the same stories, and you can't help feeling annoyance. So, you talk about the ship, about the chores, about the sea, about the weather, about the food – about the here and now. Occasionally, we fantasise about a future different to the one that seems most likely. To a future planted in soil and not sea water.

Our common defence against boredom, and the hollowness of night, was competition. We played cards. We raced each other around the deck – sprints and endurance. We'd converted one of the empty bay areas into a makeshift squash court. We'd arm wrestle. We played ping pong. Pool. It was a bottomless well of brand-new conversation. It's funny, as I was never one for sports banter. I would sneer at men in pubs who could fill hours talking about back four formations or transfer windows. I'd wince at how puerile and pointless it all was – grown men talking at such length about a game! Now I can spend hours discussing spin technique in table tennis, Bridge tactics, strategies for middle distance running.

We all know our own strengths and weaknesses in the various games we play – we know who the form players are, the top dogs. My particular thing is ping pong; I played it as a spindly youth in the community centre back in Westport when all of the cool kids were playing Gaelic Football. I was never any good at the proper sports; the ones that gave you kudos with other boys, and the right kind of attention from girls. When I was fourteen, I even reached the dizzy heights of runner up in the Connacht Table Tennis League, losing out to a fifty-two-year-old sheep farmer called Finlay O'Leary. He had a phenomenal backhand and all the attributes of a brick wall. I hadn't kept it up into my adulthood, and I'd been apprehensive when I'd first picked up a bat aboard ship; I'd been invited to play by Chen and Alon – both oilers - when I was still a mere passenger, before Armageddon. We'd been two weeks into the voyage, and I'd been pleased with both the distraction and the invitation to join them socially. I'd expected Chen to be brilliant, based purely on watching the Olympics as a child and the perception that *all* Chinese people must be pro table tennis players. The startling reality was that he was pretty appalling. Alon, on the other hand, was quite accomplished. He was a master of spin off both wings and had a mean smash. As we played, I felt my years in the ping pong wilderness melt away, and by the end, I was standing toe-to-toe with the wily Alon. Unexpectedly, both men had also opened-up as we continued to play; their shyness and reluctance to engage conversationally evaporated as we belted the tiny plastic ball at each-other.

Chen, it transpired, was effectively on the run. He had been a student in Mathematics and Philosophy at Hangzhou Normal University when he had fallen in with a group of political dissidents who had taken it upon themselves to print and distribute anti-government leaflets. Before he had quite realised what a bad idea this was, his fellow activists had been rounded up and whisked away for questioning; he had only avoided the same fate by merit of attending a family funeral at home in rural Zhejiang Province. Tipped off by a friend, both he and his parents quickly realised that his university education was over, and that without drastic action his freedom, and existence more generally, might rapidly follow suit. Being a coastal port city, the family had some connections with a shipping company and within three days he had found himself a deck hand on a Maersk ship bound for Mumbai. That had been two years ago. His time onshore was usually spent buying academic books as he continued to self-teach himself the degree that had slipped through his fingers. He had seen his time in the merchant navy as a stop-gap. His ultimate aim was to sneak into the USA, gain citizenship, fall in love and work in academia.

Alon's journey into the industry was far more conventional. He was from a long line of ship workers, going back as far as his grandfather. All the boys (of which there were five brothers) were expected to go to sea as soon as they reached their eighteenth birthday. Alon, the youngest, had done just that – signing up with the shipping agency on the very day he officially became a man. Both Alon and Chen were not employed directly by the *Thalassa's* owners, but by a third-party agency – as were most lower-ranked seaman from South East Asia. This meant that they were paid less, had far fewer legal rights and significantly less union support than their European counterparts – which had suited the major global shipping companies just fine for decades. Despite the same work sometimes attracting half the salary of a company contracted sailor, it was still seen as good money back home in Manilla, and generations of Alon's family had grown financially secure from the money sent back by its male lineage. Alon, who was the same age as me, had a wife and two children and was able to pay for schooling for both his son and daughter. He had even shown me a picture.

I'd then discovered that most of the crew members drifted in for an occasional game of table tennis. Like Alon and Chen, I found that the act of playing brought down people's guards, that they began to speak more freely about their lives, their hopes, their fears. As a writer, and a gatherer of stories, ping pong became my ally. Then came the bombs, and for a time the game – along with all games - seemed too frivolous, too indulgent. It was as if swatting a ball back and forth across a table was somehow an insult, a degradation to the memory of all those who had perished. But as time marched on, and our safe stories dried up, we again picked up the bats, and rackets, and stop-watches and cards. Competition helped fill the void.

Table tennis took on a special status. It became our 'Fight Club'. Games were played during the day, or course, but the real action took place in the small, dark hours. If you found yourself sleepless, haunted by memories, then you made your way down to the crew mess where you might find a fellow insomniac. The rules were simple – best of three sets, first to twenty-one in each set, with a clear two-point winning margin. There was a ladder league; the top spot was coveted. Days at the top of the league were recorded and compared. I continued to collect stories as the magic of ping pong continued to loosen tongues and release memories that were deemed sacred in the day-light hours.

Palvinder, our reefer from India. A left-hander. Solid backhand, weaker on the forehand. Shakehand grip. Prone to lose concentration, especially in the mid-phase of a set. Forty-three years old. Had worked in shipping all his life. Unmarried. Sent a third of his salary back home to Mumbai to his now elderly mother, and his wider family, every month. Palvinder had never learnt to swim, which was technically a breach of his contract, and had an almost crippling fear of deep water. He had a passion for pre-1980's British sitcoms, Fawlty Towers being his favourite. He was able to recite whole chunks of script.

Tanmay, also Indian, and an engine cadet. Penhold-grip. Severe spin on the serve to the deuce court. Tendency to get over excited on key points. He was the most junior crew member, effectively on an apprenticeship. He was only nineteen years old. This was his very first vessel, and he had been a member of the crew for only seven months. He had been orphaned at the age of seven, when both his mother and father had died within three months of each other – both taken by diphtheria. He had been adopted and brought up by his uncle. He had excelled at school, and like Paresh, had gone on to study engineering. His ambitions were to captain a ship, and to one-day own a horse.

Angelo. Steward. Filipino. Penhold-grip, V-Grip on the backhand. Great rhythm in rallies, inclination to over-hit serves. Forty-years-old. Married to three women simultaneously, none of whom knew about the other two. One in Manilla, one in Taiwan and one in Cebu. Father to seven children – as far as he knew. Had worried continuously about the financial implications of servicing three families. Joked that Armageddon had probably done him a favour – but at night, during our games, cried unashamedly for his loss.

Rieko. Third Officer, half-Maori. Shakehand grip on both wings. Brutal, raw strength meant he could hit anyone off the table, but possessed the finesse of a water buffalo. Easily distracted on big points. Had reached the rank of Lieutenant Commander in the New Zealand Navy aboard the frigate HMNZS Te Mana. He had served for eight years before switching to the merchant navy, citing persistent racism and the inability to move further up the ranks – in his words 'he'd tired of watching incompetent white men leap-frogging him to the position of commander'. He had got engaged two years ago and had been due to travel back to Wellington for his wedding at the end of the current voyage.

Arjun. Senior Engineer. Indian but had settled in Holland with his family. Shakehold Grip, occasional Penhold Grip on the forehand. Relative ping pong novice, but intent on improvement. Learnt quickly and would probably end up being the best. Thirty-five years old. Father to three children, aged eight, six and four. He joked that his wife dreaded him coming home because he always 'brought babies with him.' A master of origami, he made little model animals for his children and had posted them home from the major ports. Now he made them for us.

Then there was Polina from the Ukraine. A non-player, but a regular spectator and heckler. She was the Chief Steward and the only woman onboard. Women were a rarity in the merchant navy, accounting for somewhere between one and two percent of the total workforce. Most of the crew had never served on a ship with one before, but the fact that she looked and acted more masculine than most allowed them to sleekly sidestep the fact that she was a member of the opposite sex. She was brusk and bawdy, but rarely spoke about herself; her past was a closed book. She considered ping pong to be a pointless child's game and would never demean herself by playing. Arm wrestling, however, she revered as a high art.

My biggest rival, however, was Paresh. He, it transpired, had also played competitively as a child, and had even represented his university in a nationwide Indian competition. The late-night league usually ended up with us playing each-other for top spot, with me, more often than not, coming off second best. It was one such match-up by which I had made my discovery.

Like the phone incident a few months earlier, I had decided not to act on it – to again put principles of individual privacy above that of the utilitarian good. It was a decision that I, and ultimately all of us, would learn to regret.

We had arranged to play, as we often did, after midnight. I had been waiting for fifteen minutes and Paresh was nowhere to be seen. Assuming that he'd maybe forgotten or fallen asleep, I had made my way from the crew mess down to his cabin on E Deck. As always, the lights along the corridors had been switched off after midnight to conserve electricity, so I had made my way by torchlight.

I had discovered Paresh's door slightly ajar and had knocked quietly, guessing that he would be inside. There had been no reply, so I had pushed just hard enough to open it a fraction more so that I could poke my head inside. It is worth stressing here that to go into somebody else's cabin without being invited was as taboo as taboo could get – and that that had never been my intention. I fully expected to see Paresh sprawled out, asleep on the bed, or perhaps with his headphones on. Instead, all I saw was an empty cabin. I was just about to reverse and give the game up as a lost cause when something caught my eye. There was, not unusually, a storage locker on the far side of the room. The door had been left open, and from the light of the lamp that sat at Paresh's desk, I could see that the inside had been plastered from top to bottom with photographs. Again, this shouldn't have been anything out of the ordinary – most of us had private areas where we put pictures of those we had lost. What really caught my attention was how shrine-like it looked. I hovered, knowing I should go, but strangely compelled to take a closer look. I stepped back, looking to my left and right along the corridor, then took the plunge. It was wrong, but like some werewolf, the beast-like journalist in me had risen to the surface. Easing around the door, I closed it silently behind me and made my way to the locker. As I got closer, I could see that the pictures were repetitions of the same four black and white images. In the centre were what must have been the original photographs, but around them and what I had initially mistaken for photographs, were in-fact drawings. One of the images was of a family group – I could only assume it was Paresh's mother, father and younger brother. Another was what looked like a more professional portrait of just his parents. Then there was a picture of his brother, this time alone and holding a trophy. He must have been twelve or thirteen years old. The final picture was of a girl. She was sitting on a bench in front of a river. She looked directly at the camera, smiling broadly, her long hair flowing over her left shoulder. All of the drawn copies were meticulous in their detail – whether Paresh had traced them or copied them free-hand, I couldn't tell, but it must have taken him hour upon hour. This was a labour of love...or obsession.

I cast my eyes around the room. On the desk, below the lamp was another picture of the girl; a work in progress. It was only half complete in that she seemed to be melting into the brightness of the white paper. Next to the picture was an open notebook, and next to that, Paresh's dormant phone. I should have turned and left – I knew that I had already crossed a boundary, shattered an unspoken convention that had helped us to all to co-exist for this long. Instead, I moved closer. In the book were a series of dated entries. Under each, scrawled notes. I could make out names of both people and places, numbers that might have been co-ordinates. I reached forward and flicked the pages. There were at least twenty, all filled with the same spider-like handwriting. I went to the front page. The first date was from the fourteenth of November 20XX – just over two months after the bombs had rained down. I put the notebook back the way I had found it, my fingers lingering on the soft, cream pages. As I did so, I heard a sound behind me. I leapt backwards, so that I was just shy of the door. As I did so, it opened, and Paresh came in. He stopped and stared open mouthed, first at me, then at the locker, then at the desk.

'What are you doing in my room?' he said slowly.

'I just swung by to see if you were ready to play,' I said, perhaps injecting a little too much jaunty Irishness into my reply. It sounded reedy and false, even to me. Paresh looked hard into my eyes. An awkward silence permeated every corner of the cabin.

'You shouldn't go into someone else's room uninvited,' he said finally and flatly. As he did so, he inched around the bed towards the desk, his fingers searching out and closing the book. The action couldn't have been more damning, more suspicious if he had tried. He then turned, and made his way to the locker, shutting the door with determined finality before again turning and fixing me with his gaze. It was a look of betrayal, defiance and anger all rolled into one.

'So, do you still want a game? It's only 12:30.' It was lame, but I had to say something to fill the aching void.

'No, Donal. Not tonight. Maybe tomorrow.'

I backed out of the room, his eyes still boring into mine. As I left, I closed the door behind me.

The next day, Paresh was perfectly civil – his usual reverential self. He didn't mention what had happened the night before, and neither did I. When we did eventually play, he thrashed me in two easy sets.

I wasn't entirely sure what I had seen in Paresh's notebook. It had looked like a log of communications – but how could that be in a world without satellites and mobile networks, with static on every horizon?

11

Endurance

My eyes open to inky, impenetrable darkness. A part of my mind knows where I am, entombed in a four-meter by three-meter steel box, within a bigger metal box, but the solid wall of black strips away boundaries and places me in infinite space. I can smell the musk of my own sweat, feel the tussled, saturated sheets clinging to my body. I listen. Straining to hear the familiar creaks and clanks of stressed metal, but there is nothing. Then the obsidian curtain is slashed in two – white light streams into my vision, causing me to squint. It is as if I can see the individual atoms dancing, golden. I close my eyes. The atoms continue to scatter haphazardly, scorched into my eyelids. I blink them away, and now I see the source of the light. A tall sash window, one curtain drawn back. From where I lay, I can see a slate sky, pockmarked with darker clouds. As I watch, they slouch past, merging and separating, growing and shrinking. Occasionally, a pocket of blue breaks free, shouting its intent, before it is again consumed by the mediocrity of grey. It feels like I have never watched the sky like this before, with such intensity, with such a disregard for time.

Then I see her body. I have just seen it, but I know it has always been there. She lies between me and the window. The daylight falls on her, bathing her in monochrome shadows. She has her back to me, her face hidden. She's naked, aside from a cotton sheet that climbs the nape of her back and drifts over her exposed shoulder. Her pale skin looks like sand dunes in moonlight. I can see that she sleeps, the slow, rhythmic rise and fall of her rib cage. I want to reach out, to touch her. I imagine the tips of my fingers brushing her skin, the almost imperceivable rising of hairs, as fine as spider yarn. But I can't move. I am paralysed. I am a helpless onlooker.

Then she stirs. Her breathing quickens. Muscles ripple and twitch beneath her marble skin. Slowly, she sits up, her back still facing me. The sheet falls, freezing in layered peaks and troughs. I can see the subtle undulation of her backbone, the soft shadow cast by her shoulder blades. She raises her right arm, runs her fingers through her tussled hair. It is thick and luxurious, as I remember. I observe the curve of her breast, the taught firmness of her triceps as she bends her arm, the narrowness of her wrist. She guides her long hair behind her ears, as she always did. I see a glimpse of her cheek, the flutter of an eyelash, then it's gone. She stands now – an Athenian statue of beauty – and steps towards the light, partially silhouetted against the white glare. But the light isn't white anymore. It is yellow. It heaves its way through the spectrum – oranges and reds glow on the curvature of her limbs, flickering like flames. And now, I realise that the silence has been replaced by a distant roar; a sound so like silence, so all consuming, that I hadn't noticed it before. Suddenly, there is a wind that rushes through the window, forcing her to take a half-step backwards. It whips up her hair into a dervish. It stings my eyes, forcing me to blink back watery tears. The roar has become deafening. All the darkness from before has scattered. Now there is only bright, fulgent light. Then there is nothing.

I wake again. I am breathing heavily. I bring my hand to my face. It is wet; through sweat or tears, I cannot tell. My mouth is dry, haunted by the bitter taste of yesterday's coffee. I sit up, rub fingers into hollow sockets, try to push back the images that still linger. This is my nightly companion. It seeks me out in the small hours, playing out its cruelty. I have learnt that it is part of me, like an arm or a leg. It is something that must be endured.

I hear screams every night. We must all embrace endurance.

12

A reminder

The collapse of civilisation as we knew it through nuclear apocalypse was not *all* we were up-against. We were starkly reminded of this fact two-months after our first anniversary.

It had been like any other day. We had eaten breakfast, looked at the rotas and drifted out to our various tasks. I was working with Henning in the 'growing room', a contained deck area in which we had set up the hydroponic equipment. By this stage, we were beginning to reap the benefits of setting up a staggered planting schedule so that we were able to harvest new crops almost on a daily basis, but this needed round-the-clock input. Today, we were picking a new batch of ripe tomatoes, and 'planting' a new crop of lettuce. We were both fully engrossed in our work when the ship's alarm sounded.

The alarm was only raised when the Captain needed all hands on deck. It had been used sparingly, usually in response to sudden changes in weather, and once for a small fire that had started in the galley. It was the signal to meet in the crew mess.

We arrived second to last, owing to the distance we had to travel, to a room that was bubbling with nervous tension. The Captain cleared his throat, as was his custom, and asked for quiet. 'Gentlemen, gentlemen. I want to start by saying that this is not an emergency in respect to the integrity of the ship, or anything to do with adverse weather conditions. It is a somewhat different issue that I thought we should discuss democratically, before we respond. Normally, I would act according to conventional maritime protocol, but I am sensitive to possible complications that make this a group decision. We have spotted a life raft about a mile to our port side. It looks very similar to our own, so a totally enclosed model which can accommodate fifty people. I am assuming it's from a ship like ours. Its SOS beacon is flashing, but we obviously can't make contact. I can find nothing on the radio. In normal times, it would be our absolute duty to attempt a rescue. However, I am aware that these are not normal times. There is a possibility that the occupants might be hostile, or that it might harbour contagion or disease. Even if this is not the case, we must ask ourselves if we can sustain more people – potentially up to twenty or thirty. I think it deserves a discussion, then a vote. Would anyone like to go first?' Ton raised his hand.

'Captain, we are all mariners. In my view, whatever the circumstances, it is our duty to respond to an SOS.' There was a nod and grunt of agreement around the room.

I put my hand up and waited for the Captain to give me the nod. 'As the only non-mariner here, I feel that I should play devil's advocate. Can we actually sustain another twenty people? We're comfortable as it stands, both in respect to food and water, but a doubling of our numbers would put severe strain on our resources, and with strain comes tension and potential for conflict.' This time, there was no affirmation from the room. Everyone stared at the Captain.

'You are right to ask the question, Donal. Jerzy, Henning – could we feed more people?

'In the short term, yes, but beyond a few weeks we might struggle. It would just mean that we were drawing down on our reserves more quickly,' replied Jerzy.

'We aren't at full capacity yet with the hydroponics. We can still ramp up production, but it would take time. It would mean less for everyone.'

'...and we'd have to double up with accommodation, it'll be a squeeze,' added Polina.

'But no reason not to respond?' asked Ton. The question was resolutely rhetorical.

'No, it would be a struggle, but not a reason to ignore an SOS.' I felt that this was directed at me, the land-lover.

'...and the other things...the disease and piracy?' I asked. There was almost an audible intake of breath at the word 'piracy'; I'd forgotten how tetchy they all were about the term.

The Captain responded. 'We have procedures to mitigate both. We have chemical suits and masks that can be worn by those making first contact. We can set up a quarantine area if required. Ton, Dmitriy, what would you suggest in respect to dealing with any hostiles?'

'We can set up water hoses to push anyone back,' said Dmitriy.

'...and we can arm people at the deck-side with grapple hooks,' added Ton.

'Is that it?' I said. 'Haven't we got any weapons locked away somewhere?'

'No, it's against company policy. There's always been a fear that crew members will end up shooting each other.'

'What, seriously?' I said incredulously. 'That's all you've ever been given to fight off armed Somali pirates – water-canons?'

'Yes, of course.' Ton spoke matter-of-factly, as if he was answering a child.

'Okay,' said the Captain. 'Let's vote, and then we can allocate roles. Please raise your hand if you are in favour of responding to the SOS.' Everyone raised their hand. I was painfully aware that I had raised mine last. I could still see a myriad of reasons why we shouldn't intervene, but I was the only one unshackled to the rules of the sea and a sense of maritime nobility.

'Okay, we will have to launch the inflatable motor boat, and we will need two volunteers to initially drive out to the lifeboat to do the initial assessment. This comes with a certain degree of risk, gentlemen. You'll have to wear the chemical suits, so your manoeuvrability will be hampered. If there is disease involved, you will need to be quarantined for a suitable period upon your return. If anyone on board the lifeboat is hostile, you will be in danger, and there is a risk that we may not be able to let you re-board the ship. Any takers?' Ten hands went up almost immediately.

'Ton, I'd like you to lead please. Roy – thank you for volunteering, I would like you to accompany the First Officer please.' Roy was our Deck Able Bodied Seaman – a jack-of-all-trades, and one of the most-junior members of the crew. He was in his mid-thirties, heralding from Manila. 'Polina, Angelo, will you please assist Ton and Roy in preparing for the operation, and equip them with the necessary clothing. Henning, can you and your team sort out the inflatable please.

Dmitriy, Rieko, Tanmay – please can you prepare a welcoming committee for anyone hostile trying to gain access to the deck. Jerzy, Donal and Cristianto – please can you prepare medical equipment, food and clothing in case the occupants of the lifeboard need urgent assistance. Everyone else, please be on deck to assist in any way you can.'

I was grateful that the Captain had included me in one of the teams. As an outsider, and the only one to question the legitimacy and good sense of the mission, he needn't have done. As it was, I felt included, trusted.

I was quite surprised that he hadn't been the first to volunteer for the reconnaissance mission; I seemed to remember from my childhood viewing of Star Trek that Captain Kirk was always the first to beam down to hostile planets or abandoned spaceships. The reality, I realised, was that the Captain of a *real* ship was chained to it. This was an unspoken rule: accepted by all. I was also concerned for Roy. I had also remembered that Kirk, Spock and Bones were always accompanied by at least two junior members of the crew, who were invariably canon-fodder for humanoid lizards or aggressive robots.

The plan was for Ton and Roy to make initial contact with whoever was inside the lifeboat, and then to return to the ship immediately to feedback to the Captain. He would then decide on the subsequent steps to be taken. With the lifeboat drifting ever closer, the inflatable was lowered down to the lapping waves, followed swiftly by Ton and Roy, bedecked in the cumbersome chemical suits. With everything in place, we watched from the deck as the boat hopped and bumped over the waves in the direction of the craft. Those with binoculars watched in silence, whilst the Captain raised his and gave those without a running commentary of the unfolding drama.

'They have reached the lifeboat,' he said. 'I can see that they are mooring up alongside and securing the ropes. One of them – I can't see which, I assume it's Ton – is climbing the ladder to the hatch at the top. He seems to be pausing for something. He's now opened the hatch and is climbing inside.' There was a long pause. 'I can't see what is happening. Only one of the men have gone inside; the other is still standing at the top by the hatch.' We waited for what must have only been a matter of minutes, but felt like an eternity. 'Ah, there is his head. He is stepping out of the hatch. He appears to be moving quite rapidly. They are both climbing back down the ladder and getting back in the inflatable. There is no sign of anyone else.'

We could see, even with the naked eye, that Ton and Roy were making their way back. It may have just been an illusion of perspective and distance, but they appeared to be travelling faster than when they had left. As they got closer, we could clearly see that the two men were sitting at different ends of the boat, apparently as far away from each other as was possible. We waited with bated breath to discover what they had discovered, and whether their positioning was just coincidence, or by design.

Eventually, the inflatable clattered against the hull, and it was secured in place. We looked down at Ton and Roy. One remained resolutely sat at the stern of the boat, whilst the other, who had been at the bow with the motor, clipped himself into the harness and climbed the pilot ladder. When he was just level with the guardrail, Dmitriy and Jerzy leant over and pulled him over to safety. He stood and removed his hood and mask. It was Roy. His eyes were wide, and there was fear in his voice.

'They were all dead,' he garbled. 'All of them.'

'How many?' said the Captain, with a flat tone.

'Ton counted twelve in total. But, he said...he said it wasn't normal.'

'What do you mean?'

'They had lesions on their faces, around the nose and eyes... like with the disease.' We all knew what he meant. We'd seen the footage of people who had contracted the contagion released by the Russians. Early analysis had suggested it was a virulent, engineered version of Glanders, a bacterial, zoonotic disease naturally occurring in horses that spread through respiratory droplets. It caused the formation of nodular lesions in the lungs, coughing, fever and septicaemia. It the later stages, the nodules spread around the nose and eyes in a smallpox-like black and yellow rash. Incubation was thought to be between one and three days, with death coming within days of the first signs of symptoms. The mortality rate was upwards of 70%. It had been nasty enough for the Western Powers to enact the worst of retributions.

'How close did Ton get?' asked the Captain.

'He only went down the hatch ladder. He could see them well enough from there. The bodies were strapped into the seats or lying on the floor.'

'...and he didn't touch anything?'

'Apart from the ladder, no.'

'He was wearing his protective clothing the whole time, his gloves and mask?'

'Yes.'

The Captain thought for a few seconds, his brow furrowed. 'Dmitriy, what are our options regarding quarantine? I don't want Ton anywhere near the accommodation area, there is too much shared ventilation.'

'There are the storage rooms in engineering, we have some near empty containers, he could go in one of the lifeboats on deck, or Cell 1 for dangerous goods is empty...I guess he could be classified as dangerous!'

'Hardly appropriate, Mr. Dubravin,' the Captain rebuked. He always addressed his crew formally when engaged in proper seamanship, or when he needed to pull rank. 'The only option which is completely self-contained is the lifeboat. It's ready equipped with provisions and water, and we can add more. Ton could stay there for as long as needed without our contact, and still be comfortable. It is a risk, as we could be rendering one of our lifeboats unusable, but we have another. Jerzy, please could you put together a case of food that will keep Ton going for a week. Polina, can you go to Ton's room and try to get as many of his personal belonging as you can – clothes and such. We also need a bed set up. He can tell us if he wants anything else later.' He turned to Roy. 'Please could you return down to Mr. Vanderloo and tell him that he will be quarantined in the starboard lifeboat for seven days, and that we are just preparing it now. When it is time, we will bring him up, then clear the decks so he can make his way to it unhindered. Tell him that we will place a walkie-talkie inside so that I can speak with him when he is settled.'

Roy returned ten minutes later. 'Mr. Vanderloo is in agreement with your plan Captain. However, he has asked if he should do something about the other lifeboat, the one out there.' He pointed to the craft now drifting a few hundred feet from our stern.

'I understand what he means. Currently, it is a floating vestibule of disease. If anyone else were to come across it, or if it was to wash up on some untainted island somewhere, who knows what havoc it could spread.

'Sir, Mr. Vanderloo has suggested that he take a canister of fuel over to the ship and set fire to it. It would act as a suitable burial for the men inside.'

'Agreed, but tell him he must not go inside the lifeboat again. He must do everything from the upper hatch. Henning, please could you bring us a billycan of fuel please, and something to ignite it?'

As the others rushed off to complete their tasks of preparing our own lifeboat for Ton's arrival, the rest of us watched as the inflatable snaked its way back over the waves to the stricken vessel. We watched as Ton tentatively climbed up the ladder, opened the hatch and poured the contents of the can into the opening. We were close enough to see him cross himself, and the brief bloom of flame before it disappeared into the depths of the boat. As Ton hastily climbed down, back onto the inflatable and away, dense, black smoke began billowing from the open hatch. When he was half-way back, there was a small explosion, and fire leapt from the turret. Then, in a matter of moments, still pouring smoke into the sky, the little craft began to sink beneath the waves: a submarine tomb to the horrors that had befallen its unfortunate crew. Christian. Muslim. Hindu. Atheist. We all muttered a silent prayer.

13

The walls closing in

The incident with the lifeboat rattled us all. There were thoughts of the twelve men, like us in so many ways, who had survived what we thought was the worst of it and had ended up succumbing to a danger that we had all but forgotten. They had presumably been crew on a container ship like the *Thalassa*, had come into contact with someone affected, and it had spread like wildfire. Perhaps manning the lifeboat had been a last-ditch attempt to escape, little knowing that they were offering Death a free passage. They, like us, had found a way to survive, to co-exist on their little floating island. Had they answered an SOS? Had they been tempted into port? Had they been attacked by pirates, fended them off – only to be overcome by an even more unsympathetic opponent?

However, it wasn't really these thoughts that troubled us the most. For the previous fourteen months, we thought we knew what we were up-against. We thought – and hoped – that after a time, when the radiation had dimmed and life had been re-kindled and re-ignited on patches of rock and soil, that we might return. That we might start the search for a new life, for a new community, for the sparks of new civilisation. Maybe, in our search, we might be reunited with loved ones. We all knew the chances of this were slim, that surviving a world-wide nuclear meltdown, and all that came with it, was miniscule. But now, suddenly, it wasn't *just* surviving that. I, for one, had forgotten about the pathogen – it had been superseded, blown into atoms by the subsequent nuclear strikes. We'd held onto the idea that some places – remote islands, rural backwaters miles from the urban metropolises targeted by the nuclear powers – might have survived more-or-less intact, that these were the places that would become the crucible for re-birth. But now we remembered, fuelled by the closeness of our own brush with it, how the disease had spread so completely in the days and weeks before Armageddon. It had raced through airports, crossing continents and oceans in aircraft; it had breezed over country borders in cars and lorries; sped to new towns and cities in trains and buses. Perhaps, before the bombs exploded, it had found its way onto most ships. The fact remained that we all had to recalibrate our expectations. The only way to protect ourselves was to remain on the ship, and to close ourselves off completely to the outside world. The ship was now our castle, and our prison. Hope still burned, but less brightly – a smouldering coal, more black than orange. It was a time of melancholy reflection on-board. Everyone was quieter. Conversation was heavy and turgid. Time elongated. I hoped that it was just a readjustment, and that it would pass.

As well as the usual round of daily chores and duties, in the days after the discovery of the lifeboat I took to spending time with Ton. He was bored and needed the company, and I thought

I might be able to sniff out a story. As he said, it was a perfect opportunity for me to ghost write his memoires. This was said with Ton's usual levity, but I could sense it was tinged with fear – he was, after all, in quarantine awaiting the first signs of a killer disease. I would sit outside the lifeboat on a deckchair, sharing two coffees – separated by the thick fibreglass walls. We talked through the short-range walkie-talkies, which for some reason still seemed to work in our gadget-free world. Partly out of a sense of morbid interest, but mainly because I felt he needed to talk about it, I started by asking him about what he had seen on the stricken lifeboat.

'It was strange,' he said, 'even before I opened the hatch, I sensed something was wrong. There was no sound, except for the slump, slump of the waves on the side of the boat. We had been quite noisy as we had moored up, with the inflatable banging against the hull and with Roy and I shouting instructions to each other. I'd expected to hear shouts from inside, movement at least – but nothing. As I climbed the ladder, I had a sense of foreboding. I remember hesitating at the top, before I undid the hatch. I felt like Pandora and her box. I told Roy not to follow me, and opened it. It was the stench that hit me first. The mixed aroma of shit and piss and decay. There was still a light on inside. I could see a pair of legs stretched out on the floor below. I shouted, but got no response. I took a deep breath and climbed inside. I only had to climb down four runs of the ladder to see everything. Along the wall closest to me, there were five bodies, seated and slumped against each other. Further down, on the opposite side, were another four lying on the seats. The other three were on the floor, two face down, the other face up. All of them were in the same condition; their nose and cheeks were covered in yellow pustules and as these moved up around their eyes and onto their foreheads, they became a thick mass of blackened hives that covered all of their features. It reminded me of smallpox, or leprosy maybe. I called out again, but there was no movement. No movement at all. Then I got out as quickly as I could.'

'How do you know they were all dead?'

'I guess without examining them all individually, I couldn't know for sure. I couldn't hear any respiratory response, they didn't move, they didn't make any noise. What was I supposed to do, try and shake them awake?'

'Sorry, that was insensitive of me. Of course you wouldn't.' After a respectful pause, I continued. 'Why did you say 'respiratory response'? Don't most people say 'breathing'?'

'Ah, now we get into my memoires. It's a throwback to my studying medicine.'

'You have to study medicine to become a ship's officer?'

'No, but you do to become a doctor. I started off at Utrecht University studying medicine. Both my parents were medics – quite prominent ones in fact – and they expected me to follow in their footsteps. Growing up, it was always assumed that I would. Even I assumed I would.'

'What happened to Doctor Vanderloo then?'

'I hated it. Everyone told me it would get better, that the first year was the worst. So, with the help of a little marijuana, I got through the first year. Then I started the second year, but the marijuana didn't even hit the sides.'

'What did you hate about it?'

'The people. The other doctors. My fellow students. When we saw them, the patients. I just couldn't muster up the enthusiasm to treat them. The academic side of it was okay, but I guess I just didn't care enough. I didn't have the passion to make the all-nighters worth it.'

'So, what did you do?'

'Well, you know the Dutch are big on shipping. We have Rotterdam. Utrecht had a strong tradition in maritime studies, so I enrolled on that. I figured life on a ship would be fun, and it would be away from my parents and all those friends and family who would forever be looking down their noses at me as the failed medic.'

'What did your parents say?'

'I didn't tell them. I just switched courses. Medicine was a five-year course, even without the placements, and Maritime Studies was three. I figured I could be finished and out at sea before they even realised.'

'But if they were both doctors, wouldn't they have found out?'

'You'd think that, but they were both working outside Utrecht, in quite specialised areas of medicine. They didn't seem concerned enough to check up on me through their contacts. After saying that, I didn't get away with it completely. They bumped into someone at a party in my final year who worked within the medical faculty at the university, and they'd asked them if they knew why I'd quit. We had quite an awkward call that night.'

'They let you continue though?'

'They didn't have much choice. They didn't want me to drop out of two careers. Neither of them attended my graduation though.'

'Then what?'

'I got a job on a gas tanker as a cadet deck officer, and worked my way up. It's taken me nine years to become a First Officer. Next step, Captain.'

'What do you like about it, this work?'

'I see it as more than work. It's a vocation, a lifestyle even. I like the grittiness of the people who work in it. The unpretentiousness of it all. The fact that something as complex as this ship performs such a simple task – the movement of stuff from one-place to another. I like not being in Holland.

'What was the relationship like with you parents...well, before...?'

'Postcards mostly. The occasional Skype call. The odd visit. My father joined as a passenger once, from Rotterdam to Suez. It was...uncomfortable.'

'What do you think now?'

'Do you mean, what do I think now they are gone?' Ton was one of the few on board to verbalise his loss. 'I do think back on memories, especially when I was a younger child. I remember them not being there much. I didn't have any siblings, so I remember being alone a lot, to filling my own time. I miss the *idea* of them, rather than anything more tangible. I haven't cried for them, if that's what you mean.'

'Have you cried for anyone?'

'I have had good friends that I think of. Some lovers...fellow mariners, men mostly, with whom I've had brief, whirlwind romances, but I don't think I've ever been *in* love. I've lived a transient lifestyle, focused on the here and now. This is the here and now. There's no point in crying for anyone.'

'Who'd cry for you?'

'Donal, I don't think there's anyone left to cry for me?'

14

The Storm

Ton showed no symptoms, and after ten days – three more than planned – we agreed that he could be released from quarantine. He figured that as it was a respiratory disease, the fact that none of the stricken men were respiring at the time went in his favour. Everyone was still nervous though, and it was some weeks later before people stopped taking an unconscious step backwards or choosing to sit in the next-but-one chair closest to Ton. He accepted his social pariah status with good grace, and his usual geniality.

There was no doubt, however, that things had changed. A funereal blanket had descended on the ship like a thick, cloying fog. We went about our chores as usual, but there was less conversation, more unbroken silences. Increasingly, mild illness or malaise kept people in bed, unable to find the energy or heart to perform whatever menial task was before them that day. Morale dipped like a barometer in a storm. Squabbles and squalls broke out amongst the crew, words that previously would have been taken in good humour or brushed aside instead flared tempers and ignited resentment. At one point, Angelo and Crisanto, usually the closest of companions, had to be pulled apart and restricted to quarters following an argument that had quickly escalated from a verbal gale to a physical tempest. Jerzy, who had witnessed the whole episode as it unfolded in the galley, later divulged that it had been sparked by a derisory comment made by Angelo regarding Crisanto's technique for chopping onions. Jerzy, who had been instrumental in separating the pair and preventing any serious injury, had had to prise the knife out of Crisanto's closed fist whilst kneeling on his chest.

Shortly after the incident, the Captain - sensing the palpable tension and morbid atmosphere aboard – had called a special meeting of all crew members. We had gathered sombrely in the officers' mess at the allotted time and awaited his words of wisdom.

'Gentlemen, I have gathered you all here today for two reasons. Firstly, since our brush with the disease and the unfortunate events surrounding the lifeboat, there has been a noticeable shift in the atmosphere aboard ship. I think we have all felt it. It is born from a sense of us having to accommodate a new reality. Some of us, after the passage of time, had begun to believe that our circumstances might be able to change, that the risks and dangers that had kept us out at sea for so long were perhaps dissipating. We now know that there are new, possibly even greater dangers. I know this is a bitter pill to swallow. This brings me to my second reason for bringing you together. I have heard much talk amongst you of the merit of our existing strategy, that of staying out at sea. Perhaps it is my simple, matter-of-fact Danish logic at play, but this seems a contrary response to our recent experiences. However, I also appreciate that the issue of fuel supply is preying on some of your minds, and that we are reaching a point at which our future plans must be discussed if we are indeed to change course. Equally, it could just be that we have reached a point at which *something* new has to happen. So, this evening, I would like us to discuss our options, to lay the facts on the table and to hopefully draw a line under recent events...for the good of us all.' There was a nod and rumble of agreement around the room. 'As you know, the Chief Engineer and I are strongly of the opinion that we should stay as far from shore as we can.' He paused and looked over at Henning who was leaning against the wall behind the TV. Seeing the rooms' eyes swing in his direction, Henning at first reddened, then offered his affirmation with the slightest inclination of his head. 'We also believe that recent events do nothing but strengthen our argument; if the disease was to be found on a ship like ours, who knows how widespread it might be amongst survivors of the nuclear conflict. We have established a safe and healthy environment aboard the *Thalassa* and are able to sustain ourselves well into the future. We argue that this is not the time to change our strategy and to court unnecessary danger.' Polina raised her hand.

'Captain, what *is* the exact situation with our fuel?'

'Henning, could you please inform the rest of the crew of our current status.'

'Of course. We currently have approximately 1,250,000 gallons. If nothing changes, and we continue to consume fuel at the rate that we have been over the last fourteen months, we would expect to run out in eighteen to twenty months' time.'

'But we don't want to be in a situation where we just *run out* surely?' This from Jerzy.

'No, obviously not. We need to leave ourselves with around 350,000 gallons to enable us to reach land; either South America, Africa or Europe at a push.'

'Or Ascension or Saint Helena,' added Rieko, 'Which would use up far less fuel, allow us to tread water and preserve what fuel we have, and potentially allow us take more on board if the depot is still operational at Ascension.'

'Indeed, that is an option,' interjected the Captain. 'But I would still argue that this is not the time. I would prefer to leave it another eight to twelve months – stay out of danger, continue to build our own resilience and self-sufficiency and then consider our next move then. Our encounter with the disease shows that it is still virulent. The longer we give it, the better the chances of it burning itself out. It is logical to wait as long as we possibly can before we have to put ourselves in more danger.' This time, Ton raised his hand.

'Captain, I don't really understand what difference it makes if we were to sail to, say, Ascension now or in eight months' time. We could anchor off the island, and just sit and observe. What's the danger in that?'

'Ascension was an important international communications hub. It housed key US and British military defence systems. It could well be that it was targeted, in which case it could be highly contaminated. We might be putting ourselves at colossal risk of radiation poisoning, and we wouldn't necessarily know until it was too late.'

'Captain, if I may ask...' everyone turned to face Paresh, who seemed to physically shrink from the sudden attention. I couldn't ever remember him speaking in a group meeting and judging by the surprise on the faces of everyone else around the room, neither could they. He coughed self-consciously and continued, 'Have you heard anything from Ascension... or anywhere else...on the radio?' It struck me as a strange question. Paresh must have known the answer. He had been present at all the weekly briefings where the Captain reported on his and Henning's scouring of the air waves. There had been nothing but static.

'No, Mr.Kher, I have heard nothing from the Ascension Islands, or anywhere else to give me any indication of their status.'

'You are sure? Nothing at all?' Again, it seemed outrageously out of character for Paresh to be pushing the point.'

'No, Mr. Kher. As you will know from my weekly comms reports, we have heard nothing tangible, only static on all wave lengths. Why? Do you have anything to add?' Paresh held the Captain's gaze momentarily, before shaking his head and averting his eyes to the floor. Whilst everyone's focus returned to the Captain, I continued to watch Paresh. Despite no longer being the centre of attention, he still seemed tense – as if another emotion was at play. It reminded me of his calm anger when he had discovered me in his room. Although I was unable to see his whole face, I saw what I thought may have been the flicker of a smile dance across his half-hidden features. Then he looked up, his expression now a mask of opaqueness. He caught my eye, and I looked away.

'What we propose,' the Captain continued, 'is that we continue as we are until July or August...another eight months... knowing that we will then change our strategy. In the mean-time, we will discuss the various options available to us and, as a group, decide how we wish to proceed. What we need now is routine without risk, but I appreciate that we also need hope...hope that there *is* another path. All those in favour say 'I'' The room rung with the affirmative. The meeting had been introduced as a group discussion, a practical exchange of alternate views where everything was on the table. As with all consummate politicians, the Captain had skilfully guided the outcome to his preferred option, with a semblance that it was somehow a collegiate decision. 'That is excellent gentlemen. This will, I hope, give us renewed focus and a restored sense of harmony. To that ends, Ton and Rieko – I would like you to put together the case for both Ascension and Saint Helena. Angelo and Alon – I know you have argued that we should head for South America in the past – perhaps you could put together a case for that. Please consider the pros and the cons for each option. If anyone else would like to propose another course of action, please come and speak to me. We are open to exploring everything.'

From there, the meeting descended into good natured conversation and discussion – the atmosphere was as congenial as it had been for weeks. The launching of the idea that we could, and would, look at a new way forward overwhelmed the reality that, for the short term, everything would stay the same. I watched as Paresh slunk quietly out through the door, his eyes still fixed on the steel walkway at his feet.

#

The next few weeks really did seem like a return to normality. We fell back into our old routines and continued almost good naturedly with our list of daily chores. The sour, dour atmosphere had lifted and was replaced with a new surge of optimism. I made a deliberate effort to watch out for Paresh, but I saw little of him. When I did, he seemed his usual reserved, quiet self. Often, he was huddled in a group with Li and Banya, the engine cadet, but this again wasn't hugely out of the ordinary, and certainly wasn't anything to set the alarm bells ringing.

It was a fortnight after the Captain's gathering that we were hit by the storm. We had encountered relatively few in the Doldrums – it was the whole point of our being there – but when they did hit, they were bad. This was no exception. The skies had darkened throughout the afternoon, skimming through shades of grey until they were a menacing bank of granite that seemed to merge with the distant horizon. By early evening, the waves were rolling into mountainous peaks and canyoning troughs that pitched the ship dangerously from one precipitous angle to the next. The rain lashed horizontally, raking the bridge castle's windows with watery bullets, whilst the wind roared its belligerence. Everyone was on rota for the night, four hours on, four hours off. As much as anything, it was about riding it out and, in my case, holding onto the contents of my stomach.

I always found that being on duty was far easier than being off. If you were helping out in the engine rooms, being an extra pair of eyes on the bridge or even patrolling the containers on the outer deck, you at least had your mind taken off the nauseating sensation of being dragged skyward and then down towards the ocean's zenith in gut-wrenching succession. I've been to a fair few roller-coaster parks in my time, but this topped them all. Off duty was worse by a mile. Somehow, being in a smaller room seemed to magnify the magnitude of the oscillation, pitching you from angle to angle like milk in a butter churn. As well as trying to keep yourself either upright or firmly attached to a piece of furniture, you also had the added complication of trying to prevent your possessions from spinning around you like a tornado's bounty.

It must have been three in the morning. I was in the middle of an off-duty slot, desperately trying to juggle sleep with actually juggling the contents of my bookshelf, when I heard a huge bang on the hull, seemingly right next to my head. The whole wall of the cabin seemed to reverberate with the impact. I sat bolt upright and turned on the light. I sat rigidly, straining to hear anything else above the roar of the wind and the desperate creaking and straining of the steel girders, sheets and rivets that separated me from the raging sea. Just as I thought that I had imagined it, I heard another two sharp clashes of metal on metal. I remember my mind racing at the time – had we hit another ship? An iceberg perhaps? On the equator? I jumped up, and dizzily made my way up towards the bridge, bouncing off heavily lurching walls as I went.

I was met by Dmitriy and Rieko, who were manning the bridge, and the heavily dripping and mackintoshed figures of Tanmay and Palvinder, who had been patrolling the decks. They were in the process of trying to explain what had happened.

'So, we hear a crash, right – like a huge gong on the other side of the ship. I'm thinking, maybe one of the containers has come loose or something. So, I grab Palv and drag him to the port side – it's kinda difficult to make yourself heard because of the wind. When we get there, all the containers look fine – we check the restraints but everything is okeydokey. We walk up and down the walkways between the containers, but we can't see anything wrong.'

'So, I say to Tanmay, what aren't we seeing? Then it hits us both at the same time – the lifeboat is gone!'

'What do you mean 'gone'? asked Ton, incredulously. 'You mean washed away?'

'No, it's been launched. Someone's launched it.'

'Could you still see it?'

'No, we tried. It's too dark.' Ton grabbed the walkie talkie and pressed the release button. A burst of static filled the room.

'Captain, sorry to disturb you, but we have a situation. The port side lifeboat has been launched.' There was a short pause, and he continued. 'No, of course it wasn't authorised. Please may I have permission to sound the alarm. I'll meet you down in the mess shortly – we can see who's missing.'

Five minutes later, a noisy and boisterous throng assembled in the mess. The Captain quickly accounted for those that were missing – Rieko had remained on the bridge with Tanmay and Palvinder. Henning was running the engine room with Alon and Roy. Paresh, Banya and Li, however, were absent. All three were currently off duty and should have heard the alarm from their quarters.

'Ton and Donal, will you accompany me please?' commanded the Captain. 'The rest of you, please could you resume your duties or go back to your cabins. We will meet here again in the morning when the storm has abated. I will sound the alarm again when I deem it to be an appropriate time.'

We followed him out of the mess, and down the narrow stairwells to the living quarters below mine, reaching Banya's cabin first. He was nowhere to be seen. Ton checked his locker, which was practically empty of his possessions, except for a few knitted sweaters, a jacket and two pairs of trousers that hung limp and lonely on the remaining hangers. Some books, magazines and photographs were scattered haphazardly on his bed. Li's room was next – he too was gone. Finally, we reached Paresh's room. The door was unlocked. For a second time, I entered uninvited. Once again, the shelves had been swept clear of possessions. The locker, that had previously doubled as a shrine, was bare – only a uniform pattern of Blutack polka dot rectangles remained. I looked down at his desk – in place of the leather-bound log-book and the work-in-progress drawing was a crisp white envelope. On its front, in neat italic handwriting, was my name.

15

Splinters

My fingertips brushed against the silky cartridge paper. The seconds ticked by, each audibly marked by the old-fashioned alarm clock that sat on the desk. I hesitated, frozen in stasis.

'Aren't you going to open it?' Ton asked impatiently.

'Yes, sorry, of course,' I stammered. I was still trying to fathom my own reluctance to pick up the letter, to rip it open, to expose its contents.

Both men watched as I turned the envelope in my hands, and finally forced my index finger under the lip, prising it open. There were two sheets of paper inside, neatly folded in half. Paresh had only written on one side of each, the same small, uniform, italic handwriting in navy blue ink. I read it out aloud:

Donal,

You are probably wondering why I have written this letter to you...

He was right, I was.

...There are several reasons, the first being that you are not one

of them. You are not a seaman, and as such you will view things differently. You are not bound by the same loyalties or to the same conventions. You won't just view my actions as a violation of the rules, as the others might, but will give due consideration to my motivations. Perhaps you will find a way to explain them to the rest of the crew. Secondly, the time I found you in my cabin, I saw it in your eyes that you had seen it, but still, you did not break my trust...

'What does he mean?' interrupted the Captain.

'It was ages ago. I'd gone to Paresh's cabin to remind him that we were supposed to be playing ping pong. His door had been unlocked, and I'd gone in. I had been looking at a journal of some-kind that was open on his desk when he'd walked in. He'd acted strangely.'

'And what does he mean by breaking his trust?'

'I don't know. I guess he assumed I would come and tell you.'

'And why didn't you, if you had concerns?'

'I thought that it was his private business. I already felt that I'd violated his privacy by going into his room uninvited.' The Captain nodded, by way of a signal for me to continue.

...When we spoke about my family all that time ago, about why I had chosen to go to sea, I felt that you understood. That you didn't just brush my story aside as so many do. In this profession, everyone has a story to tell, but few have the time or inclination to listen. So, I am asking you to listen now.

I think you saw some items on my desk that evening that aroused your suspicion. You saw my journal, and you saw my phone. The two are intrinsically linked. You see, I had handed in my old phone to the Captain. This phone I had kept because, before the bombs, I had downloaded an app that had allowed me to use it as a two-way radio. It was something my brother and I had done...just for fun. Of course, afterwards, the mobile networks were gone, but I found that this still worked, and over time, I began to hear voices. They were indistinct at first, barely identifiable, but about six months ago they began to become more lucid. I could hear words. Initially, I thought that I was just hearing radio broadcasts, maybe recordings that had just been left to loop indefinitely, but I began to recognise different voices. They were communicating with each other. I tried to contact them on the same frequency. I repeated our co-ordinates. I spoke of our status, but I heard nothing to indicate that they had been received. Not until the 14th of May this year. That is when they first made contact. The RAF base at Ascension. They are alive, Donal. They want us to join them. Of course, as soon as I knew, I went to see the Captain with the news...

I stopped reading and looked up at the Captain. Ton was doing the same.

'Yes, he came to see me,' he said, almost defensively. 'He showed me his journal. He had written meticulous notes. He said he had made contact with a guy named Waterman, who was a comms engineer with one of the commercial carriers working on Ascension. He claimed that there was still a community of around five hundred people on the island. I asked Paresh to show me, to put me in contact with this man. We went to his cabin, but all he could produce was static. I went back every day for a week and tried again and again, but it was the same every time. Meanwhile, when I wasn't there, he claimed to have been speaking to them. He showed me the transcripts in his journal. In the end, I concluded that Paresh was delusional, that he was living out some kind of fantasy. It is hardly surprising that one of us would finally break.'

'What did you tell him?'

'I didn't want him to unsettle the rest of the crew, so I told him that if he spoke to anyone else about it, I would take his phone. I asked him to continue to monitor the communications, and to try to ascertain the intentions of those on the island. Perhaps I shouldn't have indulged him, but I thought that, given time, he might come to his senses.'

'So, you don't think there *is* a lost civilisation on Ascension waiting to welcome us with open arms?' asked Ton.

'I don't know. There may be, but I can tell you with certainty that Paresh wasn't in contact with them. His phone didn't work. Everything was in his head. Now, please Donal, continue reading.' I went back to the letter.

...The Captain was dismissive. He claimed not to be able to hear what I was hearing. He threatened to confiscate my phone if I told anyone else. I couldn't let that happen. If I lost the phone, how could I ever prove that I was right? He asked me to continue to speak to them, to gain intelligence, but I knew he was placating me. Then there was the time recently where we all gathered to discuss what we would do next. You heard the Captain say that no contact had been made. I even gave him the opportunity to correct himself, but he denied it again. He has no intention of changing our strategy; he is going to keep us out at sea until we run out of fuel, and then we won't have a choice. So, I confided in Li and Banya. I showed them my logbook; I let them listen to the communications. They believed.

Our current position puts us just over 400 nautical miles from Ascension. With enough fuel and provisions, we believe we can make it to the island...'

I stopped reading. 'Is that true, could they make it?'

'Technically,' Ton offered. 'The life raft has an engine which can give them a speed of between 10 and 12 knots at full throttle.

If they were able to navigate effectively, and if they had taken enough food and water on board to last them a month, it's feasible. But I wouldn't want to try it! There's a lot of ocean between us and Ascension, plus this storm could propel them even further away from it.'

'So, all three of them would be taking a massive risk?'

'Massive. With all the variables, I'd give them a 30% chance of success.'

'How on earth did Paresh convince the other two?

'Insanity can have an exponential impact on a man's ability to convince,' said the Captain wryly, 'Although, both Li and Banya seemed like logical, rational men.'

'Maybe they heard what Paresh had heard?' I suggested meekly.

'That is not possible,' the Captain said irritably. 'There were *no* communications. If there were, I would have heard them. What else does he say?' It took me a few seconds to find my place:

We have spent weeks gradually building up what we need and transferring it to the boat. We are truly sorry to have been forced to steal, but it was a necessity. We are also sorry to have taken the raft; we know that it makes you less safe with just the one, but there was no other way. We would have liked to have shared our plan with others...with yourself, but we knew that you would try to stop us. Others might tell the Captain, and he would have stopped us...

'Too right, I would. The bloody idiots.' The Captain, usually so stoic and devoid of emotion was visibly fuming.

Donal, this now is why I have written this letter to you. You must try to convince the crew to follow us to Ascension, not for our sake, but for theirs'. There is a fully fledged community on the island: men, women and children of all ages. They are growing their own food, building their own future but more importantly, they have the means to communicate to what's left of the World. They are working hard to make these operational – they are mostly communications engineers after-all. There's an airport – so when the World does begin to wake up, they have the means to re-join it. For now, Ascension offers society, safety and sustainability, but above all, Donal, Ascension offers hope.

'Wow! said Ton, 'He even had time for an alliterated soundbite!'

May the gods be with you. I continued.

Paresh

I folded the sheets of paper neatly and placed them back in the envelope, awaiting a response from the Captain, who stood, statue-like, gazing into the middle distance past both Ton and I.

'I guess we'll wait for the storm to settle and then go pick them up?' I proffered, as much to break the awkward silence as anything else.

'And why might you think *that* Mr. O'Brien?' said the Captain coolly.

'Well, you heard what Ton said. They've only got a 30% chance of making it. Surely, we need to go and save them...from themselves.'

'The three men have made their decision. They have stolen from us. They have put us all at increased jeopardy by commandeering the second lifeboat. They knew the risks involved with their chosen course of action. I am not going to risk the safety of any of the remaining crew on a rescue mission or expend a drop of fuel chasing a madman to Ascension. That is my final word on the matter.'

And as it turned out, it was.

16

Ruptures

The next morning, when the storm had blown itself out and the sea had returned to its regular placidity, the crew met, bleary eyed and exhausted. The Captain, like the tempest, had calmed from the zenith of his own emotions and had returned to his characteristic equilibrium of slow, stoic rationalism. He told his crew everything, even those details that reflected badly on himself. He apologised for his own actions; he lamented the opportunity he had had to perhaps turn events in another direction. He should have realised that Paresh needed help, not mollification. He considered that the loss of three crew members to be a weight on his own shoulders: his own failure. The remaining eighteen shipmates listened in solemn silence. Finally, the Captain explained, in much the same way as he had with Ton and I, why he would not sanction a rescue mission. His words had the same finality as the night before. There was no opening for discussion, no leanings towards a communal decision. Then, after communicating the day's rota, he excused himself and left the room.

The room remained bathed in silence for a few seconds more, incredulity seemingly sucking the words from the stunned crew. Then, as if a button had been pressed or a knob turned, it erupted into babelism.

'We can't just leave them; it's tantamount to murder!' shouted Arjun. 'They are all members of my team, what am I supposed to do, just wave them goodbye?'

'It's hardly murder, Arjun, but I agree that doing nothing doesn't sit well. It feels wrong,' retorted Polina.

'Like a betrayal,' added Angelo.

'Hang on, hang on!' said Jerzy. 'Just wait a minute. Who's done the betraying here? It's them that stole from us, that have put us at increased risk by disappearing with one of our only two life rafts.'

'Yes, they've made an error of judgement, but is that any reason for us to leave them for dead?'

'We are already talking as if their fate is inevitable; they still have a chance of making it to Ascension!' interjected Ton.

'But a much greater chance of *not* making it!' said Arjun, 'You said that yourself.'

'And who says they have made an error of judgement? We only have the Captain's word to go on.' This, an uncharacteristic contribution from Palvinder, who was usually mute during group discussion. 'What is there to say that Paresh didn't make contact with Ascension? We know that the Captain doesn't want us to deviate from his strategy of staying out here, at sea - indefinitely. It is within his interests to deny all knowledge of the communications, to cast Paresh as a madman. Donal, you saw the journal, didn't you?' All eyes turned on me.

'Yes, I did. Fleetingly.'

'And what did it say?'

'I only had the briefest of moments. I didn't really read it. There were just a series of entries and dates. I'm afraid that just my seeing it doesn't give it any validity.'

'But there must have been more to it for both Li and Banya to join him. They must have heard it too; why else would they risk everything?' continued Palvinder.

'Maybe the Captain doesn't want us to find them, in case they tell us the truth,' added Roy.

'This is ridiculous!' said Rieko firmly, 'The fact is that we haven't a clue where they are, anyway. The storm could have sent them in any direction. As I see it, the Captain is doing his job; he's trying to protect us, his remaining crew. We could spend days and days, and huge amounts of fuel, chugging around fruitlessly trying to find them. Without radar, or our normal means of communications, it would be like looking for a needle in a haystack.'

'We could at least head for Ascension. If that is where they are heading, then surely we'd have a chance of finding them! I thought that was what you wanted anyway, to go to Ascension?'

'It is, but on our terms, not on some foolish rescue mission.'

'To me,' said Tanmay slowly, 'it is all becoming clear. If it were three Europeans who had left the ship, then it would be all-hands-on-deck to enact a rescue.'

'Or three officers!' added Roy.

'But as it is just a bunch of low-ranking Asians, then any idea of a rescue mission somehow becomes *foolish.* It looks like our State of Thalassa is as bigoted, prejudiced and hierarchical as our old World!'

It was then that I looked around the room. It wasn't that

I hadn't been watching the faces of my companions before, but I had been guilty of looking without seeing. Whether this had been the case when we had first gathered, or if people had drifted and gravitated since the Captain's departure, I couldn't say, but there was now a definite, physical demarcation of personnel. On the one side of the central sofas, and dotted sporadically on chairs, were the Asian contingent: the Indians, Filipinos, the Indonesian, the Chinese. All, except for Arjun, below officer level. On the other, were the Europeans; a Dane, a Dutchman, a Russian, a Ukranian, a New Zealander and a Pole. All with positions of rank. Had it always been such? With this realisation came a sense of danger. Without diffusion, the situation could easily escalate. I was perhaps not the only one to recognise this as a pivotal moment, not just to the current harmony aboard ship, but perhaps to our very existence. Then I remembered Paresh's words in his letter, his reasons for addressing it to me. I cleared my throat. 'Look fella's, I think this is getting a little out of hand. We don't want to be starting anything here that we can't stop.'

'Says another white westerner,' snapped Palvinder.

'Now, hang on just a second. Don't forget I'm an Irishman; our whole national persona is rooted in being at the painful end of bigotry, prejudice and hierarchy! 'As was my usual defence mechanism, I was hamming up the jaunty Irish charm; this was a moment, if ever I'd known one, for disarming levity. 'I mean, this maybe isn't the time to give you a potted history of Ireland, but do you know the shit we lived through at the hands of the English? Now, here's another important thing. I'm not a merchant seaman, with all your conventions, weird superstitions and strange, near religious attachment to rules. I'm a bloody writer of all things...and not a great one of those if my CV is anything to go by. The fact is, guys, that Paresh – whatever state of mind he was in – wrote that letter to me because he knew. He knew that I'd be able to offer a different perspective...' There was an almost tangible silence in the room, and I paused, sucking in air like a goldfish.

'Which is?' asked Arjun.

'You guys live in a world that requires reliance. You pit yourselves everyday against the most ardent powers of nature. The only way you can win, that you can overcome it, is to work together...unflinchingly, unquestioningly, unswervingly. That's why you guys always get so jumpy with the word mutiny; it's the absolute Ying to your Yang. Whether you are trained to think like it or think like it naturally and levitate towards this life, you are programmed to act as the ultimate team. And that 'team' extends to anyone else who happens to be at the mercy of the sea. Look at how you all worked together last night! Look at how you all, without exception, voted to help those poor souls in the life raft, despite the obvious risks. I'm from a very different world. In my world, we live and die by our own decisions. There's no collective safety net: we make our own beds, and we sleep in them. I think that's what Paresh meant. He hasn't done this as a cry for help, or to attract attention. For whatever reason, he...and Li and Banya, felt that this is what they needed to do. I don't think he wants us to chase after them. If, at some point, we follow their intention, then sobeit, but this isn't about a rescue mission. Despite the risks, he wanted to be cut loose. This is his bed...' There was a brief pause, a moment of reflection. 'And I don't think any of this is about who's an officer and who's not, or where in the bloody world you're from. We can't allow ourselves to start thinking like that, or we'll all be doomed. You guys...' I nodded towards the

Southeast Asian side of the room, '...you were closer to them than the rest of us. Maybe in the heat of the moment, you're not able to look at it as objectively.

'I think he's right...,' said Henning. He paused, allowing all eyes to fix on his. He seemed to somehow hold us all in his gaze at once, '...the Irish really do have a massive chip on their shoulder.' It was exactly the right thing to say, at precisely the right time and it shattered the tension like a hammer to glass.

We dispersed to do our various chores, but the seeds of discourse had been sown. Despite my own reasoning, despite my own words, I couldn't help returning to Palvinder's assertion; in all of this, we did only have the Captain's word to rely on. There was no other evidence to support or disprove his version of events.

17

Ripples of doubt

It was a week later. On the surface, life had continued as before – the same routines, the same endless list of jobs, the same food, the same sense of a world standing still, but beneath the veneer there were new layers of tension. There had been no subsequent 'them and us' talk – not communally or in my earshot at least – and seemingly no more discussion concerning the rights and wrongs of the Captain's decision. The crew continued to function as a unit, to express civility towards each other in the running down of each day's clock, but this civility seemed somehow more brittle; like old cut flowers in a vase, you sensed that the slightest jolt might induce an irreversible cascade of papery petals: something that had been vibrant and colourful reduced to an ugly skeletal shadow.

I found myself on painting duty with Dmitriy. This time, we were tasked with painting the deck railings that ran the length of the ship. We'd managed to find enough tins of the same colour for us to work in tandem, but in doing so we'd had to compromise on a bubble-gum pink which somehow gave the balustrades a semblance of inside-out flesh. I hadn't spent much time with Dmitriy since the storm, and I was keen to explore his thoughts, but it was he who first broached the subject.

'So, do you still think Captain made right call?'

'You mean with Paresh and the others?'

'No, on decision to paint railings pink. Yes, of course!'

'I don't know, I can see both sides. It's the Captain's job to make difficult decisions, and he has to do what is right for his crew as a whole.'

'You think that was what he was doing?'

'Yes, at least that's how he rationalised it. The logistics of a rescue were too...variable. He couldn't justify the increased risk to the remaining crew, or the use of fuel.'

'What risks were those do you think?'

'Well, I don't know. Launching the inflatable maybe – getting to and from the life raft if we found it?'

'All risks he was prepared to take when we found other life raft...and this time we know that those inside don't have disease.' Dmitriy's disregard for determiners was as prolific as ever.

'Okay, so maybe he was more worried about the fuel.'

'Perhaps....' Dmitriy left the word hanging, like a maggot on a line.

'What do you think then?' I took the bait.

'The Captain is scared. Here we are, safe out at sea and he is scared of making a decision that changes that. Or maybe he's scared of something else.'

'Like what?'

'The unknown. He likes what he can control. Going to

Ascension, to Saint Helena, to anywhere else but here means sailing into unknown where he cannot guarantee our safety, our lives.'

'Not unreasonable. If that is the case, I can empathise.'

'Yes, but it is not a decision he can put off indefinitely; our fuel dictates that. In which case, why not make that decision when it may also have meant being able to save three members of crew?'

'So, you think the Captain made the wrong decision?'

'All I say is that I would have made different one.'

'You should have shared that view with Arjun, it may have taken the wind out of his sails about the decision being racially motivated.'

'Arjun has point. The shipping industry *is* racist, there is no doubt about it. Europeans sometimes get paid twice as much as crew from the East for doing same job. We are employed by the shipping companies and are supported by unions: they are not. They are recruited by third-party agencies who offer them practically no rights. We know it, they know it. There *is* a class system onboard ship, and it permeates everything, it always has. You heard conversation, it was the white, European officers who were supporting Captain's decision.' Dmitriy's brush work was becoming more violent as he spoke, and I found my shoes spattered with bright pink paint. He stopped mid-stroke and stared at my feet with an intensity that I found somewhat unnerving. 'Sorry!' he said finally.

'No problem, I'll just put in an Amazon order, get some new ones. They were shit anyway.'

'No, I am sorry for getting angry.'

'Not anger, Dmitriy, passion. There's nothing wrong with a bit of passion.' He continued to stare at my feet.

'I liked them you know, Paresh, Li and Banya. They were good men. Whatever their motives, we shouldn't have just cut them adrift.'

'Look, you're talking as if they are one hundred percent dead. They had a chance of making it. They might get picked up by another ship, like us.' Dmitriy just shook his head.

'Maybe,' he said whimsically. We both looked out to sea, across the flat expanse of ocean towards the distant horizon. It was as featureless as ever. High cirrus clouds peppered the duck-egg blue sky like daubs of white paint. I thought back to the times when the skies would be criss-crossed with streaks of white as jets etched their trajectories into the troposphere. It was only now that I realised how desensitized I'd been to such miracles, how blinded I was by the banality of the extraordinary. The sea, now, was an impenetrable blueish grey, the gentle undulating waves yielding the occasional pearly-white breaker that briefly threatened to become something more substantial before dissipating into a frothy glaze. Despite all this time as its hostage, I still found the ocean endlessly mesmerising. I wondered if Dmitriy felt the same. After a few minutes of comfortable silence, I raised the subject that had continued to haunt my own thoughts.

'Do you believe the Captain, about Paresh and his communications with Ascension?'

'Henning told me that he'd been there in the comms room when the Captain had been trying to find them. He'd heard nothing but static also. Not just the once, either.'

'And you believe Henning?'

'Do you?' Dmitriy knew that I had spent a lot of time with Henning in the hydroponics farm, and as such I should know him as well, if not better, than anyone else. It was as good as an answer. 'Actually, the thing that confuses me is why Paresh took time to write you letter, but didn't give any details...he didn't tell you frequency of channel, or any examples of the communications? Why not leave you his journal, or at least some pages?'

'I've asked myself the same questions,' I admitted. 'Could he really have been deluded enough to imagine the whole thing, and if he did, how on earth did he convince Li and Banya? I wouldn't have jumped ship unless I'd had concrete proof... certainly more than some scribbled entries in a journal. Which brings me right back to the Captain's version. Henning was never there when he and Paresh were together.'

'Have you spoken to Henning about this?'

'Yeah, he confirmed that he'd been with the Captain every day during the period that he says he was trying to verify Paresh's claims. They used the same radio as they always did. He said that, in retrospect, the Captain seemed more agitated than normal, as if he had something on his mind. He didn't tell Henning anything at the time: about Paresh or the alleged contact with Ascension.'

'What does that tell you?' prompted Dmitriy. I thought for a second. I'd been trying to order my own thoughts for days, but this was the first time I'd verbalised them.

'As you say, I've no reason to distrust Henning. I know he's Danish as well, but I don't think he'd lie for the Captain just to satisfy a shared heritage; he's far too pragmatic for that...which just leads me back to the same question. Do I believe Paresh's version of events, or the Captain's? Henning was never witness to Paresh using his phone to make contact, he only ever saw the Captain using the usual equipment. The Captain could have deliberately avoided the frequencies in front of Henning or been safe in the knowledge that he knew the ship's comms wouldn't pick up whatever Paresh was hearing on his phone.'

'Or...there was nothing to hear, and Paresh had gone cuckoo.' Dmitriy helpfully illustrated his point by tapping his temple with his index finger and going cross-eyed.' 'Look, fact is you are never going to know for sure. The only two people who know truth are Captain and Paresh, and Paresh is somewhere out there in small life raft.' He prodded his paintbrush in the direction of the distant horizon. Another large globule of paint dripped onto the toe of my shoe. 'Sorry,' he said, apologetically.

'Then maybe someone needs to confront the Captain, put him under some pressure. I know you lot can't...or won't because of your weird conventions and sense of hierarchy that can't be questioned, but I can!'

'Great, then go for it, big man! I'm sure he'll...what is it you say...spill beans if you ask him nicely.' I fully understood Dmitriy's cynicism, but I knew that I would be unable to move on unless I at least did something to try to alleviate my nagging doubts. As this realisation settled, so did another. It was true, I wasn't a member of the Captain's crew, I wasn't bound by the same etiquette or training, but I *was* just that little bit scared of him. He had an aura of authority like a Victorian headmaster or Mother Superior, and the thought of confrontation produced unwanted stirrings in the pit of my stomach.

18

Blind faith

I knocked on the solid steel door and waited. My palms were surprisingly clammy, and I felt a sense of nervousness that I hadn't experienced since my last job interview. Just as I was about to turn away and give it all up as a lucky escape, the door swung open to reveal the Captain, mid-shave. He was using a cut-throat razor.

'Mr. O'Brien, with what do I owe the pleasure?'

'I'm sorry to disturb you Captain. If this is a bad time...' I attempted to gesture towards his half-finished ablutions with my eyebrows.

'Not at all, this is as good a time as any. Please forgive me though, whilst I finish up.' He beckoned me into his cabin and pointed in the direction of a battered leather couch that ran the length of the hull-side wall. 'Why don't you take a seat, I'll be with you in just a minute.' He stepped across the room and into the bathroom; from my vantage point, and with the door wide open, I was able to watch the smooth movement of his elbow as he guided the razor across his face. I heard the splash of water, and a moment later he re-emerged, a rolled towel wrapped around the back of his neck.

'Coffee?' he asked.

'That would be grand.' We'd been fortunate to find some crates of coffee amongst the cargo, but by no means enough to make it part of our everyday lives. It was rationed, and as such still a luxury. The Captain had one of the old-fashioned percolators sitting on top of a filing cabinet in the corner of the room. The machine itself was held in place with black duct tape, and the glass jug wedged inside it with a thick rubber band. He opened the top draw and brought out two mugs and poured the dark, steaming liquid into both.

'I'm afraid I have no milk, but I do have sugar if you would like some?' I didn't usually take sugar, but I felt a sudden craving for something sweet.

'Please, that would be grand.' I couldn't help myself. I'd always had a habit of descending into Irish caricature when I was nervous, wheeling out the same twee phrases again and again. I took a deep breath. 'I mean, that would be great, thanks.' As he busied himself, I looked around the cabin. We were currently sat in what was a relatively large reception room. Beyond us, was an open hatch that led to his bedroom, and another to the side that he had already shown to be the bathroom. A desk and a solid metal chair sat to our right, behind which were hung the cage-like shelving that we had in all our cabins. These contained a collection of books, mostly about trains. In the top-most shelf sat three solid looking models of steam engines, each fixed to a polished mahogany plinth. 'I like your trains!' I said, stupidly. I cringed inside.

'Thank you. Those ones, up there, are all American engines...

from the time of the great expansion west in the 1880s.'

'You made them yourself?'

'I did. They are a great distraction. I find it very calming.'

'Grand.' I was at it again. There was an awkward silence.

'I doubt you are here to quiz me about my trains, Mr. O'Brien. How may I help you?' As he spoke, he manoeuvred himself around the desk, and sat sanguinely in the chair, facing me directly. His steely blue eyes bore unblinkingly into mine.

'No, you're right. Not trains. I wanted to talk to you about Paresh.' The Captain straightened and pulled the mug of coffee closer, cradling it between his clasped hands. His newly clean-shaven jowl wobbled slightly, and his piercing eyes narrowed.

'I am quite surprised that it has taken you this long...as the recipient of the letter, that is. It must have all been very confusing.'

'Yes, I found the whole incident quite...confusing.'

'And what is it that you would like to discuss Mr. O'Brien?'

'It's gone around and around in my mind, and I still can't fathom how Paresh would have convinced the other two to go with him...not without hearing concrete proof that there was something to go to.' He stared at me for a long time before answering, raising his coffee to his lips and taking a gulp. My eyes flickered momentarily to his prominent Adam's apple, which dipped briefly as he swallowed. I thought of pistons on steam engines.

'So, you must be thinking that they heard something on Paresh's phone, and if they did, so must I...' I was taken aback by the speed at which we'd reached the epicentre of my uneasiness. His eyes continued to bore into mine, and I was forced to look away. '...and if I did listen to Paresh's Mr. Waterman on Ascension Island, then I must be lying to you, and the rest of the crew? And if I am lying, you must be asking yourself *why* I am lying?'

'I guess, in a nutshell, yes!'

'Are you a religious man, Mr. O'Brien?' The question took me by surprise.

'Yes...no...I mean, I was as a child, but not really as an adult... not now.'

'No, nor am I. I've always found religion too shrouded in dogma, and deeply religious people too unquestioning, but I have always found the concept of religion fascinating.' As he spoke, he rose from his chair and made his way back to the filing cabinet, where he poured himself a second coffee. 'Another?' he raised the jug in my direction.

'No thank you, I'm fine.' This time, he walked back over to the couch and sat down heavily, resting the steaming coffee mug on the arm. Subconsciously, I shrank a little further into my side of the seat.

'How can perfectly normal, rational people...many of whom are highly successful in other walks of life...' he continued, '...politicians, judges, scientists even, just believe in something that is so irrational, so unprovable?'

'Faith?' I proffered.

'Indeed, faith. I can understand it, back in the past when religion was used to fill gaps in knowledge, but in our modern era? In our age of medicine, space exploration and genetic engineering? How can there still be room for blind faith?'

'You're asking the wrong man, my faith bubble burst years ago.'

'I guess it must be that there are always unanswerable questions,' he continued. 'We know, for instance, exactly what happens to the body in death; the degeneration of cells, the decay of fats, the breaking down of proteins, but we still can't be one hundred percent sure what happens to our sentience, our ego. We can't quite believe that it just evaporates into the rest of the organic puddle. Nobody can prove or disprove the existence of a soul or speculate definitively on what happens to it after our biological demise. Neither can we prove or disprove the existence of Gods. For some, faith is the blind eye we trade for a sense of comfort, an antidote to despair.' He took another swig of his coffee, fixing me with his steely gaze. I was a little bemused as to how we'd lurched so quickly from steam trains to the fundamentals of theology, and how any of this in any way answered my question. 'In some circumstances, where the unanswerable cannot be answered, or the unprovable cannot be proved, we must rely on faith, however illogical and unsatisfying it may be.' The penny dropped.

'So, you are saying that we should have faith...faith that you are telling us the truth. That's how you've answered my question?'

'Mr. O'Brien...Donal...I can't prove to you that I didn't hear the communications from Ascension on Paresh's device, because we no longer have it. I cannot provide evidence that his Mr. Waterman doesn't exist, as much as I can't disprove that Li and Banya didn't hear him. I could show you that my radio picks up nothing but static, but you could argue that I have withheld the true frequency from you. I could let you spend a week doing nothing else but meticulously searching the airwaves for Mr. Waterman, but if you were to find something, I would say that you had succeeded where I had failed. If you failed, you could say that my radio was useless, but that perhaps Paresh's device was not. Do you see, the only option available to us is faith. The alternative is to live with constant suspicion, with anger and despair. That is no way to exist, not in a community as small as our own.'

'You're asking me...us...to just close off part of our minds. To never question.'

'No, Mr. O'Brien. I would be very disappointed if you were to *never* question, especially in your line of work. What I'm asking you to do is not question the unanswerable.'

'And your decision to stay here, out at sea rather than head for land, is that unanswerable? The crew don't understand it, they are restless.'

'Firstly, we don't talk of 'restless crews' out at sea Mr. O'Brien, especially to the captains of those crews: it has certain connotations. Secondly, it is indeed my decision to continue to avoid contact with what was once civilisation. We just don't know enough at this point to allow us to change this approach. I have yet to make any meaningful contact with anyone beyond this ship to make me feel that we have another safe option. The only contact we have had is with those poor souls in the life raft and that has strengthened my resolve to stay put until we either have another concrete option, or we no longer have a choice. Believe me, I would have been the happiest man on this ship if Paresh had been able to prove to me conclusively that Ascension was a credible, viable option. Alas, he could not.' He stood again, this time placing the coffee mug on the desk, before turning to face me. He perched on the edge, folding his arms. It felt like he considered the conversation to be at an end, or at least that it was my turn to respond, but I could see his point, and the futility of arguing. If I were to plough on with a critique of our current strategy of floating in the Doldrums, then I risked sounding churlish at best, and insubordinate at worst. He'd heard all the arguments before; what could I add?

'The radio...,' I said, finally.

'What about it, Mr. O'Brien?'

'Your offer of having it for a week.'

'It wasn't an offer as such, more of an adjunct to my reasoning.'

'Yes, but what would be the harm in letting me, and the rest of the crew, use it? We could set up a rota, so it could be manned 24/7; we might find something useful. If we do, then as you say, we would have been lucky. If we don't, then...well...' I didn't feel the need to finish the sentence. His brows furrowed as he considered my request.

'I fear it will raise hopes, only for them to be dashed.'

'Perhaps, but the men need hope now, even if it is just a short window, and if we draw a blank...'

'*When* you draw a blank!'

'Okay, when we draw a blank, they will better understand why we need to stay here, out at sea.' He stood again, this time walking to his bedroom. He disappeared for a short moment, before reappearing clad in a regulation blue shirt, the shipping company logo emblazed on the breast pocket. He slowly did up the buttons, apparently lost in thought.

'I see no harm in it,' he said eventually. 'I will ask Henning to set the radio up in one of the rooms near the mess; I want it to be as accessible and public as possible. I'll create a rota and include it in my morning briefings. Two men at any one time, so there is always someone to verify anything that is heard. I want you to do the lion's share. Let's say it is your project, Mr. O'Brien.'

'Thank you,' I said. 'It will be a welcome distraction.'

'Indeed, but the problem with distractions is that they tend to be short-lived.' I sensed that it was time to leave. I stood and made my way to the door. 'Mr. O'Brien...!' I turned to face the Captain again. 'Thank you for coming to see me. I appreciate your candour. Thank you also for pointing out the restlessness amongst the crew. Sometimes, as captain, it is difficult to see the wood for the trees.' It's funny sometimes how one's mind works. I felt an inexplicable lump in my throat as I turned the door handle and stepped into the corridor. I couldn't help thinking that I hadn't seen a tree for nearly a year-and-a-half.

19

Waterman

I began to hear static in my sleep. It followed me from the radio room, hissing in my ear like a demonic snake. It sat with me whilst I ate; it walked with me on deck, competing with the crash of waves and the wail of seagulls; it filled the darkness of my cabin late at night.

The Captain was true to his word. He and Henning requisitioned one of the storage rooms close to the main mess, cleared it out and set it up as a radio room. It was open to anyone who wished to enter, at any time of day or night regardless of whether they were scheduled to be on radio duty or not. The Captain courted transparency, warming to the idea that this was a route to at least a partial vindication of his actions. Between us we manned the radio 24/7 for a full seven days. Each member of the crew, barring the Captain, did a rotated four-hour shift with either myself or Palvinder. I chose him deliberately to co-lead the effort because he was both non-European and relatively low ranking; it was essential to ensure that this exercise didn't become tarnished with accusations of racism or elitism.

We methodically scrawled through the frequencies, back and forth, riding the waves of static that peaked and troughed in volume and intensity. It was as if there was *something* there, but it was hiding on the other side of an impenetrable wall. Sometimes, after hour upon hour of the same crackling monotone, I could have sworn that I'd heard voices. Each time, my companion, whoever it was, would confirm that they had heard nothing; it was evident that we were incapable of suffering concurrent delusions. Our own senses tricked us, our hopes driving us to hear phantoms that whispered to us from another world. I began to understand how Paresh might have succumbed to such susurrated sirens, how his imagination might have filled in the gaps. But what of the other two? How could he have convinced them?

There had been a sense of hope at the beginning; that we were taking our destiny back into our own hands. However, from relatively early on I had felt that this had been tempered by a degree of cynicism from most of the crew. This had been unspoken; nuanced in silences and sighs, raised eyebrows and barely vailed indifference. Palvinder was the only member of the Asian crew who had shown any great enthusiasm, and I wasn't sure if this was because I had offered him an elevated role, or perhaps why I had subliminally offered it to him in the first place; I couldn't determine the chicken or egg. Ton, Dmitriy, Rieko and Jerzy had all thrown themselves into it with gusto, at least initially: the only 'westerner' who openly questioned the point of the whole exercise was Polina, but this was because her preference had always been to stay out at sea. She had said that she had joined the merchant navy to avoid land, and all that came with it, so why would she want to seek it out now. We assumed that, by ‘land’ she meant whatever skeletons lay in her closet; a closet that she kept tightly shut much to our collective frustration. Years of late-night speculation had Polina down as anything from an ex-gangster’s moll on the run from the mob, to a serial killer on the run from the law. She always remained tight-lipped. Whatever it was, she had deliberately chosen a life of relative reclusion, in an industry almost entirely dominated by men.

It wasn’t until a late-night shift at the end of the fifth day that I discovered the true feelings of the Asian contingent. It was three in the morning, and I was sharing a shift with Angelo. He had been particularly disengaged throughout, peppering me with questions about my previous relationships in between overly graphic descriptions of the sexual proclivities of his three wives delivered in his characteristic pidgin English. Some of these he had kindly illustrated on the table with a ball-point pen. Eventually, I had had enough.

‘Angelo, we really do need to try and concentrate on the job in hand!’ He stopped, mid-pen-stroke, leaving me guessing as to what the hell he was drawing. It could have been a foot, a face or a genital; it was impossible to tell. He looked at me quizzically.

‘How long you been doing this now, Irish boy?’

‘You know how long, it’s our fifth day,’

‘No, how many hours *you* done? In total?’

‘I don’t know, maybe fourteen hours a day...so, what, seventy hours!’ Angelo snorted, a gesture so unmistakably dripping with disdain that it demolished all language barriers. ‘What was that for?’ I said, I was trying to keep it light-hearted, but I couldn’t help a hint of anger creeping into my tone.

'Why you waste your time?'

'What do you mean?'

'The radio is broken. The Captain, he make sure. Why else he let us use it after all this time?'

I thought for a moment. 'Is this what you've always thought, right from when we started?'

'For sure!'

'And is this what you all think?' He nodded; a smirk stretched across his face.

'Of course.'

'Then why did you agree to be part of the rota?'

'What choice we have? It keeps you white boys happy.' He seemed to lose interest in the conversation and went back to his drawing. I felt crushed. Not only had I heard nothing of substance in seventy hours of frequency surfing, but my hopes of creating some kind of solidarity around the Captain had been sunk before we had even started. Half of the crew were as, if not more distrustful of him than before. I had to blink away my disappointment. I found myself watching Angelo's sketch take form. It was then that I noticed his pen for the first time...not that it hadn't been in plain sight for the last two hours, but now I really took it in. It was a nice pen; the barrel was a sort of mottled brown and black tortoiseshell, the nib, clip and trim all gold. It looked well balanced, expensive. Oddly, it sparked a memory.

'Nice pen, Angelo,' I said. 'Where did you get it?'

'It was Paresh's. He give it to me day before he go.' He stopped drawing and passed it to me, finial first. I took it, balancing it between my thumb and index finger. I was right, it had an exquisite feel, the feel you only get from luxury brands. I brought it closer to my face so that I could examine it more closely in the dim light of the radio room. It had the maker's name engraved around the golden centre-band. In a clear classic font, it said: Waterman.

20

Saboteur

The Captain took full advantage of my discovery, placing me centre-stage at the next morning's crew meeting. My disclosure was met by a dumbfounded silence as everyone weighed up the probability that Paresh's contact on Ascension Island just happened to share the name engraved on the pen he used to record his conversations. With a politician-like verve, the Captain gave it just enough time for people to begin to come to their own conclusions before launching into a monologue. He explained that this, along with our failure to find anything on our radio vigil, was proof that Paresh had been in the grips of a psychotic, delusional episode. We still knew nothing of the state of civilisation on land, Ascension or otherwise, and that with our recent brush with the horror of the disease, he still believed that our current course of action was the correct one. We would stay put, protected by the ocean, until something material changed – either irrefutable contact with the outside world, or a lack of fuel or supplies. Buoyed by the weight of evidence behind him, he wasn't in the mood for discussion. After communicating the day's rota, he left.

No one seemed eager to move as they absorbed this new bombshell.

'Shit! said Jerzy. 'I guess that proves it. Paresh really had lost it.'

'And you had seen the same pen on Paresh's desk, by his logbook?' asked Arjun, directing the question at me.

'Yes. I remembered as soon as Angelo showed it to me. It was so distinctive.'

'Maybe he was using the name Waterman as a code...a pseudonym for his real contact?' suggested Tanmay.

'Why would he do that? Who would he be protecting his identity from?' retorted Rieko. 'Look, I think we are just going to have to accept it. There's no point in us clutching at straws trying to come up with some spurious explanation. The facts are that we spent a whole week trying to make contact with Ascension and came up with nothing. Paresh's supposed contact shares the name of his pen; subliminally, this must have filtered through to his subconscious. We still haven't made any contact with the outside world; we don't know what's out there. As such, I don't think there is any other option but to stay put. To keep ourselves safe.'

'But maybe we aren't hearing anything on the radio because of our position? Maybe we're in a black spot?' said Crisanto.

'Or maybe the radio just doesn't work, in which case we'll never hear anything,' added Tanmay.

'Gentlemen,' said Henning, making one of his rare interjections. 'I will talk to the Captain about us shifting position, to see if that affects the operation of the radio, but ultimately we just have to get on with it. We need to work together again.

To support each other. My God, we've seen what can happen if you become isolated, insular, paranoid. We've already lost three members of our crew. We can't let this be a downward slope, we only have each other.'

The room emptied, there was nothing else to add.

#

The days trickled into the next week. Henning's words seem to have resonated with the crew, and life had returned to a semblance of equilibrium. I worked with everyone at some point or another, and no one spoke of Paresh, or indulged in speculative theorizing. We were living in the present, turning our backs on the past, and shielding our eyes from the future. Perversely, this collective resignation lifted the cloud of melancholy that had hung like a shroud over the ship for the past month. There was more laughter, more lightness of spirit. The tensions, especially those between the 'western' and 'eastern' contingents of the crew, seemed to dissipate. Then, one morning, it all changed again.

As I did every morning before the daily briefing, I had swung by Henning's cabin before making our way to what we had glibly christened 'Sea View Farm' – otherwise known as the hydroponics room. Each morning, we spent an hour and a half harvesting, tending to the growing crop and planting new seedlings before dropping off the produce at the kitchens in time for breakfast. It was a hugely cathartic exercise, and despite the need to get up at the crack of dawn, it had always put me in a good place before the start of the day. The radio project had taken me away from this routine, and I had sorely missed it.

As we approached the bay along the narrow corridor, we both sensed that something was amiss at precisely the same moment. The door, which we always kept closed to keep the environment as thematically regulated as possible, was open. We slowed, glancing at each other.

'Did you forget to close the door yesterday?' asked Henning, accusingly.

'No, I don't think so. Did you?' He left the question unanswered. Nobody else usually entered the room: it was our domain.

'Maybe someone from the kitchen came down for something,' he speculated, as we quickened our pace, reaching the open door at the same time. Inside, was carnage. Four of the towers, with the most mature plants, had been virtually stripped bare. A carpet of wilted, crushed leaves was strewn across the deck. There was a strong smell of kerosene permeating the room, which must have been poured on the floor to ensure nothing remained edible. As we moved down the rows, we could see more and more damage. The tomato plants had been overturned; the fruit crushed to a pulp. Saplings had been ripped from their casements, cases of seeds emptied on the floor, scattered and mixed into an assorted jumble.

'I think there are some seed boxes missing,' I said, the words sticking in my throat.

'How many?'

'I don't know, three or four maybe. Enough to feed us for months, that's for sure.'

'As it is, we're going to have to ration what we have in the short term. There's hardly anything left. Even the mid-growth plants have been severely damaged.' Henning was almost in tears.

'Who'd do this?' I asked rhetorically. 'Who'd be so stupid as to disrupt our own food supply?'

'I don't know. But it's a finite list of suspects.' He was right. I knew that I hadn't done it. I couldn't imagine that Henning, with the tenderness he demonstrated towards his plants, could ever indulge in such wanton vandalism. Putting the food supply in jeopardy would go against the Captain's every engrained instinct. That left just sixteen people.

'Do you remember what the Captain said at the meeting where you told everyone about the pen?'

'He said lots of things.'

'He said that we would stay put, until we either made contact, or ran out of fuel or supplies.'

It was clear that somebody had decided to force the issue and take our future into their own hands.

#

The Captain sounded the alarm for an emergency meeting. When he shared the news of the sabotage, the crew looked shocked, then angry. He asked if anyone had seen anything. No one had. Rieko and Alon, who had both been on night watch, were quizzed. Alon claimed to have been in the engine room all night, which Rieko confirmed as best he could. He had, himself, patrolled the length and breadth of the ship, passing the hydroponics room twice; once at approximately 02:00 and again at 04:00. On both occasions, the door had been shut. This pointed to the destruction taking place somewhere between 04:00 and 06:15, when Henning and I arrived. Without any clues or evidence, we had hit a dead end.

The Captain spoke calmly and authoritatively. He reiterated

his determination to keep his crew safe and from harm's way, and that he would not be swayed from this mission by any act of sabotage. We would remain in the Doldrums as planned. The only thing the saboteur had achieved, he said, was to make his fellow crew members go hungry. He then went on to pass a new edict that the hydroponics room would be always locked, along with the main provisions store and the rooms housing the desalination pumps. The keys would have to be collected from him and signed in and out. He also decreed that, for the time being, four of us would be on night-watch, working in pairs. He said that this was for our own safety, but we knew that it was to ensure that no one person was left alone at night. We were to keep a close eye on each other.

As he spoke, furtive and mistrustful glances were exchanged around the room as we tried to remember past conversations and thrown away comments – anything to shed light on the possible culprit. Our brief return to comradery and conviviality had been shattered, crushed and pulverised along with our life-sustaining crops. Suspicion spread its long tentacles, reaching out, probing; dragging us down to new, unfathomable depths.

21

Polina

I was back in the hydroponics room with Polina, working through the mess of remaining seeds that we had managed to rescue from the floor. Henning was busy doing something in the engine room, so Polina had volunteered to help. It was a surprisingly ataractic task; sifting through the mass of tiny pods, trying to filter out the tomatoes from the peppers, the lettuce from the rocket. It required optimum concentration, and we mostly worked in silence. Occasionally, coming up for air, we talked. I'd always liked Polina: she was a constant. She always spoke her mind, never sugar-coating her opinions. She called a spade a spade, and I respected that.

'When we find out who did this,' she said, sitting back and rubbing her eyes, 'I am going to break both of their arms.' Polina was a solid, strong, fifty-something year old woman – I had no doubt that she would, and she could.

'When we find out who it was, we'll gladly let you.' She sat, contemplatively, and stared at the small seeds.

'This reminds me of when I was a child. In the early autumn, I used to sit with my grandmother and separate the seeds left from our harvest. We had a smallholding, and she used to grow all sorts of fruits and vegetables. She would always dry a portion of her crop, and we would sit at her kitchen table and organise all of the beans and seeds into little pots, ready for the next year.' I'd never heard Polina talk of her childhood, or her past in general. The journalist in me sensed an opportunity. I ventured a question, knowing this might cause her to clam up, to retract back into her cocoon.

'Where was this Polina? You are Belarusian, right?'

'No. I was born and grew up in the Northeast of Ukraine. I moved across the border to Belarus when I married, to a village called Milashavichy. Back then, the border meant nothing – we were the same people.'

'I never knew you were married!' I saw it flicker across her face, a moment of indecision. Had she said too much? Was it time to re-erect the barriers, or would she continue, and open the flood gates? I don't know what it was that made her decide to finally break her silence, but she did.

'I met him in my final year of college. I was studying Hospitality: he was training to be a teacher. Gregori. He was a sweet man. Different from the rough, sullen farmers back home. He was a Belarusian, from Stolin. We fell in love and shortly after, we married. For a while, we lived in Minsk; I worked in several hotels, moving up the tiers of management. Gregori got a job in a high school, teaching English and History. We were happy, like any young couple trying to make their way in the world. Then I got pregnant, and we decided to move back to Gregori's hometown so that we could get help with childcare from his family. He secured a job in the school he had attended as a child, and a few years after the birth of our daughter, Alina, I got a job as the manager of Stolin's only internationally owned hotel. Over the years, we tried for more children, but it never happened. It didn't matter: we had Alina. She grew up. We suffered those trials and tribulations that all families go through: moving house, trying to make ends meet at the end of each month, overcoming minor illnesses and accidents. We spent most of our time running Alina around to her never-ending list of activities and interests: swimming, dancing, ice-skating. She was really good at ice-skating – she was so graceful. Then she hit thirteen and almost overnight she became more interested in boys, and arguing and black eyeliner. Just like any other teenager. Gregori and I found her infuriating. We would sit in the evenings with a bottle of vodka and ask ourselves what we had done to deserve this.

Then, one day – it was Tuesday the 18th of June 20## at about 10:50 in the morning - it all changed. I was walking through the foyer of the hotel when I noticed a small huddle of people around the TV screen opposite the concierge. It was always tuned in to the rolling news channels. I think it was CNN – one of the American networks. It was a story about a shooting in a school; like the ones that seem to happen every few months in the USA. There were pictures of grey, concrete school buildings, lines of children running, hunched, towards the perimeter fence. There was shaky amateur footage showing the terrified faces of students as they poured out of a set of double doors; the sound of automatic gunfire intermittently drowning out the sound of screaming. Tragic, but I'd seen it all before. I was about to move on, to return to my end-of-month spreadsheets, when the ticker-tape news feed at the bottom of the screen appeared. It took a while to register. Far too long. This wasn't happening in some distant US city, or some Canadian leafy suburb. It was happening in Stolin. It was happening at my husband's school. Alina's school.'

She paused, staring into the middle distance as she rolled a seed between her thumb and forefinger. Her face was a mask, emotionless. I waited patiently for her to continue.

'I went home as quickly as I could. I thought Alina might be there. It was empty and silent. I went to the school. Once they realised that I was a parent, and the wife of a teacher, I was taken into the church that sat opposite the school, along with all the other dispossessed parents. We were the ones who still hadn't heard from our children. There, we were shielded from the media, protected from the journalists who circled like vultures. We were told very little. They said that they didn't want to speculate, not until they had the big picture. At various points in the day, names were called. People were told that their children had been found safe. They were led away, tearful reunions guaranteed. It wasn't until mid-afternoon that the police finally came in to speak to those of us who remained. There were twenty-two families. We were taken away separately, each with an assigned liaison officer. I was told what had happened in a police interview room at Stolin Police Station. I remember looking at the large mirror on the far wall opposite and wondering if it really was two-way – like in the movies.

Maksym Bondarenko was a thirty-two-year-old Ukranian. He was the same age as me, from my own mother country. He was a soldier, who had fought against the Russians in their failed invasion. He'd survived the war, but whilst he was away fighting to protect his family, a Russian missile had gone astray and hit a civilian tower block in his home town of Korosten, northwest of Kiev. His whole family, including his three children, had been wiped out in an instant. At that time, the Belarusian political elite had sided with the Russians. The Belarusian border was closer than the Russian, so Maksym made his way to Stonin to exact his revenge. They said afterwards that he had been treated for severe PTSD, caused by the horrors of frontline war, and the guilt of not being there for his family. The inequity of his survival, and their deaths. I don't know anything about that, but he must have been broken inside...shattered to pieces and hardened by pain to do what he did that day.

At 10:19, he walked into the school reception. CCTV footage showed that he was holding a large duffle-bag over his shoulder. He spoke briefly to the receptionist, a woman called Sveta; a lovely woman who had worked there for over twenty years. I knew her well. She had babysat Alina when she was younger. There was no sign of confrontation. It all looked very civil. Then he coolly placed the bag on the ground, bent down and unzipped it, still in conversation with Sveta. When he stood, he was holding an automatic rifle. She was his first victim.

For the next twenty-three minutes, he methodically made his way around the school, stalking the corridors and forcing his way into classrooms. He indiscriminately shot anyone who got in his way. Twenty-two children dead. Fourteen boys, eight girls. The youngest only eleven years old. He also shot dead four members of staff, all who had been doing their best to protect the children. A further sixteen children and adults were shot and injured. When he had caused enough carnage, and the easy pickings had dried up, he pulled a pistol out of his back pocket and shot himself in the head. I didn't know it at the time, but by 10:42 that morning all my hopes and dreams, the version of the future that Gregori and I had mapped out, went up in smoke with the cordite of Bondarenko's Kalashnikov. It's funny...well, not funny, but strange. I know, looking back, that at that *precise* moment in time I was thinking about a missing crate of toilet tissue that had disappeared from the hotel's inventory. Something so insignificant, so banal.'

She reached up to wipe away a single tear that had been slowly following gravity along the heavy lines that sat beneath her eyes. Now she was welling up, and her face looked flushed. I sensed that this was a release of years, if not decades, of repressed emotions.

'So that was it. I couldn't stay there anymore. Not Stolin, not anywhere. My family were victims, ultimately, of politics, of ego, of ethnic tensions, of history. I had to get away from all that. So, after the funerals, I left. I travelled to the port of Gdańsk, where I rented a small room, and I applied for every stewarding job that came up; I reasoned that my background in the hospitality industry was not that far removed. At the time, there was a big push to improve the gender balance in shipping, so I got a job quickly. I've never looked back. I've never wanted to look back. I live in the present, that's all there is, especially now.'

'And that's why you want to stay here, on the *Thalassa*?'

'Yes, partly. I ask myself, what can be left out there? Just more hatred, more chaos, more cruelty. No, I know a good thing when I see it. This, what we have here on this ship is a good thing. Simple. Pure.' I reached across the table and placed my hand on hers.

'I won't tell anyone. Your secret is safe.'

'Thank you,' she said. 'I know.' She wiped her eyes with the back of her sleeve, then flicked her long greying hair away from her face, and over her shoulder. She straightened. 'Let's get this done. We have food to grow.'

That was it. Like the brief glimpse of a shooting star or the abrupt, bright flash of burning magnesium, the window into Polina's past was closed. Back to the present, and the mending of our current wounds.

22

Stalagmite

Trust. I'd never really thought about it before, not deeply. Is it an ostensibly black and white concept; you either have it, or you don't? Is it possible to trust somebody a little? Can you *mostly* trust someone? Or does it depend on the circumstances in which you find yourself placing your trust? Can you trust someone to do one thing, but not another? If trust is broken, is it irreversible...unmendable?

What I'd learnt over my sixteen months aboard a merchant ship – both before and after the bombs and pestilence – was that trust was as essential to successful seamanship as oil was to an engine: without it, the moving parts grind to a screeching halt. With such small teams of people sailing such Levithan vessels, each individual has to be able to trust one-another not just to perform their own job properly, but potentially with each other's lives. Part of the reason that the chain of command existed, and continued to exist even when the corporate bodies who created them no longer did, was trust.

Each person within that chain had a function to perform, and they were trusted by others to do it. An oiler was trusted to maintain the engines. The galley staff were trusted to cook wholesome food. The Captain was trusted to make the right decisions, to protect the ship and its cargo from danger and, ultimately, to put the safety and interests of the crew above all else.

Despite everything that had happened with Paresh, and perhaps because of more recent events, the Captain still seemed to have the trust of his crew; somehow, he'd weathered the storm. Or so we had thought, until the attack on the ship's fresh food supplies. This showed that one or more of us *had* lost trust in the Captain, to such an extent as to try to force his hand and, in so doing, put the whole crew at risk. But it was worse than that; to lose faith in a leader is one thing, to lose trust in all those around you is infinitely more dangerous. As none of us knew the culprit, we had to be suspicious of everyone. Distrust spread like a mould, the spores infiltrating every conversation, every facial expression, every hand gesture. It built tension. Now you questioned everyone's actions...and inactions. You looked for clues, past or present, of their trustworthiness. Everyone was on perpetual trial, and everyone knew it. You began to overthink what you said and did, choosing words more carefully, worrying about lapses in concentration which might herald incriminating mis-speak. Interactions became exhausting, so you tried to limit them. Chores were performed wordlessly, conversations shrunken to monosyllables. In downtime, you chose to spend time and space with those that you thought you trusted more, and who you second-guessed trusted you. The crew became more factional than ever before, but the fraction lines remained steeped in the past. When you are desperate to find threads of trust, it is natural to seek out those who share commonality of origin, of language, of socio-economic background. Thus, the disintegration of our little State of *Thalassa.*

Such a simple act. Pushing over a few growing towers, the scattering of seeds, the crushing underfoot of leaves and fruit, the sprinkling of kerosene. It couldn't have taken long, minutes perhaps. I wondered if the perpetrator had had any wider understanding of the destruction that they would cause. Not to the stoma and mesophyll, the chloroplasts and epidermis, but to the fabric of our community, to our chances of survival together.

I think the Captain realised the danger. He called more meetings. He spoke at length of the importance of coming together, despite the traitor in our midst. He offered an amnesty to the culprit, to anyone with information. He said that it was better to come forward, for us to be able to *move* forward. He increased the number and frequency of container forages (there were still nearly five hundred that we hadn't searched) not only because we needed to find a wider assortment of food, but because he knew it was everyone's favourite task. Good for morale. He hoped, I guess, that any great discoveries might again foster a sense of camaraderie, that the sense of achievement might help re-build bridges. Yet, he was cautious with his pairings – unwittingly demonstrating his own hierarchy of trust. Undoing the good he was trying to do.

Life limped on. We went through the motions; we did what had to be done. I thought that with time, and no further acts of treachery, we might sail out of our ship-bound doldrums unscathed. That we might be able to forget the act of sabotage, to pass it off as a moment of madness. With the passage of time, I hoped that trust might be regrown, like a stalagmite, one drip at a time.

23

Warm coffee

I'd slept badly, even by my own low standards. I'd had my usual dream: waking up in bed; Beth; the searing light at the window; the maelstrom of wind, then nothing, as if a TV screen has been switched off. But tonight, it blinked back on. A new scene. The interior of a church, the light leaking through the stained-glass windows dimmed by dark Irish skies. I look down at my hands; the hands of a ten-year-old child. I sense the congregation behind me, but I stare straight ahead to the wooden casket that sits on a table below the altar. The hinged lid is wide open, and I see verdant green fabric bubbling up from within, threatening to overflow across the lip. I feel my mother's hand in mine, but I can't look at her; I must look at the casket. Dust particles, the skin of the living and the dead, dance sombrely through the weak sun beams, reflecting the grey light. I step forward, pulled by the hand that I cannot see. I close my eyes tight, seeking to shut out the vision that I know is coming. I'm guided to the casket, my hand placed on the edge of the box. Now I feel the soft material, the silky-smooth velvet juxtaposed against the slick varnished wood, as cold as ice, life and death. If I open my eyes, I know what I will see. My father. Waxen skin. Sunday best. A look of peace, contentment even, as if he is pleased that it is all over, the trauma of living. I know if I open my eyes, I will experience a wave of rage; how dare he look so becalmed, so at ease with his release? Why isn't his face scarred with the anguish I feel? I stand there a moment longer, in my own darkness, protected, but I know it can't last for ever. I open them, but it isn't the benevolent mask of my father that greets me, but the face of the Captain. His eyes are wide open, but unseeing, blue like polar ice, iridescent. His face is expressionless, like he is a shell of himself, an empty vessel. He wears his regulation company jacket, his sky-blue shirt with the embroidered logo. His hands are crossed over his chest as if in silent prayer. I stare down at his still form, watch in terror as his face begins to turn. Water dribbles from the side of his mouth, until it becomes a steady torrent, a Biblical flood. The casket is filling. His vacant, unblinking eyes meet mine.

I wake, breathless.

#

We were assembled in the mess, awaiting the morning briefing. There was already an undercurrent of murmured conversation, mutterings that come with a deviation from the norm. Usually...no, not usually, *always*...the Captain was first to the meeting. He was in the room when the first of the rest-of-us arrived. This morning, he was not. The minutes ticked by. He still didn't appear. Eventually, Ton cleared his throat.

'Has anyone seen the Captain this morning?'

Everyone looked at each other. They shook their heads. There were negative affirmations. No one had seen him, but we were all able to see the Captain's morning routine in our minds-eye. He rises early, if he is not on the night shift, and walks the entirety of the upper deck, starting with the bridge to check-in with those on duty. He doesn't rush. It can take him from anything from fifteen to thirty minutes to complete his rounds. He then pokes his head into the galley to wish Jerzy, and whoever else is on breakfast duty, a good morning. There he collects a mug of black tea, before making his way to the mess.

'Dmitriy, Tanmay – you were on the bridge last night. Did he not stop by this morning?'

'No,' says Dmitriy, 'There was no sign of him. We thought maybe something else had come up.'

'And you didn't think to mention it, to me?'

'We came straight here; I am mentioning it now.' Dmitriy always took the offensive when he was on the back foot.

'What about you Jerzy, did he come by the kitchens?'

'No. I thought it strange. I bought his cup of tea with me, I thought he'd be here.'

'Okay. Donal, come with me. We'll go to his cabin. Maybe he's ill or something. The rest of you, stay here until we get back.'

We left the hubris of the mess behind and made our way down to the living quarters. When we reached it, his cabin door was closed. Ton hesitated, then rapped on it three times with the back of his knuckles. If there was anyone inside, they would have heard. We waited. There was no movement, no sound from within. Ton gave me one last look, puts his hand on the handle, and pushed. Despite the sabotage in the hydroponics room, and our restricted entry to certain other rooms, we still hadn't started to lock our own cabins. The door swung inwards. Ton checked himself, keeping it only half open.

'Captain, are you there?' His question was met by silence. He opened the door fully, and we stepped inside. The room was as meticulously tidy as the last time I visited. The only thing that appeared out of place was a half-drunk mug of coffee on the desk. I walked over to it and pick it up, as Ton poked his head first into the bathroom and then the bedroom. 'No sign of him. His bed is made. I'm assuming he slept in it.'

'This coffee is still warm. He must have had it this morning,' I said.

'Then where the hell is he? He can't have just disappeared.' As soon as the words left Ton's lips, we both knew their absurdity. Of course you could. On the one hand, we were on a huge container ship; if you slipped or fell down some steps or a ladder, you might lay undiscovered for hours. On the other, the even more stark reality that we were also on a comparatively tiny metal box floating in a vast ocean. Fall off the box and.... a cold shudder passed through me as I remembered my dream.

'Where does he keep his coat? He always wears it when he does his morning rounds,' asked Ton, breaking my own train of thought. 'If it's gone, it at least shows us that he followed his normal routine.'

'In the cupboard I guess, on the back of the door?' We both searched, but it was nowhere to be seen.

'Okay,' said Ton, as much to himself as to me. 'This is what we're going to do. We'll section off the ship, put everyone in groups and search it. One of us with one or more of them.'

'What do you mean?' I asked, 'Us and them?'

'One of us...officers, European...'

'And one of them...non-European! Are you sure we should be making those distinctions now?'

'Look, I don't trust them. Even before the hydroponics room was ransacked. Now the Captain's gone. I just want to keep an eye on them, that's all.'

'It won't go unnoticed.'

Ton shrugged his response. As First Officer, he was next in command after the Captain, but I couldn't help feeling a sense of dread at the pit of my stomach. This would be a statement, a reinforcement of a long-established hierarchy that even in the old, real world had fostered simmering prejudice and resentment. It had been smouldering already, like the core of a long-extinguished fire, threatening to re-ignite. I feared that Ton's plan, even though born from crisis, might lead to an uncontainable conflagration.

We returned to the mess. I was expecting hysteria, or at least a high degree of turmoil, but to my surprise the atmosphere seemed subdued. Low, dulcet conversations filled the room. Tanmay and Roy were playing cards. I'd forgotten that these were people who dealt with crisis as a matter of course. All eyes turned to us as we entered.

'Right, everyone, he's not in his cabin, but it does look like he left it this morning – we can only assume he was following his normal ritual. We need to search every inch of the ship, whilst also enacting the Person Missing Procedure in the assumption that he might have gone overboard.' Everyone knew what that meant, even me. If you fell overboard, and were fortunate enough to be spotted, you had a tiny chance of being picked up alive. You'd have to survive the 60-metre fall well enough to be able to tread water, without the help of buoyancy aids, for however long it took to be recovered, and hope that hypothermia didn't set in before you were rescued. As it was, we have no idea when and where he might have fallen – it would be like looking for a needle in a cluster of haystacks.

'I guess we are looking at any time between an hour and an hour-fifteen since he's been missing. That means we could have drifted...what...one, two miles,' continued Ton. 'Henning, can you fire up the engines and turn us around. We'll need a Williamson Turn.'

'Of course, but we should do a visual around the perimeter of the ship first. If he's anywhere near the outside of the hull, I don't want to risk sucking him into the propellers,' said Henning.

'Right, good call. Rieko, Tanmay and Alon – you take the starboard side of the ship. Check all the walkways, ladders, containers...everything, but also keep your eyes peeled on the sea. Jerzy, Alon and Crisanto – you do the same on the port side. Donal, you go with Palvinder and Roy and check the bay areas, then the stern...take some binoculars and scan the water in our wake. Polina - can you and Luis search the accommodation areas; that includes the cabins. Henning and Arjun – the engine rooms please; look in every nook and cranny. Dmitriy and I will check the waterline either side of the ship to make sure we are safe to turn...I'll send Dmitriy down to the engine room to let you know, and I'll make my way to the bridge. When you are all done searching the ship, that's the meeting point. If we can't find him onboard, then we are going to need as many pairs of eyes as we can to try and spot him out there.'

Perhaps I was looking too hard, putting meaning into something that didn't deserve any, but as Ton issued his orders and announced the task teams, I couldn't help noticing a look pass between Arjun and Alon. It was after Ton had indicated the final group – with each-and-everyone being 'led' by a European. A realisation, also, that there was not a single all Asian team. It was a look of resentment and, I feared, rebellion.

24

Shipwreck

We found nothing. He had vanished. We executed a Williamson Turn to starboard, enabling us to loop around and follow our previous path. We then did the same to port, to be sure we hadn't left any stone unturned. At different vantage points around the ship, we all stared into the green-grey abyss, scanning the undulating, shifting waves for any anomaly. From the hull waterline to the horizon, and back. Repeat. A dizzying sweep of white horses and breakers that conjured spectral hallucinations. A fleeting glimpse of a waterlogged torso, the sheen of wet hair, the white paucity of exposed flesh. Then gone in a blink. Nothing more than the perpetual shifting of currents, the wind-whipped salty froth of sea water.

By noon, we had completed our figure of eight. If the Captain was in the ocean, that was to be his final resting place. He would have begun his final journey to the depths, drifting further and further from the light, spinning serenely in his suspended state. His eyes open but unseeing. The sea would slowly strip away his modesty, then his water saturated skin, leaving the underlying tissue to the fish, crabs and sea lice that would nibble away at his flesh. Perhaps the cold of the deep water would facilitate adipocere, where body fats transform into a soapy shell that stalls putrefaction and creates waxen images of the dead. Maybe he would lie on the ocean floor, in the black, gathering silt and his own ecosystem: a shipwreck. It would be his final sacrifice to the sea.

Once we had acknowledged the Captain's death overboard, we had to turn to his possible resurrection *onboard.* Was his unconscious body lying in some yet unsearched cavity? Had he, for reason unknown, entered a container and fallen or been crushed? The afternoon was spent searching the unsearched and the already searched. By early evening, we were able to say with some certainly that he was not on the ship. He was gone.

The mood at dinner was sombre, dominated by the now undeniable fact that we had lost another. Nineteen down to eighteen. Attention now turned to the future. Ton cleared his throat:

'Gentlemen...Polina...we have to accept that we have lost the Captain.' I had to battle to suppress a smile, a sudden bubbling up of mirth born from a cauldron of emotions: horror, sadness, exhaustion. The statement seemed so absurd, so comical; as if he was ours to lose, like a wallet or an umbrella. 'Thank you all for your efforts today. I am sorry that we have nothing to show for them.' As one, eyes were cast to the floor. 'As much as it pains me to say it, we must now look forward, to what happens now. As First Officer, company protocol dictates that I take over as captain and command the ship. I feel it is my duty to do so...'

'Aren't we a little *over* 'company protocols', since the company no longer exists?' This from Arjun, who sat on a table with Palvinder and Tanmay. I looked around the room with fresh eyes. There was a divide, whether by design or coincidence; European crew sat on one side, across two tables, the non-European on the other, across three.

'What do you mean?' said Ton.

'I mean, shouldn't we be looking at a different way of making decisions that affect us all? Something more democratic? We don't need to be tied to archaic conventions any more. The corporation, the culture, the colonial history that made you First Officer and Alon an oiler don't exist or matter now, not in this world.'

'So, you're suggesting that we, what, vote for our next leader?'

'No, I'm suggesting that we don't have a leader. I'm saying that we all have an equally weighted say in how we run the ship...*where* we run the ship. We all have a vote on any major decisions.'

'We run ship by committee?' interjected Dmitriy, incredulously. 'There is good reason why hierarchy developed in navy. Decisions need to be quick, you can't wait to hear everyone. What do we do in typhoon, sit down and chat about what we do, have a little vote?'

'I don't think that is what Arjun is saying,' said Henning. 'If you will forgive me, Arjun, for perhaps putting words into your mouth, I believe what you are saying is that decisions that affect us as a whole crew – issues about our day-to-day lives, our strategy, our future plans should be put to a vote. The running of the ship must be done according to the skill-set of those on board. We must continue to have trust and faith in each other's abilities. For instance, in the engine room, Arjun will largely listen to and act upon my reasoning, by merit of my more extensive experience.'

Arjun nodded his agreement. 'Yes, that is true to a certain extent, but you and I have a mutual respect. I know that you will listen to me if I have an idea or an opinion. I have known you to change your mind on many occasions because of something I have said. That is a measure of you as a man, Henning. Not everyone is so magnanimous in spirit.'

'Meaning that I'm not!' said Ton, irritation edging into his voice.

'Look,' said Henning, 'Ton is the closest we have to the Captain in respect to his training, his experience and his leadership. I, for one, would trust him to command the rest of us during a storm, to make the right decisions when it came to protecting us and the ship from harm.'

'Protecting some of us,' interjected Angelo.

'Meaning?' said Ton, irritation turning to anger.

'Meaning that you would make the right decisions to protect the interests of some crew members, those with white skin and European accents.'

'What are you talking about? Are you trying to say I'm racist?' Ton stood, resting his hands on the table, enraged. 'How *dare* you suggest that my judgement might be clouded by such things!' I was sitting to Ton's immediate right, and I felt a globule of spittle land on my hand.

'Then why you put all of us with 'European' *minder* this morning?' said Alon. 'Why weren't any of *us* leading the search groups? Where is trust, eh?'

For a second, Ton was lost for words. For the briefest of moments, he shot me an accusatory look, as if my premonition somehow made it my fault. Before he could reply, Jerzy spoke up:

'Before we can mention trust, maybe we have to discuss the elephant in the room.' He paused for effect, courting everyone's full attention.

'Which is?' asked Rieko, on behalf of us all.

'Which is, how exactly did our captain happen to fall overboard? You must all be thinking it, surely? The seas aren't rough, it's like a mill pond out there. People, especially experienced mariners, don't just fall off ships. You all know that, right?' We all looked at each other. Over the duration of the day, we'd all asked ourselves the same question. 'And look, a mere week ago, somebody tries to sabotage our food supply...to force us back to land. The Captain kyboshes that idea. Back to square one. It doesn't take a massive leap of imagination to guess what might happen next.'

'So, someone here's murdered the Captain?' stated Polina matter-of-factly. 'That is quite a progression from destroying some salad leaves!'

'We all know his morning routine,' continued Jerzy, 'we know the exact route he follows, and when. We all know when he'll be alone and out of sight. Any of us could have done it. Hit him from behind, push him overboard...'

'Then, coincidentally, we start having discussions about democratic votes to decide our future strategy,' interrupted Ton, pointing his finger at Arjun. 'You lot have always opposed the Captain's approach, arguing that we should head for land at any given opportunity...and you know full well that you outnumber us. How democratic is that?'

'So, you're accusing me of murder, is that it?' said Arjun, his voice now rising to match Ton's.

'To be fair, Ton,' added Polina, 'you argued alongside Rieko not that long ago that we should head for Ascension. It was probably the strength of your argument that set Paresh off on his obsession.'

'...and what do you mean by that?' said Ton.

'Nothing, nothing at all. Only that we've all opposed the Captain about something. We've all disagreed with his approach at some point. Just because Arjun voiced opposition, doesn't make him a murderer...'

'But *someone's* a murderer,' added Jerzy. 'One of *us* is a murderer!' It was a chilling thought that momentarily silenced the room. Trust, once again, was the secondary victim. Henning cleared his throat:

'It is a sad fact that this might indeed be the case. We may have a murderer in our midst. I must ask the question; beyond finger pointing and conjecture, did anyone witness anything unusual this morning, did anyone see anybody else acting suspiciously? If so, now is the time to say.'

Nobody spoke.

'Then we have a possible crime, with no witnesses. As unlikely as it may seem to us, we must also consider that an accident befell the Captain, until we can prove otherwise. We cannot let this uncertainty tear us apart, we must look forward. I suggest we sleep on it: we are all exhausted, and it has been an emotional day. I will sit with Ton and Arjun now and we will produce a rota for the next few days. We must continue with some semblance of normality. In a few days-time, perhaps we can discuss our next moves.' There was a nod of agreement around the room and a collective sense of relief that someone had taken control. We stood to leave. 'But gentlemen...Polina...,' added Henning, 'please be vigilant. Watch your backs. Keep yourselves safe.'

I thought about Henning's closing words as I made my way along the corridor to my cabin. Rieko was ahead of me, Arjun and Jerzy behind. It was an oxymoron, to watch one's back, but doubly so when you had no idea who to trust. If someone had killed once, would they kill again? Might it depend on what decision, collectively, we made next about our future? In which case, did we now really have any other choice but to set course for the uncertainty of land and what might be left of civilisation?

25

Suspects

The following day was like every other. We met in the morning, we ate, we went through the rota, we departed to do our allotted chores. When we were together, as one, nobody spoke of the previous day's events. Conversation was hollow, functional. Henning had said that we would discuss next steps in a few days' time, so we clung to that reprieve.

In our rota pairings, in our chosen social groups that evening, it was a different matter. There were whispered, conspiratorial conversations; theories of guilt were shared, speculation bubbled and fermented. We'd all spent the previous night playing back through our memories, searching for incriminating words and actions, dissecting our past interactions with our fellow crew members. What did we know of each other's pasts that might provide a precedent for murder? What didn't we know? The rising sun and the dawn of a new day had burnt gaping holes in these theories that, in the darkness of the early hours, had seemed so logical and opaque. Without any real, tangible evidence, all we were left with was guesswork and gut feeling, which left the bitter taste of treachery in our mouths as we whispered our poison.

Ton blamed Arjun.

Arjun blamed Ton.

Jerzy accused Angelo and Crisanto in unison, on the grounds of a conversation he had once overheard in which they had cursed the Captain's intractability.

Tanmay pointed the finger at Jerzy, who he said had acted churlish and reproachful once when the Captain had reprimanded him for being reckless with the food supplies, although he freely admitted that this was months in the past.

Angelo was also convinced it was Ton, who he said had the most to gain from the Captain's demise. His description of Ton as a crazed megalomaniac was a little different from my experience of the man.

Roy thought it was Rieko, who had once squared up to him after a game of poker, accusing him of cheating; he claimed to have seen something in his eyes that day, something malevolent and violent; a sign of what Rieko was capable of.

Rieko accused nobody and kept his council.

Alon thought it was Dmitriy on account of him being Russian.

I still couldn't believe that any of these people with whom I'd lived with cheek to jowl for the best part of sixteen months could stoop to such a thing. Perhaps I was being naïve, but I couldn't see it in any of them.

After dinner that evening, I went to Dmitriy's cabin to play cards. Polina joined us. Unlike me, Polina was unequivocal in her view that each-and-every one of us was capable of murder; with my own insight into her history, I could quite understand why. Dmitriy couldn't.

'Why is your heart so dark?' he asked her. 'To take another's life, you have to have screw loose. Do you think *I* could do it?

'For sure, if the circumstances were right. Would you not defend yourself, your family?'

Dmitriy thought about it for a second, before placing down a card. 'Yes, but that is different. That is in heat of moment. There is no premeditation. Whoever killed Captain must have given it great thought. Planned it. Chosen right time.'

'What if you thought that someone was putting you or your family in danger, if it was just a matter of time. Would you not plan a pre-emptive strike, nullify that danger before it was a real threat?'

He again focused on his hand of cards, seemingly distracted. 'No, what if I was wrong, what if there was no threat?'

'But what if you knew for sure, knew it was coming? Could you plan then? Pick your weapon? Pick your time?'

'Yes, I suppose. But this is still different. The Captain was not threatening our lives, he was trying to do opposite.'

'That's your belief, but what if you felt strongly that by staying out here, our lives were at risk?'

'I come back to what I say before. You would have to have screw loose.'

Polina tutted by way of response, shuffled her cards and placed down a straight flush.

'You have a pact with Devil!' said Dmitriy sulkily, slamming his own cards on the table. It was Polina's fourth win on the trot. She smiled smugly. 'Look, I have not told anyone of this before,' he said, suddenly sitting up straight, an earnestness entering his tone. 'I want to know what you think.' He leant forward, looking first at me, then at Polina.'

'Go on,' I said, 'don't keep us hanging!'

'The morning that Captain went missing, I was on bridge with Tanmay. It was 6.35 a.m. – I know because I looked at my watch. It was time that Captain is usually on his rounds. He said that he needed to pee, that he had been holding it in for hours. He left and did not return until 6:52. That was seventeen minutes.'

'That's a long time for a piss,' said Polina,' even taking into account the walk down to the toilet and back.'

'Yes, that is what I have been thinking. I even did it myself before dinner; I went to the bridge and walked it through. It took eight minutes, and that was going slow.'

'He could have gone for more than a pee?' I ventured.

'Have you asked him?' questioned Polina.

'What, if he went for a shit, and if that was why he was so long! No, it will sound as if I am accusing him. Also, he might just say that yes, he was taking a shit; then what? Worse than that, he may then point out that whilst he was taking shit, I was alone for seventeen minutes.'

'Okay,' I said, 'then what do we do?'

'Speak to Henning?' suggested Polina, 'See what he makes of it?'

'Sure, but it will also make him think about me.'

'Look Dmitriy, you are in no worse a position than the rest of us. We were all alone, without any witnesses at the time. What you *are* saying though, is that at a time that potentially matches the Captain's disappearance, Tanmay deliberately excused himself from your company; *his* witness.'

It was a concrete lead. That is, if my friend and confident, Dmitriy, was himself to be believed.

26

South

It was kept simple. One-person, one-vote. Stay in the Doldrums or set sail for Ascension Island. It was decided that it would be a blind vote, so that no-one else would know how anyone else had voted; if nobody knew, nobody could be targeted. Before we voted, Henning reiterated the list of risks and unknowns associated with sailing south: we had no idea if Ascension had been targeted in a nuclear strike owing to its status as a US-UK communications hub; we had no real way of telling, until it was too late, if radiation levels were dangerous; we didn't know if the pestilence had reached the island; if the island was still populated, we had no way of knowing how they might have coped over their months of isolation, and whether or not they would be friendly or hostile; there could be other ships there, that might increase our exposure to the disease or represent a threat; we would be using up valuable fuel. We cast our votes: a cross in one of two boxes, each paper folded neatly to conceal its contents, then placed in an old biscuit tin. Henning read them out, one-by-one: five for remaining, thirteen for going. Ascension it was.

I could guess most of the Remainers: Polina, who had always been unequivocal about her desire to stay at sea; Henning out of a sense of practicality and risk averseness; Ton out of a posthumous sense of loyalty to the Captain and a new sense of responsibility for 'his' crew. Then there was me. A strange one, you might say, that the person with the least attachment to the sea might vote to remain marooned within it. I had honestly planned to vote the other way, to make haste for Ascension, until the very last second. Then I found myself crossing the other box. I'm not even sure why. I don't think it was out of fear of the unknown, or even a sense of life preservation. Maybe it was because I was the newest to this life, that it was still all relatively novel, and that fatigue hadn't set in. All I know for sure is that, as my pencil hovered above the two boxes, Polina's words came into my mind – *what we have here is both simple and pure.* I thought that, with the chaos and destruction that had been wrought on the outside world, perhaps we could savour what we had for just a little longer.

I wasn't sure of the fifth and final Remainer. Dmitriy maybe? I was never one hundred percent sure what was going on in his head. Jerzy perhaps? Rieko? The one thing I was sure of was that it wouldn't have been any of the Asian contingent; they had made their stance crystal clear.

So, it was decided that we would set sail in three days' time, to give us an opportunity to prepare the ship for a longer voyage. We would be sailing south-south-east for co-ordinates 7°56'S 14°25'W, a distance of approximately 520 nautical miles from our current position just north of the equator. There would be no need to sail flat-out, we weren't in a rush. At a reduced speed of 15 knots, to conserve fuel, and sailing during the daylight hours only, Ton estimated it would take just five days.

27

Us and them

I thought that the new sense of purpose might bring the crew closer together. I was wrong. It started with Angelo, Arjun and Palvinder refusing to work any shifts with Ton, on the basis that he was racist at best, and a homicidal maniac at worst. Despite being outraged, Ton agreed in the hope that it would defuse tensions and avoid further conflict. Buoyed by his colleagues' success, Roy then requested not to be put on shift with Rieko. Ton had no option but to acquiesce. In complete contrast, Dmitriy asked discretely to be paired up with Tanmay as much as possible; he planned to watch him like a hawk for any incriminating behaviour.

Then, the day before we were due to set sail for Ascension, the Asian contingent abandoned the Officer's Lounge, our agreed communal recreational area since the bombs. They arrived in the morning to view the day's rota, then left. At supper, they briefly appeared in the dining room, took their food, and retired to the crew mess opposite, closing the door behind them. After dinner, the rest of us went to the officers' lounge as normal, but we saw nothing of them for the rest of the evening.

'This is absurd,' commented Ton. 'Donal, go and find them will you, and try to talk some sense into them: they seem to have less of a gripe with you than they do the rest of us.'

I figured that they would still be in the crew mess, on C Deck. As I made my way down, I came across Alon and Roy coming out of Arjun's cabin. Arjun, now that Paresh was gone, was the only one of the group to be quartered on the officers' corridor. They were both carrying boxes full of what I could only assume were Arjun's possessions.

'Hey guys, what's going on?' I asked. They both turned abruptly, a shared look of shock that they had been caught red handed.

'We are helping Arjun move his stuff,' said Roy, a little too hesitantly, as if he was unsure as to whether or not he should be speaking to me.

'Oh yes, where to?'

'To Banya's old cabin.'

'On D Deck, right? I guess that means that you'll all be on the same level then, eh?' They nodded uncomfortably. 'Can I give you a hand, lads?' I asked. They looked at each other, unsure if in this new regime of us and them, such an offer of assistance was permissible.

'I guess,' said Alon.

I stepped into Arjun's room to find only two more boxes and a pile of clothes remaining. I picked up the nearest box, filled with an assortment of books, questionable DVDs and a ragged looking potted plant, and followed Roy and Alon along the corridor and down the double flight of stairs that led to D Deck. Banya's cabin was three-in from the stairwell. I trailed in behind them, to find Arjun hanging clothes in the locker and Palvinder sitting on the bed. They turned as Roy and Alon entered, and sensing that something was amiss, fell silent as I came into view.

'Hi fellas, how's it going?' I said, awkwardly. Arjun flashed Alon an accusatory look. 'Arjun, Palvinder, I was just wondering if I could have a wee word?'

'Sure,' said Arjun. 'Thanks for your help,' he said, turning to Roy and Alon, 'I'll get the last few things myself later. We'll see you in the mess.' Realising that they had been excused, they left, closing the door behind them.

'What would you like to discuss?' asked Palvinder when we were alone.

'What's going on guys? What's with all this separation, moving cabins, avoidance?'

'We decided that we would prefer to keep ourselves to ourselves,' said Arjun.

'Well, that much is obvious. Why though? We've been getting on just fine until now.' They looked at me as if I'd lost the plot. Upon reflection, it wasn't the keenest observation, not on recent evidence anyway.

'You mean, apart from being treated like second class citizens, accused of treachery, murder? Of not being trusted to work alone without a European chaperone?'

'Well, there is that!' I admitted. 'But really, is it worth all this segregation? There are so few of us already.'

'You mean, what, safety in numbers?'

'Yeah, I guess.'

'That's the point, we don't feel safe,' interjected Palvinder, 'not when one of your number has stooped to murder. If they're prepared to kill the Captain, what chance do we have?'

'And you're so sure that it *is* one of us?'

'Well, it isn't one of us.'

'How do you know?'

'Because we do trust *each other.*' It was a fair point, a mirrored view of E Deck above: the Europeans were equally convinced that the traitor in our midst had to be one of the Asians.

'But this is crazy. We can't go on like this indefinitely.'

'In five days, we'll be at Ascension.'

'Then what? Are you just hoping to step off the ship and start a new life? We don't even know what's waiting for us there?'

'We'll see. Until then, we prefer to be left alone. Of course, we'll do what we need to do to sail the ship, but beyond that, we'd appreciate being left alone. We'll stay here on D Deck, and eat in the crew mess on C. We can work out a rota for the other facilities, like the gym and the games room.'

'Is it Ton?' I said in desperation. 'If it is, I'll speak to him, see if he'll agree to take a low profile for a while?'

'Ton is just a product of everything that is corrupt and broken in the shipping industry. He's the embodiment of centuries of prejudice and exploitation, of a corporate model born from indentured labour and colonialism. Ton, and the rest of them, have just shown that even the end of the world isn't enough to change things. It's time that we take what-ever future we have into our own hands.'

'And Henning, do you tar him with the same brush?'

'Henning is a good man, but he too belongs to another age.'

I took a deep breath. I was getting nowhere. I could also understand their stance; this was born from a poison so engrained, so deep rooted that it was perhaps impossible to purge. 'I'll talk to the others, 'I said. 'I'll try to make them understand, to give you all some space.'

'Thank you, Donal. This must be difficult for you. You come from another world.'

'Perhaps, but my world also ripped itself apart because of distrust, for a failure to appreciate each other's culture, for a need to redress perceptions of power. That's why we're in the mess we are now. I was hoping that we might do better.'

#

I returned to the Officer's Mess and tried to relay the conversation as closely as I could. I couldn't help thinking that the sense of outrage, the inability to shift perspectives did little but underline Arjun's argument. As it was, they agreed to abide by their wishes, although the pervading view was that it would all blow over, that it was all an over-reaction to recent events. They didn't seem to realise that this very act of infantilisation encapsulated everything that was wrong with the status quo.

'I don't mind what they do, as long as they stop coming into my stores and taking whatever they fancy?' said Jerzy.

'What do you mean?', asked Ton.

'Just this morning, when I was preparing breakfast, I came out of the galley to go to the dry provisions store and I saw one of them disappearing up the stairwell. The door to the store was wide open – I know I'd left it closed just minutes before.'

'I thought you were supposed to be locking them?'

'Yeah, at night, but not when I'm on shift. I haven't got time to be messing with keys every five minutes.'

'What was taken?'

'Not much, I think I must have disturbed them. A few boxes of dry cereal, some tins of fruit. Some of the cardboard boxes had been ripped open, as if they were looking to see what else there was inside.'

'Who was it?'

'I don't know, I only saw their back, and even then, only for a second. They were small, slim – so I guess it might have been Luis...Angelo perhaps? Tanmay?'

'Tanmay!' exclaimed Dmitriy, suddenly showing interest in the conversation. He had been lying on the couch, apparently engrossed in solving a battered Rubiks Cube which had lost at least two of its corners. 'You think it was Tanmay?'

'Well, it might have been, or one of the others.'

'Why would Tanmay be stealing food?' Dmitriy said, as much to himself as to us.

'I said it *might* have been Tanmay,' added Jerzy, 'Don't go rushing to any conclusions.'

'Why the particular interest in Tanmay?' asked Ton.

'No reason,' said Dmitriy, a little too airily to avoid further suspicion. To make it even worse, he couldn't help himself from throwing a barely concealed conspiratorial glance at both myself and Polina.

'What's going on Dmitriy?' asked Ton, wearily.

'You'd better tell him, 'I said, knowing that there was now no way of re-corking the genie. So, he did: a detailed retelling of the missing seventeen minutes on the morning of the Captain's disappearance, and his observations of Tanmay's movements and behaviour since. Of the latter, there was little of significance, although disturbingly Dmitriy had taken to timing and recording all of Tanmay's toilet visits on shift.

'His average is 8 minutes 20 seconds across six different visits,' he said triumphantly, as if this was irrefutable proof of Tanmay's guilt.

'But surely it depends where you are on the ship and how close the toilets are?' said Rieko.

'That is why I also go to toilet after him, and time myself...so I can do direct comparison. My average is 8 minutes 30 seconds.'

'Which tells us...what?'

Dmitriy looked at Rieko as if he was stupid. 'It tells us that on the morning of Captain's disappearance, Tanmay's toilet break was more than twice as long as normal. He had time to kill Captain.'

'There are plenty of reasons why someone might spend more than normal in a toilet, Dmitriy...I'm not sure you can extrapolate that one fact to prove Tanmay's guilt,' said Ton.

'But one of us killed him,' added Jerzy. It's more than we've got on anyone else. I don't see why everyone is making out that Dmitriy is wrong for following a lead. Has anyone heard or seen Tanmay do anything out of the ordinary?'

'What, like pushing people overboard?' said Polina acerbically.

'No, you know, anything out of character?'

'I can't say I've really been focused on him enough in the past to be able to tell what was and wasn't normal behaviour. He's always been kind of invisible,' said Rieko.

'How can you live with just twenty-two people on a ship for nearly a year-and-a-half and say that one of those people is 'invisible',' said Polina.

'Right, you tell us all about Tanmay then,' retorted Rieko, irritably.

'He's from India...'

'Where in India?'

'No idea...but it's more than you know.'

'He's from Mumbai,' I said. Everyone turned in my direction.

'He's nineteen and was brought up by his uncle after both of his parent's died. He studied engineering at college and is the first one in his family to ever join the merchant navy. He's very intelligent...when you speak to him.'

'Okay,' said Ton. 'So, you know him better than us, have *you* seen any out of the ordinary behaviour?'

'He's had less to do with me in recent weeks, but then again, so have all the Asian guys. He usually likes to get out on deck when he's not on shift, but I've seen less of him out there. When I've seen him with the others, he appears to be a little more confident, but then again, he's mixing solely in a peer group that he's more comfortable with, so I guess he's bound to. Let's face it, none of us have been acting completely in character recently...' I deliberately threw Dmitriy a glance, '... so I wouldn't say that Tanmay's acting any more weirdly than anyone else...not enough to pin a murder charge on him, anyway.'

'Except stealing food,' added Dmitriy.

'*Maybe* stealing food,' corrected Jerzy.

'If I was a suspicious man...' said Ton, '...I'd be asking why you were trying so hard to convince us that it's Tanmay. After all, if Tanmay was alone for seventeen minutes, so were you.'

Dmitriy looked at both me and Polina in turn with his one good eye. 'I tell you this would happen,' he said. He thrust himself out of his seat, his bear-like hands in tight fists, and glowered down at Ton, his face colouring. 'I know that I didn't kill Captain, that is why I focus on Tanmay. He was gone when Captain went missing, that is good enough reason for me. Instead of doing nothing, like you, I try to find more evidence. You all act as if you don't care that Captain is dead. You...' he said, pointing his finger at Ton, '...are not fit to clean shoes of

Captain, let alone step into them.' With that, he turned and stormed from the room.

'What the hell was all that about?' asked Ton, breaking the deathly silence that had filled the void created by Dmitriy's departure.

'He'll calm down,' I said. 'We all know how passionate he can be, especially about what he perceives to be an injustice. The Captain's disappearance has hit him hard, he just can't get his head around it. He needs to apportion blame to somebody, and for now, that somebody is Tanmay. I'll speak to him later when he's had a chance to cool off.'

A voice came from the back of the room. It was Henning, who, until now, had kept his council. To be honest, I'd forgotten he was there. 'We must keep an eye on both of them, especially Dmitriy; we've seen first-hand what obsession can do to a man. As for Tanmay's missing seventeen minutes – it can all be explained rationally, but it does raise a question mark.'

'Why don't we just ask him outright, get it all into the open?' asked Polina.

'I think that with relations as they are at present, it would be unwise. It would only make things worse. Let's just do what we need to do to get to Ascension, try to remain as civil as we can, but continue to be vigilant. Thank you, Donal, for your attempts to broker a peace, it's good that there's somebody who has the trust of both camps. I thought that Arjun and I would be Okay, but beyond a working relationship, he has closed himself off. It's a great shame.' He seemed to disappear into himself, shaking his head slowly, his eyes closed. After a few seconds, he eased himself out of his seat, his knee joints cracking like snapped bamboo. 'Gentlemen, Polina, I think it's time for me to go to bed. I'll bid you a good night. We have five days until we reach Ascension. I just hope that we can make it there without killing each other.'

28

Single Malt

Over the next two days we made steady progress. As we slipped out of the Doldrums, the winds and waves picked up, colluding together to test the mettle of the ship. She creaked and groaned under the onslaught, ever complaining as she cut through the rising swell, the engines providing a constant monotone accompaniment to the steel percussion of grinding metal. The skies darkened, the clouds bubbling into brooding cumulonimbus that gathered on the horizon, biding their time. A constant drizzle rained down. As much as we could, we avoided going on deck: there was no way of knowing how laced with death it might be. So far, we still had the ocean to ourselves, aside from the occasional seabird that took refuge from the lonely skies.

The atmosphere on board reflected the changes around us; there was a sense of increased danger, a ratcheting of tension that mirrored the worsening weather. The linear distinction between both groups remained, as tangible as that between sea and sky, blurred only by the necessities of sailing the ship. We ate separately, spent time separately, entertained ourselves separately; two communities within one nation...or perhaps three. Dmitriy had increasingly spent his time alone, either physically or by creating such an aura of unapproachability that he had devised his own isolation, even within the communal areas. This only changed on day four of our journey, following a wholly unexpected find from a container forage.

We had kept up the foraging throughout and were now down to the last few hundred. Occasionally, amongst the commercial containers used to haul finished goods and components from one continent to another, we found one which was being used to transport an individual's life – their furniture, clothes, ornaments, electronic goods, children's toys – everything that had been an intrinsic part of their existence in one place, bagged up and transported to another. These were often the most lucrative and rewarding containers, and always filled us with a surge of delight when we stumbled across them. They usually represented a great opportunity to upgrade our means of entertaining ourselves, heralding books, magazines, DVDs, sports and gym equipment, as well as useful gadgets and nostalgic keepsakes of our old lives. Along with the excitement though came a certain amount of trepidation; a sense that we were encroaching into someone's tomb, defiling all that was sacred to their memory by picking through their personal affects.

I'd found one once, alongside Paresh. As we'd squeezed through the gap we'd managed to create between the container's doors and cast our torches into the darkest recesses, we'd quickly realised what we'd found. Through the disturbed dust that cascaded like snowflakes through the beams of light, we tore open boxes and rummaged through chests-of-drawers. After the initial assessment and plundering of what was useful or desirable, I'd settled into a pattern for some weeks afterwards of visiting the container alone, to explore the personal and sentimental. I'd create a space in the middle, set out a chair, put a rug on the floor – created a living space within the debris. I sought out those things that were only of value to the treasure-trove's owner: photographs, letters, journals, trinkets. Again, maybe it was the journalist in me, but I desperately wanted to build up a picture in my own mind's-eye of who this person was: their history, their present, their intended future. Like Howard Carter delving into the majesty of Tutankhamun's tomb, I wished to scrape away at the layers of time, to construct an epitaph built from chattels alone. Even when I'd bored of it, I had still taken away a memento: it was a small, framed photograph of a family group, a mother and father smiling, a child of about three between them. The parents were around my age. It was set against a Mediterranean background: Italy perhaps. I don't know why I took it. The woman looked a little like Beth, I suppose. It was an image of what might have been.

Dmitriy's treasure was far, far simpler. In a dramatic break from his recent sulk, he burst into the mess that afternoon with an air of exultation. In his arms, he carried a cardboard box that clinked enticingly as he laid it down carefully on the table. Polina traipsed in behind him, her face difficult to read.

'Look what Dmitriy has found!' he boomed.

'Well, actually *I* found it,' said Polina stoically. Ignoring her, Dmitriy reached into the box and pulled out a bottle of whiskey.

'This is just six...there are *many, many* more. It's not cheap rubbish either, it's really good stuff.'

'There are two full crates,' added Polina. 'There must be thirty of forty bottles in each crate, all boxed up and protected with bubble-wrap. I don't know much about whiskey, but someone has gone to a lot of trouble to keep them safe.' Henning had ambled over, and gestured for Dmitriy to hand over the bottle that he was holding like a baby. He took it in both hands, stroking the label absent mindedly with his thumb.

'This is a Glenfiddich 30 year-old single malt. It must be worth thousands of dollars.' He peered inside the larger box and pulled out the remaining boxed bottles one-by-one. 'A Willet Family Estate Bourbon, Teeling 32 year-old Irish single malt, Kurayoshi 25 year-old Japanese malt, Glen Scotia 25 year-old single malt, an Avaonside-Glenlivut blended whiskey. These six bottles alone must be worth ten, maybe twelve thousand dollars.' Jerzy let out a high-pitched whistle.

'This guy must have been a serious enthusiast. Why'd he risk putting it in a container?'

'Maybe he was trying to avoid it being taxed. What was the other stuff like in his container? Any Picassos? Maybe a couple of Stradivarius violins?'

'Nope,' said Polina, 'Just pretty standard stuff. Nothing really fancy. I guess whiskey was his thing.'

'What are we going to do with it?' I said.

'Whatever we want, I doubt the owner is going to ask for it back! Plus, I'm pretty sure the bottom has fallen out of the whiskey asset market. What we've got here is some really, *really* good booze,' said Ton.

'We'll, I say finders keepers...,' said Dmitriy, '...and I invite you all to my party. We should ask the other guys too. Maybe we can have reconciliation.'

'Technically, if we're calling finders-keepers, its mine, but I'm not going to argue against the idea of piss-up...and Dmitriy might be right, maybe we can use it to build some bridges,' said Polina.

'Please, you can't call it a 'piss-up' with whiskey of this quality. Let's call it a *tasting*,' rebuked Henning. 'Donal, why don't you pay Arjun and the rest a visit and explain to them what we've found. Invite them to the Captain's Office on F Deck...neutral ground. We'll suspend all shifts this evening.'

#

I was convinced that the invitation would be rejected out of hand, but to my surprise the lure of alcohol, denied for so long, proved too powerful. Not that there wasn't an attempt to have their cake and eat it.

'Can't we just have some bottles down here?' asked Arjun.

'I don't think it's that kind of thing, guys. This is a peace offering as much as anything else. They are trying hard to put things right; to draw a line and start again.'

'Can we discuss it...alone?'

'Of course, be my guest.' I stepped out of the mess and paced the corridor for what turned out to be a surprisingly short time. There couldn't have been much discussion. The fears and insecurities that Arjun and Palvinder had shared with me a mere three days previously apparently evaporating as quickly as the first breath of alcohol from a freshly opened bottle of Scotch.

'We will come, but this changes nothing,' said Arjun, as he opened the door.

'Of course not!' I said, wondering how he was reconciling the duplicity of the statement, 'But maybe you'll feel differently later with the warmth of some whiskey in your belly.' The men followed Arjun one by one out of the room, and we snaked our way up the stairwell towards F Deck in a silent procession. I sensed a nervousness, a reluctance even, but equally a resignation that they were helpless in the face of such a powerful lure; like ancient mariners dragged to the rocks by the siren's song.

When we arrived at the Captain's Office, they filed in awkwardly only to be met by cheers from Dmitriy, Jerzy and Rieko who beckoned them over to the table upon which stood six bottles, now clad from top to bottom in aluminium foil, and a forest of glasses.

'We're so pleased you came?' said Polina, with genuine warmth.

'Here!' said Henning, handing out a small square of paper and pencil to each person. 'We thought it would be more fun if we made this a blind tasting. I've written down the name, age, origin and some tasting notes from the labels of each. You have to match them to the numbered bottle.'

And it *was* fun. To begin with. Before long, the icy atmosphere had thawed. There was laughter, the sharing of theories as to which liquid treasure was which, a rise in volume as inhibitions were loosened by the first waves of inebriation. It could so easily have been the triumph we had all hoped for, the reunification that at least some us craved. If it hadn't been for Tanmay and Dmitriy.

The party was in full swing. We'd moved beyond the tasting notes and the first six bottles and had just opened a seventh and eighth. I had noted that Dmitriy was merrier than most, and by 'merry' I mean tanked. After being the life and soul, he'd just entered a quieter and more circumspect phase where his one good eye lurched belatedly from the mouths of those around him as he desperately tried to keep up with the conversation. He was sitting in a group with myself, Rieko, Palvinder, Roy and Tanmay. Discussion had found its way to the shores of Ascension Island, and our expectations of what we might find. Tanmay had himself gone through a metamorphosis, shedding his shy demeanour for something bordering on brash. He had become loud and opinionated.

'I don't care what we find...' he said, 'whether it is scorched to the ground or overrun with zombies, it can't be worse that being imprisoned on this damn ship.' A combination of his own volume and a momentarily lapse in the conversation of the others around us turned all heads in his direction. I had been watching Dmitriy, and I noticed his roaming eye lock on to Tanmay with a solidity I hadn't seen for some time.

'I mean,' continued Tanmay, now with the ears and eyes of the room on him, 'why the hell has it taken us this long? We could have done this months ago...a year ago. All that time wasted...cleaning, painting, greasing, oiling. All so we were ready to sail the ship, but then not sailing. Floating in the Doldrums. For what? All I can say is, thank God the Captain is dead, otherwise we may never have escaped.' He stopped, only then seeming to realise that he was the centre of everyone's attention. Silence reigned, as he looked from one face to the next. 'What?' he said into the void, 'You must all think the same. He was an idiot, and I'm pleased he's dead.'

What happened next played out in slow motion. Dmitriy, defying the sluggishness of his recent movements, exploded from his chair and threw himself at Tanmay in a flailing maelstrom of rage. Before anyone could even move, he had thrown Tanmay across the room and was in hot pursuit. Tanmay hit the table harbouring the whiskey bottles, causing it to overturn and scattering the bottles across the floor in a shower of broken glass.

'You damn little shit,' he bellowed as he scooped up a half-broken bottle by the neck and lunged towards the cowering Tanmay. By now, the rest of us had recovered from our shock and drink-induced paralysis – Ton and Jerzy were moving rapidly to put themselves between the two men, and the rest of us had stood up. This had given Tanmay a split second longer to scramble unsteadily to his feet, and stagger towards the door, using the wall as support. A small dribble of blood ran down his cheek from a cut above his eyebrow. He disappeared through the exit, a wide-eyed look of abject terror on his face. Dmitriy, meanwhile had swung his jagged weapon in a wide arc, forcing Ton and Jerzy to take a step back. Seeing his chance, he bowled forwards, charging through the open door in pursuit.

As one, we all scrambled after them. I was first to the door and was just in time to see Dmitriy disappear down the stairs to our right. I could hear his howls of fury echoing from the stairwell. As I followed, I quickly began to appreciate my own unsteadiness, my movements were slow and uncontrolled, my senses dulled by my overindulgence. I clung onto the railings as I made my way down the stairs, my head swimming. The others followed close behind.

Down through E Deck, to D Deck where a hatch led to the covered BBQ area and then the deck walkway that ran down the length of the ship. I stumbled out, the rest of the crew cascading out of the opening like scree in my wake. We stood, taking in the diorama before us. Dmitriy had finally caught up with Tanmay. He had him pinned against the balustrade, one hand around his throat, the other holding what was left of the bottle in the air above him. One of Tanmay's hands was wrapped around Dmitriy's thick wrist, trying to relieve the pressure on his neck, whilst the other tried to stave off the jagged glass blade. But that wasn't the only scene that met us.

'Look!' cried Arjun, pointing beyond the tangled forms of Dmitriy and Tanmay and confirming to us all that it wasn't our own personal, drunken hallucination. In the sea behind them, as real as could be, was a bright orange lifeboat.

29

Reunited

To our starboard side, no more than half a kilometre away, our missing lifeboat bobbed sanguinely in the ocean's gentle swell.

'It is ours, right?' said Alon.

'Can't be sure, but it looks like it,' slurred Rieko. We all stared past the frozen scene of Dmitriy and Tanmay. Tanmay still had his eyes tightly shut, his facial features contorted in anticipation of the expected blow, his throat pinned to the railing by Dmitriy's massive fist. The broken bottle in Dmitriy's other hand hovered in the air. His gaze swung like a metronome from the crumpled body of his captive to that of the bright orange craft that taunted us from the waves. Slowly, he brought the weapon down until it rested limply by his side. He released his grip on Tanmay and took an unsteady step backwards. A look of dismay now rested on his face; his eyes wide, the crimson rage blanching rapidly into an alabaster grey. The bottle slipped from his hand and shattered on the deck. Tanmay, who was still too much in the grip of terror and confusion to know what was happening, opened his eyes and sensing the opportunity to escape, scurried along the railings, scrambling and half-crawling to put as much distance between himself and his assailant. Roy and Angelo stooped to help him, guiding him to a position of safety behind them.

'I...I am sorry,' stammered Dmitriy. 'I don't know what came over me.'

'A bottle and a half of whiskey, I'd say,' said Henning matter-of-factly.

'Let's forget about that for now,' said Ton, 'we have a more pressing issue to address. We need to salvage the lifeboat.'

'If it is ours, could they still be alive?' asked Arjun.

'It's been six weeks. I guess it depends on how much food and water they took with them. It's definitely possible,' said Henning.

'Then what are we waiting for?' asked Angelo.

'I'm not sure if any of us are in a fit state to perform a salvage operation,' said Ton, casting a glance towards Dmitriy who was now slumped in an untidy pile on the floor, his back against the wall, 'I can't risk any injuries. Let me ask, has anyone *not* been drinking?'

No one put their hand up.

'Anyone think they haven't drunk much?' Chien, Arjun and Palvinder put up their hands.

'How much?'

'Three small glasses,' said Palvinder.

'Two glasses,' added Arjun and Chien in unison.

'All I want to do at this stage is secure a line to the lifeboat, so we don't lose it...and to confirm that it is ours. If it is, we know what we are dealing with. If it isn't, then there are all sorts of other things we'll need to consider. Do you three feel that you could get over there in the inflatable? I'd need one of you on board to look after the winch, and the other two to ride out.'

'Yeah, I can do that,' said Palvinder. The other two nodded their agreement.

It didn't take long to prepare the inflatable and lower it down to the waterline. Palvinder and Chien were then securely attached to the safety ropes, and then climbed down the pilot ladder before setting off towards the lifeboat that had been drifting ever closer to the ship. We watched as they attached a line to a cleat on the hull, then towed the vessel until it was within twenty metres of the *Thallasa.* They then secured their own line to one we had lowered from the ship; we now had the lifeboat safely tethered. It was close enough now for us to confirm, with the naked eye alone, that it was indeed our own. Ton leant over the railings and gestured for Palvinder and Chien to return to the ship. Palvinder was clearly shouting something, but his words were whipped away by the sound of the waves that sloshed noisily against the hull. We watched as he and Chien then wheeled the inflatable around and rode back out to the lifeboat, securing themselves to its side.

'What the hell are they doing?' said Ton irritably. 'I told them just to secure it.'

'Maybe they heard something from inside?' suggested Rieko.

'It doesn't matter,' said Ton, 'an order's an order. They should wait until we are all in a fit state to take part.'

'Palvinder's using his own judgement, we have to trust him.'

We watched as he clambered up onto the turret of the lifeboat, whilst Chien remained in the inflatable. He opened the hatch and peered inside – appearing to then reel backwards, covering his face with his sleeve. He seemed to compose himself, then turned and lowered himself into the hatch feet-first before disappearing from view. We waited with bated breath.

Within a matter of minutes he re-emerged. He meticulously closed the hatch, and tentatively made his way back down the outer ladder to the inflatable where Chien guided him aboard. The two men huddled together for a short while, presumably to allow Palvinder to share his news, then they detached themselves from the lifeboat and travelled the short distance back to the hull of the ship. Once they were secured to the guide rope, Arjun winched first Palvinder, then Chien back onto the deck.

'What did you find?' asked Rieko, as soon as Palvinder was safely over the railings. 'Are they still alive?'

'Li's alive, but he's very weak. He's barely breathing. Banya is dead.'

'What about Paresh?'

'That's the strange thing. Paresh isn't there.'

30

Hallucination

'What do you mean *he's not there*?' said Ton incredulously.

'Just that. He's not on the lifeboat,' replied Palvinder.

'Did Li say anything?'

'I had to check his pulse to make sure he wasn't dead, I don't think he'll be telling us much for a while.'

'We can't be leaving him alone on the lifeboat if he's that bad, 'said Polina. 'Not even if it's just until morning.'

'Chien and I have already discussed it,' said Palvinder, 'we'll go back with a medical kit, food and water, and stay with him overnight. If he does say anything in Cantonese, Chien will be able to understand it.'

'You'll need some blankets as well...both for him, and you. I'll go and get some now,' said Polina. 'I'll pick up a medical kit too. Jerzy, come with me and we'll sort out a provisions pack.'

'Once we've got Chien and Palvinder safely back on the lifeboat, the rest of us need to sleep, so we're in a fit state to recover it in the morning. It's nine fifty now. Let's say that we'll start the salvage operation at six thirty.' There were nods of agreement all round.

We busied ourselves helping Palvinder and Chien as they prepared to re-board the lifeboat. When they had everything they needed, we lowered them back down to the inflatable and they made the short journey over to the craft. After securing the inflatable, they both climbed the external ladder to the hatch and disappeared inside. The wind had dipped and for the first time in days the relentless drizzle had relented. Collectively, we began to drift to our cabins; eager to start the clock on the purging of the worst effects of the alcohol before morning. The burst of adrenalin following Tanmay and Dmitriy's altercation, and the discovery of the lifeboat, had miraculously cleared my head and returned me to a surprising level of sobriety, but as this began to wear off I was starting to feel terrible. My head was throbbing, and I felt dizzy and nauseous. Judging from the pale faces and sweat drenched clothing of those around me, I wasn't the only one. Tanmay was looking particularly green. His plight as the victim of a physical assault had been somewhat overshadowed by subsequent events, but I noticed that he had remained on deck. He leant on the outer railings for support and gazed out to sea. I caught Polina's eye and gestured for her to follow me over to him.

'Tanmay, are you Okay?' I asked.

'I feel sick,' he said, 'I don't think I can go inside yet.' I noticed that the cut above his eye was still oozing fresh blood. I wondered if he might be suffering from concussion as well as the after-effects of so much whiskey.

'Did you hit your head?' Polina asked, as if she was reading my mind.

'Maybe, I don't know. It all happened so fast.' He brought his hand up to the cut, and winced as he touched it. He seemed to pale even more when he saw the crimson on his fingers.

'I think we should patch you up before you go to your cabin. Do you think you could come with us to the mess whilst I get a medical kit?' He nodded, and I held his arm for support as he backed away from the railing. I was surprised how small and weightless he seemed, like the carcass of a bird. Slowly, we made our way down to the Officer's Mess, whilst Polina went ahead to prepare the medical kit.

'I can't believe that Banya is dead,' he said suddenly, 'and Li not far off it. I mean, we thought that they *might* be dead, but I always thought that they may have made it. Somehow.'

'I know. We could always convince ourselves that their odds were better than they were.'

'And where's Paresh? It doesn't make sense.'

'I don't know. Maybe he'd gone outside for some reason and lost his footing. Perhaps he'd died earlier, and the other two had thrown his body overboard.'

'Perhaps...or maybe he wasn't on board the lifeboat at all.' I stopped in my tracks at his words.

By this time, we had reached the mess. Polina was sat inside, anti-septic wipes and band aids at the ready. I guided Tanmay to the chair next to Polina and sat him down.

'I haven't mentioned this to anybody because I thought I was seeing things. I thought you'd all think I was crazy.'

'What are you talking about?' said Polina, trying to catch-up with our conversation.

'Paresh,' I said. 'Tanmay was just questioning whether he was ever even on the lifeboat.' Polina raised her eyebrows but said nothing.

'It was on the morning that the Captain disappeared. I was on shift on the bridge with Dmitriy, but I'd needed the toilet. I'd gone down to my own cabin on D Deck, because I prefer to use my own. I decided to get the elevator back up. Whilst I was waiting, I looked down the corridor to the stairwell, wondering if I'd be better off walking. The door was open. For a fleeting moment, I thought I saw him.'

'Paresh?'

'Yes, he was framed in the doorway. It was if he was looking right at me. I blinked, and he was gone. I ran down the corridor to the stairwell and onto the landing. There was nothing, not even the sound of footsteps above or below me.'

'Why didn't you say anything?' said Polina.

'Would you?' asked Tanmay. 'I thought I was seeing things. If I was questioning my own sanity, what would everyone else have thought? So, I convinced myself it was just a figment of my imagination. I'd been up all night. I was just tired.'

Tanmay grimaced as Polina wiped his cut. 'This is quite deep,' she said. 'I think I'm going to have to staple it to stop it bleeding.'

'Do you still think it was your imagination?' I asked, ignoring the practicalities of his treatment. Tanmay shrugged.

'Who knows? He wasn't on the lifeboat. Maybe he's been on the ship all along.'

My head throbbed even more with the myriad of questions this raised. Was it possible that Paresh had been on the *Thalassa* all this time without any of us knowing? Could he really have concealed himself from us so completely, and if so, why? Why had he written the letter professing to have left with Banya and Li, and how could they have ended up on the lifeboat alone? I thought about the desecration of the hydroponics room, the Captain's disappearance, Jerzy's reports of thefts from the galley stores.

'I guess we might find out more tomorrow when we recover the lifeboat,' said Polina. 'Perhaps Li will recover enough to tell us what happened.'

We all came to the same realisation at once. If Paresh was onboard, he would be desperate to make sure that that didn't happen.

31

Invisible

The salvage operation in the morning went smoothly. Palvinder had towed the lifeboat so that it sat directly below the winching system, leaving Chien onboard to tend to Li. The thick, steel cables had been attached and the vessel had been slowly raised until it once again rested securely within its cradle.

Chien and Palvinder reported that Li was still unresponsive. His breathing was shallow and his pulse faint. Twice in the night Chien had woken suddenly and hearing no sound from Li, had feared the worst. Both times, Li's lungs had heaved back into action, his ragged breath competing against the moans and groans of the boat. Chien had dripped water onto his chapped, crusted lips and tried to make him as comfortable as possible with the new supply of blankets.

'Li is showing signs of radiation exposure,' reported Palvinder. 'He has obviously been vomiting a lot, and his hair has been coming out in clumps. There is no sign of them having any Thyrosafe Tablets – no empty boxes or anything. They must have been mad; why wouldn't they have thought to take any with them?'

'Also, no food,' added Chien. 'Banya starve to death. Li not far behind.'

'But how can that be, Paresh said he'd filled the lifeboat with provisions? Are you sure?' asked Ton.

'There is no empty packaging, no boxes, no tins...nothing. Unless they'd been dumping all their rubbish overboard, it looks like they didn't have any food. The lifeboat would have been stocked well...there should have been enough for three people for a month, especially if they were careful with their rations.'

'What are you saying?'

'I don't know. It doesn't make any sense.'

'Also, both Banya and Li only have one set of clothes. What they were wearing. Nothing else. No bag either,' said Chien.

'And absolutely no sign of Paresh?'

'No, nothing. It's as if he was never on the lifeboat at all.'

Polina shot me a look. 'In that case guys, you might be interested in hearing what Tanmay has to say.' Everyone looked from Polina to Tanmay, who visibly shrank back, a rabbit in headlights. 'It's alright, Tanmay,' she said, 'just tell everyone what you told us. No one's going to think you're crazy...this whole thing is crazy, after all.'

Everyone listened intently as Tanmay retold his story. Dmitriy, who looked considerably worse for wear anyway, seemed to wilt even further as Tanmay explained the reason behind his extended absence on the day of the Captain's disappearance. He hung his head and avoided my eye contact. When Tanmay had finished, there was a communal pause as everyone contemplated the same question: could Paresh really have been on the ship, among us, all this time?

'So,' said Rieko, breaking the silence, 'we're saying here that it was Paresh who killed the Captain? Wrecked the hydroponics room? Who Jerzy saw stealing from the provisions store? *Could* it have been Paresh you saw, Jerzy?'

'Well, I didn't exactly factor him in as a possible contender before, but yes, I guess. He was...is...the right size and build.' There was another pause, as people took this in.

'But, when the Captain disappeared, we searched everywhere,' questioned Arjun. 'Why didn't we see him then, or any sign of anyone living rough on the ship.'

'It's a big ship. There were only nineteen of us, it would have been easy for Paresh to keep hidden. Think of how many places there are to hide, especially if it was premeditated,' I said. 'It would be easy to remain invisible. Plus, we were looking for the Captain, who we thought was unconscious somewhere. We weren't tuned in to looking for someone who was deliberately trying to conceal themselves. I'm not sure I would have picked up on any subtle signs of someone going commando.'

'So, what do we do now?' said Ton, 'Do another sweep of the ship?'

'I don't see the point. If he's hidden from us for this long, I don't see how he'll allow us to find him now. As well as all the nooks and crannies in the ship itself, we're looking at thousands of containers to search.'

'Also, he doesn't know that we know that he's on the ship,' added Henning. 'If we make a big thing of searching, we'll alert him to the fact that we are aware of his presence. This might make him more desperate, more dangerous.'

'So, what, we do nothing?'

‘I think the best we can do is stay vigilant. As much as possible, work in pairs. Avoid being isolated, alone. Lock our cabins at night. After all, aside from the Captain, who he saw as a barrier to reaching Ascension, he hasn’t attacked anyone else. He would have had plenty of opportunity.’

‘Plus...,’ said Henning, ‘...we’re on our way to where he wants to go, why would he do anything to jeopardise that?’

‘What about Li?’ said Palvinder. ‘Paresh will know that if he regains consciousness, he could tell us what happened on the lifeboat. He might think that his secret is safe if Li was out of the way.’

‘Li needs to be watched 24/7 anyway. We’ll all do four-hour shifts. If we move him to his old cabin, we can keep the door locked from the inside and only open it as we do a changeover,’ said Ton.

‘What about when we get to Ascension?’ asked Arjun.

‘He’s going to have to try and get off the ship somehow. That’s when he’ll be more vulnerable. We might have a chance to apprehend him then.’

‘Of course, this is all assuming that he *really* is on the ship. We still don’t know for sure. It all still seems too far-fetched,’ said Rieko.

‘I agree,’ said Henning, ‘the whole idea seems preposterous, but recent events, coupled with Tanmay’s evidence make it a very strong possibility. We would be foolish to be tempted by complacency and discount the improbable.’

#

The process of removing Li from the lifeboat, cleaning him up and making him comfortable turned out to be far more problematic than the retrieval of the vessel itself. I had volunteered, alongside Dmitriy, who was seeking some kind of penance, Polina and Chien to clean him up the best we could and strap him into a stretcher so that he could be lifted up and out of the hatch. The inside of the boat was putridity personified. Although Banya's body had been covered with a thick tarpaulin sheet, the stench was almost overwhelming. Coupled with the smell of Li's soiled clothing, and the swill of vomit and faeces that surrounded both men, it was difficult to maintain focus. How Chien and Palvinder had spent a night on board, I just didn't know. Li was non-responsive; covered in a veneer of tepid sweat, he was limp and pallid, clinging onto life by a fingernail. His clothing was crisp with dried bodily fluids, a camouflage of dark stains and filth. We removed what we could and wrapped him in a clean blanket before transferring him to the stretcher. Once he was secure, he was raised inch-by-inch until he was finally free of what, even a day later, might have been his final catacomb.

One by one, Polina, Dmitriy and Chien climbed the ladder towards the sanctuary of the sweet-smelling sea air. As I placed my foot on the first run, I took one last look around me. It was barren, a fibreglass bubble in which two men had rattled, possession-less, for over a month. This was where they had slowly starved. Where their flesh had been gradually poisoned by the air around them. Maybe they had counted down the days to their salvation, ever expectant to feel the tell-tale swell of an approaching ship, to hear heavy boots above them, of familiar voices. When had they given up hope? What kind of deprived thoughts had entered their minds as they contemplated survival – two men, flesh and blood, trapped in a watery desert? Had Li had to battle temptation after the life had finally leached from Banya's body? Had he had the mercy of being too weak himself to act on such temptation?

Li was taken to his old cabin, where his body was washed and dressed in clean clothing. Medical equipment on board was rudimentary; normal procedure - back when things were normal - was to airlift the very sick to hospital. What Li needed was an intravenous drip – fluids to rehydrate, antibiotics to clear the infection from the weeping sores on his skin. We had neither. His wounds were dressed, and anti-septic creams applied. He was fed a water-sugar solution through a tube into his mouth. He was stable, yet catatonic. Polina began our vigil over his body and soul, the door locked behind us.

From the living to the dead.

I felt shame, but I was inwardly relieved when Roy, Alon and Crisanto volunteered to retrieve Banya's body and prepare it for a burial. I don't think I could have done it. They too cleaned his body and paid him the respect of a fresh set of clothes for his final journey. From somewhere, they found a sheet-sized Indonesian flag and wrapped him in it before strapping his remains onto the stretcher. He was winched up and out of the lifeboat and placed on deck. Words were said, before the stretcher was raised and tipped, committing his mortal form to the sea.

I couldn't help wondering if somewhere beyond us, in the crags and crevasses of metal or the deep shadows that separated the containers, Paresh was watching.

32

Parasite

We were three days from Ascension – approximately two-hundred and eighty nautical miles. Despite the onset of a new chapter in our lives and the prospect of a return to a semblance of civilisation, we continued as before – slaves to an engrained routine. Up at 7 a.m., exercise for those of us so inclined, breakfast and then the morning rota meeting. Then the carousel of chores to keep the vessel ship-shape and our minds and bodies occupied. The only difference now was that we had returned to doing all of our work in pairs - and that we had a new task to perform, namely the care and protection of Li.

Strangely, none of us really talked about Ascension. It had been looming in our mind's eye for so long, a metaphor for change and an antidote to our oceanic dependence, that one might have thought that it would have been our only focus of conversation. I think it was the uncertainty that stopped us, the notion that all our expectations could come crashing down. For all we knew, the island might have been targeted with a nuclear strike to eradicate the Western World's Trans-Atlantic communications. It might have been ravaged by the disease. It may have descended into a post-apocalyptic anarchy in the face of its isolation. If there was anyone there, how would they react to a motley crew of mariners and a one-time journalist rolling up? Would they see us as saviours, with our bounty of lawnmowers, fashion wigs and tinned ham, or as superfluous, temporary custodians of a floating supermarket whose tenure had come to an end? Had Ascension long before become a magnet for people like us, a wild west of waifs and strays dragged to its shores out of curiosity, desperation and boredom? Would it all be some Darwinian, Lord of the Flies-like dystopia where only the strongest and most morally bankrupt might survive?

So, with our destination off the conversational menu, we focused our attentions on the next best thing, namely the unhinged, homicidal maniac potentially living amongst us. Tanmay's public confession of sighting Paresh had induced a tsunami of similar stories. Alon claimed to have seen him on deck one evening. Cristanto had fleetingly seen him at the top of the stairs leading to C Deck. Angelo had seen the back of someone at two in the morning, who he had thought at the time was Arjun, coming out of the crew mess clutching a paperback. Arjun, now confronted, said he had been on shift on the bridge on the night in question. Whether any of these were genuine or not didn't matter – they merely fuelled the mythology of a killer in our midst. With this came an almost perpetual feeling of being watched. It made us all nervous, jumpy even. We had previously roamed the entirety of the ship, scuttling worry-free along the walkways and corridors, climbing up and down isolated stairwells and navigating our way around the maze of containers like termites in a mound. Now, every rat-run was a potential scene of ambush. You took an intake of breath every time you turned a corner, felt the hairs on the back of your neck rise as you passed a shadowed alcove. We travelled in numbers.

It was against this backdrop of hysterical paranoia that I had sought out Henning's company. I had a hunch that he would be in the hydroponics room. I wanted to wrap myself in his blanket of rationality, to dodge the feelings of danger and chaos that so occupied the rest of the crew. Our crop had recovered well since the assault, and we now had a fresh batch of green salads ready for harvest. Henning was planting new seeds – an odd act, I thought, bearing in mind our imminent arrival on terra ferma.

'No room for complacency,' he said, reading my expression. 'We need to carry on as before, mitigate against all possibilities.'

'What brings you here?' I asked. 'You're off rota, like me, aren't you?'

'I suspect that I am here for much the same reason as you. I was craving a little order. Some calm. Where better than amongst nature.'

'Can you call something that is so man-made 'nature'?'

'Of course. We're not *making* it, we're *facilitating* it. We have just created the conditions for it to flourish.' I looked along the neat rows of saplings, each row at a different stage of growth. We had provided light, water and nutrients. Nature had done the rest – the machinery of photosynthesis, stomata to facilitate respiration, the engineering to turn CO2 into oxygen, the miracle of reproduction. 'It is a little like our own situation, don't you think? Here we are, on this ship, blessed with the building blocks to allow us to survive in a hostile environment that has made it impossible for others. Regardless of what happens on Ascension, we still have this ship. That thought gives me much solace.'

'And what of Paresh? Isn't he a blight that threatens our ability to survive?'

'Not a blight, Donal, no. A 'blight' suggests contamination, infection. If Paresh is here, and he has done what we think he may have done, his poison won't spread – we won't succumb to his madness. He is more like a symbiont, leeching from us, sucking from our resources...our resourcefulness. Most symbionts in nature are opportunistic, they are parasitic. We just need to ensure that we don't give Paresh the opportunity to damage us further. Like all parasites, he can be flushed out – it just isn't always a very pleasant experience.'

We spent the next hour in comfortable silence, broken only by conversation relating to the needs of our plants. We finished by picking a basket-full of green-leaf salad, rocket and a punnet of ripened tomatoes – the first we had had in weeks – and prepared to take our harvest to the galley. As we locked the door behind us, we both jumped as the ship's alarm sounded. We looked at each other, then made our way to the meeting point in the Officer's Mess.

We were the last to arrive. The room was a throng of voices and confusion. My attention was immediately drawn to Angelo, who was sitting, slumped in one of the arm chairs, clutching a bloodied bandage to the back of his head. Polina was kneeling next to him, speaking to him quietly. Ton was standing to his right, his hand resting on his shoulder.

'Gentlemen,' he said, above the general hubbub. It took a

few seconds, and a repetition, for the room to fall silent. 'As some of you know already, I am sorry to say that there has been another incident. I regret to inform you that Li is dead.' There was an audible gasp around the room. It was perhaps no major surprise that Li had lost his battle to survive, but the term 'incident' flooded the room with trepidation. 'Angelo had been sitting with Li when he had heard a knock on the door. It was a few minutes before the end of his shift, so he thought that Rieko, who was relieving him, had arrived a little early. He remembers opening the door, and that there was no-one there. He stepped out of the room to look down the corridor...and then doesn't remember anything else. When Rieko arrived, he found Angelo unconscious on the floor with a wound to the back of his head. It looks like he was hit from behind. He went into the room to find Li still in bed. His throat had been cut.' The sense of shock was almost tangible. 'I think we have to assume that our theories about Paresh are correct...I can't imagine why anyone else here would have wanted Li dead. We also have to assume that Paresh is highly dangerous and that his insanity has reached new depths. To push someone off a ship is one thing, but to slit someone's throat in cold blood is another level of depravity. I think the time has come for affirmative action – we can't just continue to Ascension and hope that we'll all make it in one piece. We need to hit him where it hurts and flush him out into the open. Henning, Palvinder – I want you to shut the engines down; we're not going anywhere until we've found him...and I want him to know what we're doing, so we'll put up notices around the ship. I want a constant guard on both lifeboats, but keep it subtle – I want to catch him if we can. The rest of us are going to arm ourselves with whatever we can and do a sweep of the ship –

and keep doing a sweep until we find him. He can't hide from us forever.'

'What do we do with him if we come across him?' asked Alon.

'Use whatever force you think is necessary. Above all, you need to protect each other, I don't want to lose anyone else.'

#

The engines are silenced. We search the ship. One group sweeps from the stern inwards, the other from the bough. Four of us surreptitiously slink into the shadows around the lifeboats, two on each, waiting. The first sweep of the ship takes hours and reveals nothing. So does the second. We are not just looking for a needle, but a moving needle that doesn't want to be found. Night falls again. Darkness envelopes great swathes of the ship, fighting and winning against the artificial strobe lighting. Somewhere, out there, we know that eyes are watching us.

33

Atonement

Static. The screen blinks on again. From my bed, I see shapes in the darkness. I can't yet determine what they are, but there is a familiarity to them. A dim, moon-dipped light fights against the thick material of curtains to my left. As my eyes adjust, I can just make out a swirling pattern of concentric circles and loops. Below the covered window, is a black rectangular block. I know it to be a chest of draws made from a dark, deeply grained wood. It is old and battered: a hand-me-down from a hand-me-down age. I know, instinctively, that the middle draw sticks. Beyond this, on the far wall, I can make out a gallery of posters, their images consumed by the gloom. There are five. I can picture, but can't see, what each depicts. The first, the largest, is a film poster from the 1973 classic, *Soylent Green*: Charlton Heston running headlong from a lorry piled with bodies, his eyes wide. There are two equally sized posters to the left; they are both vintage Guinness adverts. My favourite depicts the famous Guinness Toucan. Around these are a collection of small squares: I know that these are my collection of beer mats, each stuck perfectly equidistant from each other with small balls of Blu Tack. To the right of the central poster is another, marginally smaller: a second film poster, this time for *Reservoir Dogs.* The final image below that is a black and white illustration of a nuclear mushroom cloud. At the bottom, in stylised block capitals it says, 'BAN THE BOMB!'

In the corner of the room, I can make out the outline of a guitar, the black hollow of its belly staring at me through the darkness. On the far wall, a long bookshelf hangs; a silhouetted cityscape of books run along its length. Next to this, a second curtained window.

I have not set foot in this room for seventeen years. No. 12 Iona Road, Dublin. I lived here as a student, the single tenant of Mrs. Maeve Finnigan, a 62-year-old widower who all but adopted me as the son she never had. She had passed in my second year, taken by cancer. I had had to move out as her family had picked over her possessions.

I push myself into a sitting position, pulling the crisp sheets and blanket to one side. I can smell the familiar faint odour of carbonic soap. I swing my legs around and place them on the cold, wooden floorboards. They feel hard and hostile against my skin. The darkness is still all pervasive, and I have a sudden urge to pull the curtains and smother the room in moonlight; I want my eyes to catch up with my mind. I stand unsteadily and make my way to the largest window. I grip the thick material, one curtain in each hand, and pull them apart. Where I should see a midnight scene of semi-detached Victorian villas with neatly trimmed privet hedges, I see the deep grooves of corrugated steel. I reach out, confused. I feel the stone-cold metal, the tips of my fingers brushing against the peeling paint.

I turn and rush to the other window. Again, I tear the curtains apart. I am met by the same scene. Half-inch sheet metal. Panicked, I turn again, and this time run to the door. The door should be set in a wooden frame. It should be unpainted pine, with a tarnished brass knob. Instead, it too is made of steel, a thick bolt mechanism running from top to bottom. I look around me with fresh eyes. The absence of windows should mean there is no light, but for an inexplicable reason the darkness is lifting. Where there should be thick striped wallpaper, deep maroon and green, I now only see the alternating lined shadow of the metal walls. I look up. I expect to see whitewashed plaster, an ornate acanthus leaf ceiling rose in the centre, a deep crack running lightning-like across the furthermost corner. Instead, there is the same closely undulating sheet metal. Then, out of the corner of my eye, I notice something else. I notice it, because it shouldn't be there, not in this room. On the chest of draws is a framed photograph. I walk over to it. I can't remember it being there before. They stare up at me, the two strangers. Smiling. The child between them smiles too.

#

I wake again, my eyes snapping wide open. I am momentarily disorientated, but I sense that I am in my cabin. As I should be. I can feel the cool sharpness of a blade at my throat, the prickling sensation that it is a shadow away from drawing blood. I hear fast, ragged breathing that is not my own.

'Keep still, Donal. Don't try to move,' whispers a voice close to my left ear. I can feel the hairs on my arms rising to attention, try to suppress this new wave of panic. My heart quickens, thumping like a piston in my chest. The thick vein in my neck throbs against the knife's edge. 'You just need to listen,' rasps the ghost voice. 'I need to explain.' I can smell the heavy scent of sweat, of stale breath. 'They are there, on Ascension. Waterman told me. I have spoken to them.'

'Who?' I manage to whisper, although my throat has tightened.

'My parents. My brother. Samira. They are all there. They are waiting for me.'

Samira, I think, must be the girl in the pictures. I have so many questions for him. How can he think this is in the realms of possibility? How and why, amongst such global carnage, could his family have been supplanted from New Delhi to a tiny island in the middle of the Atlantic? I want to grab him by the shoulders, to shake him back to rationality. But my tongue is fat and turgid, the air trapped in my lungs, my limbs frozen by fear.

'I had to get them off the ship. They were about to spread their lies; I heard them speaking to one-another. They refused to listen to Waterman, just like the Captain. His voice was as clear as day, but they refused to hear. They were going to go to the Captain, to say that they thought I was insane; unsafe. Waterman told me what I should do, how I should prepare. I took provisions from the lifeboat – just a little each day and built myself a store. I drained the fuel. I wrote the letter. Then, the storm came...and I was ready. At its height, I told them both that the Captain had ordered that we should prepare the lifeboats. They didn't even question it. They got inside to check the systems, to make sure everything was ready. I closed the hatch and launched them. Then, in the confusion that followed,

I went to their cabins and packed some of their possessions into bags. Later, when I had an opportunity, I threw them overboard.'

'But...' I managed to squeeze out the single word before I felt the blade press deeper into my flesh; imagined the first beads of blood.

'No, Donal. I don't want you to speak. I just need to explain. To make you understand why I had to do these things.'

I think of making a sudden move for the knife, of trying to twist away. Paresh is small; surely, I could overpower him! However, my head is already pinned against the pillow and the cold blade is unrelenting; in the time it would take me to raise my hand to his, it would all be over. I blink away my false courage.

'Although I'd said in my letter that I didn't want you to follow the lifeboat, I was disappointed that you didn't: did our lives really mean that little? Waterman was right though. He said that the Captain would refuse, but that was fine; we weren't ready to go to Ascension yet. So, I disappeared into the fabric of the ship, watching and listening. I lived off the lifeboat rations. I found that I had become invisible. Then, when a few weeks had passed, and the lifeboat was long gone, he told me it was time. It was my idea to destroy the hydroponics crop; he was sceptical. He'd told me to go for the Captain, that with him out of the way the rest of the crew would agree to set sail for Ascension. I convinced him there was another way, but in the end he was right. So, I had to do it. It was the only way. It wasn't easy...making myself do it, but not the act itself. I was shocked by the simplicity of it. I hit him from behind with a wrench. He staggered to the railing. I grabbed his leg and lifted, tipping him over the side. There was no resistance. It was over in four seconds; he didn't even make a sound as he fell. It was almost an anti-climax after the time I had spent deliberating. This had been my third attempt; every other I had stood in the shadows, frozen, and watched him walk past. It was only after the second that Waterman had let me speak to Samira. Her words gave me courage. She said it was the only way we could be reunited.'

I feel the pressure on my neck slacken. Either fatigue is setting in, or he is losing himself too much in his own story, his concentration ebbing. I think again of resistance, of trying to overwhelm him, but my indecision filters through my muscles and he seems to sense the danger. His grip re-tightens.

'Don't do anything stupid Donal, I don't want to kill you.'

He might not want to, but I have no doubt that he is capable.

'Why not?' I manage to say. 'You killed the others. You murdered Li.' As soon as the words are out, I regret my confrontational tone.

'You and I, Donal, we have always had a...connection,' he says calmly, either choosing to ignore or failing to hear my reproach. 'We are not like the others. I sensed it the very first time we met. You were interested in what I had to say, my thoughts, my opinions. Nobody had ever asked me what I thought of the shipping industry before, or asked about my family, or my motivations.'

'I'm a journalist, Paresh. It's my job to show an interest.'

'No, it was more than that. I felt it. That's why I decided to write you the letter. That's why I'm here now.'

'Why *are* you here, Paresh? What is it you want? Do you want my absolution, is that it?' I had found my voice at last, my words flowing freely like water from a breached dam.

'Absolution? Yes, perhaps. But I need more from you than

that. I need you to convince the others that I am dead.' He let the words seep into the darkness. 'It's the only way they will stop looking for me; the only way they will re-start the engines and continue to Ascension.'

'Why me?'

'Because you are the one they all trust. If you say it, they will believe.'

'Even if that *is* true, why would I do it?'

'Because if you don't, I'll kill one of the others. Polina, maybe? Henning? Dmitriy? Their death will be on your conscience.' As he made his threat, I felt the point of the blade twist slightly against my skin, causing a new, warm bead of blood to trickle down my neck, pooling in the indentation between my sternum and clavicle. I considered my options. As I saw it, I had few.

'How?'

'Tomorrow, when Henning starts the engines to maintain our position, go to the stern of the ship. Go running, like you usually do. You'll say that I attacked you, and that you managed to fight me off. Say that in the struggle, I lost my footing and fell overboard. With the engines on, I could easily be sucked into the propellers. I have a jacket here; it is the one Tanmay saw me wearing when the Captain disappeared. It is distinctive, he will remember. I have torn it to shreds. You must throw it into the sea. If they decide to retrieve it from the water, they will think it was ripped from my body.'

'Then what?'

'Then I will disappear. You won't see me again. I'll make my own way onto the island when we get there.' He waits for my answer, the seconds filled by his heavy breathing.

'Okay,' I say. I'm not sure if I mean it – I need time to think it through, but what else can I say with a knife against my throat.

'Good, I knew that you would help me.' He sounds triumphant, excited even, as if I have agreed with my own free will. 'Tomorrow then, as I described. Don't forget the jacket.'

I nod my agreement, forgetting the knife. I feel a sharp intensification of pain.

'Now I need you to turn on your side, facing the wall.' I do as he says.

'I am sorry to do this Donal, but I can't risk you following me.' Before I can register his words, brace for whatever he intends, I feel an abrupt impact, then a searing pain in my right flank. I arch backwards, consumed by agony. I imagine he has punched me or used his knee, but I fear he has used the knife. My hand flashes to my injured side. I anticipate wetness, a slick of blood. I reach for the light switch above my bed, expect to see the smear of scarlet as the darkness is banished. To my relief, there is nothing. Then I remember Paresh. I roll over so that I am facing the door, but he is gone. Only the pain lingers.

Then my gaze falls upon the desk to the left of my door, and to the small photo-frame that sits upon it; the family stolen from the container. They smile back at me. Then the realisation that I hold a trump card beyond Paresh's wildest comprehension: I know where he is.

34

Prophet

I had been ten years old when I had what I consider to be my first premonitional dream. I had dreamt that my father had sold his heart to a travelling magician in return for a packet of Woodbines. The magician had placed the still beating organ into an ornately decorated casket which then proceeded to shrink to the size of matchbox, leaving my father gasping for breath like a beached salmon. I had woken in a fit of terror, my mother comforting me and cajoling me back to sleep. Unbeknown to me, she had received a telephone call an hour later from hospital telling her that my father had collapsed in the pub with a suspected heart attack.

It was only in the days after the funeral that I finally recounted the details of the dream to my mother, partly as a confession for my perceived role in his demise. It was then that she had confided in me that prophetic dreams where somewhat of a family trait; she had been afflicted, as had her mother, and her mother's mother before her. This was the first time, in her knowledge, that it had manifested itself in the male line. Despite the numerous cases of anecdotal evidence that she shared, I was torn between thinking it was either an elaborate rouse to make me feel better or the more romanticised notion, craved by all ten-year olds, that I had been lavished with a superpower. After she had explained that I was unlikely to dream the name of winning racehorses or lottery numbers, and that our dreams were often so cryptic that any meaning rarely showed itself until after an event, I had decided that if it *was* a superpower, it was a pretty pathetic one.

I had had many such dreams since. Usually, I only made connections retrospectively. My dream about Beth had started two weeks before everything had gone nuclear. I had considered it to be the product of guilt-fuelled separation anxiety, a metaphor for being left behind, and leaving her behind. Imagine my surprise.

Often, the details that linked my dreams to future realities were the most infinitesimal: an object of such insignificance that it barely registered; a person I hadn't seen for years or hadn't seen yet; a single word or phrase yet to be uttered; a room or landscape unknown. Then, days or weeks later, in a warmth of deja vu, there it was. It had always been utterly useless, a past-tense superpower that was intriguing rather than practical. Until now.

I knew where Paresh was hiding; I had never been so convinced of something in my life. He had been with me when we had found the container. He had helped me to unpack some of the boxes, move the crated furniture, salvage the objects that we deemed to be most useful. Maybe he too had felt a connection, a longing to immerse himself in the vestiges of an ordinary life that now seemed so alien. It was well positioned in the middle of the ship, in a section of containers that had already been searched and audited; as such, it was unlikely to attract unwanted visitors. I had visited it so many times after our initial discovery that I knew precisely where it was.

It was now 3.20 a.m. In four hours time, Paresh expected me to have performed my subterfuge and declared him dead. I suspected that he would be bedding in and keeping a low profile until the deed was done; I couldn't imagine him risking being out anywhere where he might be seen, and my...his... story compromised. As such, I had a window of opportunity. The question was, should I go it alone or take someone with me? The latter was tempting: it would make sense to share my whereabouts and recent brush with Paresh with someone in case something happened to me, as well as improving my chances if we did run into him. On the other hand, I'd have to explain why I knew where he was and convince someone of my psychic tendencies at three in the morning. As much as I'd like to have had the towering presence of Dmitriy at my side, I decided that it was better to keep things simple. As an insurance, I wrote a quick note describing Paresh's visitation, and my guess at his hiding place (minus the explanation) and placed it in an envelope on my desk; if I didn't return, the rest of the crew would be able to pick up the trail.

I dressed in the darkest clothing I could find and rummaged around in some draws until I found a torch. I opened my door as quietly as I could and crept out onto the corridor of E Deck; the fulgent light from the fluorescent bulb stinging my eyes. I crept down the stairwell as far as B Deck, overly aware of the sound of my feet on the galvanized steel steps.

My first port-of-call was the galley; I was hoping to find a knife or similar implement to defend myself – not that I had ever wielded a knife at anything more dangerous than a cucumber. As it was, Jerzy had done an excellent job in keeping such weaponry out of the reach of would-be psychopaths by locking the cutlery cupboards. The best I could manage was a heavy-duty wooden rolling pin. I looked at my watch; it was now 3:40.

I made my way out of the accommodation tower and down the port-side deck walkway, towards the metal steps that led down into the foredeck container hold. It was a still night and the waxing moon peeped out from bubbling clouds. The constantly shifting ocean reflected the dull light, creating a kaleidoscope of monochrome jewels. There was a cool breeze that lifted the hairs on my arms. As I turned into an unseen alcove, I collided solidly into a wall of flesh. Stumbling backwards, I waved the rolling pin pathetically in front of me. I heard a deep chuckle from the shadows that masked the huge form that had halted my progress so completely.

'Please don't hit me with your scary kitchen tool!' it said. A smirking Dmitriy materialised out of the gloom, his one good eye glinting in the moonlight.

'What the hell are you doing out at this time of night?' I hissed.

'And what are you doing out at this time of night, with a rolling pin?' asked Dmitriy.

'I asked first.'

'I couldn't sleep. I thought I would creep around ship and try to find Paresh. Daylight search was useless, I thought night-time might be better. And you? You have sudden urge to make pastry?'

'Surprisingly, not.' I lowered my weapon. 'Look, Paresh broke into my room tonight. He said some things that gave me an idea of where he might be hiding; I was on my way to test out my theory. I was going to do it alone, but you're here now. I could do with a bit of muscle.'

'Sure, I come. I have nothing else to do.'

'But Dmitriy, we must be careful. He's dangerous: he held a knife to my throat...' I pointed to the dried blood that I hadn't had time to wipe from my neck. 'In this state, he is capable of anything.'

'Then it is just as well you have rolling pin.' It was the first time that I heard Dmitriy utter more than a few monosyllables in days – since his altercation with Tanmay he had kept a low profile. Even when he had helped to remove Li from the lifeboat, he had barely said a thing. It was strangely comforting to hear his deep baritone and stilted dry wit.

I whispered my theory, and the semblance of a plan to him as we made our way to the ladder, all the time sticking to the safety of the shadows. My plan, if it could be called that, was vague and based on a myriad of variables. I also told Dmitriy what Paresh had asked me to do, and that if push came to shove and I had to go through with it, that he was to play along. It all depended on what we found in the container.

Dmitriy's choice of weaponry was far more practical than mine. He had armed himself with a sizeable crowbar and had also thought to bring some rope and plastic tie straps with him in the event of having to immobilise Paresh. He had also brought along a head-torch. I also imagined that, somewhere on his person, he might be concealing a huge, bone handled hunting knife used for skinning bears in the Russian forests. Whatever, I felt considerably safer with him than without him.

We reached the ladder that led down to the cargo bay and, one at a time, descended the thirty or so feet down into the utter darkness of the hold. In normal times, these bays were illuminated twenty-four-seven, but in an attempt to conserve as much energy as we could, the Captain had decided to disconnect all unnecessary lighting. As it was unlikely that we would ever need to check the containers at night, the holds were prime candidates for such efficiencies.

When we reached the bottom, we stood for a few moments, allowing our eyes and senses to adjust to the wall of black.

'Shall we use torch?' whispered Dmitriy.

'We haven't got a hope in hell of finding the container unless we do.' We both switched them on at the same time, cutting narrow beams of colour into the blanket of darkness. The reds, greens and blues of the containers flashed before our eyes as we scanned our surroundings. 'I think it's this way,' I hissed. 'From now on, we should keep talking to a minimum,' I added. Dmitriy nodded.

I hadn't really thought about it before, but I was suddenly aware that by choosing to search now, at night, with flash-lights, we were practically broadcasting our presence. If Paresh was out and about here somewhere, he'd know we were coming well in advance. Still, my hunch was that he'd be in the container, and that our approach would be shielded.

We were looking for Bay 14, Row 4, Tier 1; about as close to the middle of the ship as you could get. We'd searched this segment of the hold well over eight months ago, and it had probably seen few visitors since. As we reached the bay, with the narrow access point running between rows 4 and 5, I gestured for Dmitriy to switch off his torch, then put my hand over the bezel of my own to stifle the light. My hand glowed red, giving just enough light to read the row numbers. Row 1. Row 2, Row 3....

The container had seen better days. Even in the obscured light from the torch, the curls of peeled green paint were obvious, as were the streaks of rust. The doors were closed, but not locked. Would I have left it like that all those months before? Why wouldn't I, there was nothing to steal, and nobody to steal it. I wavered in a moment of indecision; should we just wait, see if he came out...and try to take him then? What if I was wrong, and this was all a wild goose chase? I could hedge my bets; leave Dmitriy here, on guard, whilst I went back and prepared to stage Paresh's death...as he'd planned. But now that I was here, I felt a compulsion to see it through. Had I interpreted my dream correctly, or was I too succumbing to delusion and insanity? Perhaps it was a selfish decision, born from irrationality and ego, but I slowly opened the door.

The interior of the container was not how I had remembered it, to the extent that I immediately doubted that we had found the right one. There was a wall of crates and boxes, stacked from floor to ceiling two feet in from the doorway. It didn't make sense – I knew it by heart – Bay 14, Row 4, Tier 1. This had to be it. I took my hand away from the torch head and scanned the full expanse. It looked impenetrable. Dmitriy tapped me on the shoulder and pointed down at a large, rectangular box at the very bottom of the pile, another boxes' width from the wall of the container. I could see what had grabbed his attention – it was jutting out a good two inches more than any of the other crates. He crouched down, putting his fingers either side of the exposed edges and pulled. The box began to slide out with surprising ease, like a loose tile in a game of Jenga. He awkwardly shifted his huge bulk so that he was able to pull the box clear of the wall, and push it to one side, out of the way. I eased my way around him, knelt and illuminated the black cavity with the torch. The beam stretched out before me, before finally hitting another vertical expanse a good five or six metres deep into the container. I could see other shapes dotted around the open space that broke the beam. I turned to Dmitriy.

'There's a cavity behind the wall. A room,' I whispered. I moved to one side, so that he too could kneel and look into the gap. As he did so, he switched on his own headlamp, momentarily leaving me blinded as my eyes took the full-force of the sudden light. Before I could blink away the supernovas etched onto my retina, he was half-way in. How, I didn't know; Dmitriy's dimensions and that of the hole seemed incompatible. I watched as his feet disappeared, listening to his muffled grunts and groans as he manipulated his colossal frame through the entrance, like a cat entering a mouse hole. I crouched down to follow, cursing noiselessly as my knee scrapped against the crowbar that Dmitriy had left behind. I tightened my own grip on the rolling pin.

I crawled out and stood, my gaze following Dmitriy's line of vision as he too took in the scene around us. My description of the space as being a 'room' was startlingly accurate. There was a minimalist 1970s style couch sat against the right-hand wall of the container, and a similarly designed reading chair to the right of that. A sleek teak coffee table with an inset glass top sat between them, a collection of books and magazines neatly stacked on its top. An intricately decorated Persian rug lavished itself in the centre of the floor, a chaos of swirls and concentric shapes. A standing lamp stood next to the reading chair, a wire snaking across the floor to a car battery that hunched in the darkness. A fully stocked bookcase sat opposite the couch on the far wall. A small wooden table, the type that could be extended by pulling up two flaps each side of the central tableau, crouched on the other side of the room, flanked by two simple dining chairs. There was an opened tin of peaches on the table, next to a single plate and spoon. The whole ambiance was very 1970's British sitcom. Aside from the wall decorations.

I raised my own torch and swept the walls. They were covered in familiar pictures; the light reflected off the Sellotape that had been used to secure them in place. One, a family group – a mother, father and younger boy; Paresh's brother, Charun. The portrait of his parents. Then there was a picture of his brother, alone and holding a trophy. The final picture of Samira, sitting on the bench in front of the river. There must have been dozens of replicas of each image, of various sizes and detail. Dmitriy, perhaps forgetting himself, let out a low whistle. I threw him a look.

'What?' he said, still in a low whisper. 'He's obviously not here.'

'Don't you think there's something missing?' I hissed.

'Three ducks on wall? Vinyl record player? Wooden TV set?'

'No, I mean, where is he sleeping? Where's the bed?' We both scanned the room again, expecting it to suddenly leap out at us. It was then that I noticed that the wall opposite us mirrored the fake wall of crates that we had crawled through, although this time it didn't span the whole width of the container – there was a two-foot-wide gap on the far side. It was hidden in shadow, making it less noticeable. I quickly tried to do a mental calculation of the length of a container, trying to ascertain if this could be another false wall – a final hiding place.

What happened next, even as I recall it now, felt like it happened in slow motion. I had turned towards Dmitriy, pulling the beam of my torch with me, with the intention of pointing out the gap in the wall with my next sweep. As I did so, I thought I saw a grey shape materialise from the darkness. The next thing I knew, I was sprawled on the floor, winded. I had dropped the torch and it had rolled to the corner of the room, illuminating a small square of steel. I could hear a struggle going on behind me, the grunts of physical exertion. Light from Dmitriy's headlamp danced around the container walls like strobe lighting – in my dazed confusion, I was unable to hold onto an image long enough to form a picture of what was happening. I heard a crash, the sound of breaking glass, and a heavy exhalation of breath like the expulsion of air from a pair of bellows: then it all went dark as Dmitriy's headlamp snapped off. The only light remaining was the postage-stamp sized glow from my torch in the corner. Then there was a pause. I could hear ragged breath, but I couldn't be sure that it wasn't just my own.

I tried to roll over but felt an intense pain in my shoulder. I reached up, my fingers exploring. I felt something protruding – something hard and metallic. Then I felt pressure on my leg, and a hand gripping my knee.

'Get out!' It was Dmitriy. He sounded breathless. 'Get out, now. Go get others. You must lock door, so he can't escape.'

'What about you?'

'I stay.' That's all he said.

I struggled to get into a crawling position, feeling the stab of pain in my upper back. I slithered more than crawled to where I thought the entrance should be – navigating through the dull glow of the torch in the opposite corner. I felt the rough fabric of the Persian rug beneath me, feeling it slide with my movement. I reached the crate wall, using it to guide me to the gap. Then my fingers hit hollow space. I dragged myself through, forgetting the object lodged in my back – it scraped against the crate above, sending fingers of pain across my shoulders, down my arm. I collapsed, prostate, and used my hands to slide myself through the hollow.

When I was free enough to be sure of not dislodging the knife again, I heaved myself into a crouching position and used the container wall to help me stand. The crowbar still sat where it had been abandoned, and I stooped to pick it up. Staggering outside, I turned and closed the two doors behind me. I tried to turn the handles, to engage the locking mechanism, but they both rattled loosely and uselessly – Paresh's insurance against imprisonment. I raised the crowbar and wedged it horizontally between the two vertical struts that went from the top to bottom of each door. Nobody would be getting out until I returned.

Torchless, blind, I used my hands to guide myself back along Row 4 and into the narrow corridor that ran the length of the bays. As I neared the metal ladder, I could see the dim dawn light filtering down from above. I had to raise the alarm as quickly as possible; I knew that Dmitriy's life might depend on it.

35

Ascension

I only have fleeting first-hand memories of what happened next. The others, later, did their best to fill in the gaps, to the extent that I find it difficult now to recall my own experiences from theirs.

I do remember the climb up the metal ladder from the hold to the main deck as being excruciating; with the knife in my shoulder, I was unable to bare any weight on my right arm. Somehow, I made it up but was so dizzy and nauseous with the pain that I had to spend a few minutes on all fours trying to muster the inner strength to move on. My aim was to go to the bridge to raise the alarm, but the prospect of making my way along 150 feet of deck, then up six flights of stairs now seemed unsurmountable. Using the deck rail as a crutch, I dragged myself towards the accommodation tower. The back of my shirt was slick with blood, but I remember thinking that it was far from being a flood, and that perhaps I had been lucky and the knife had missed any major blood vessels. As such, I was keen to minimize any unnecessary arm movement to keep it that way.

As it was, I didn't have to negotiate the stairs single-handedly, as I virtually collided with Alon and Tanmay as they burst out of the E-Deck corridor on an early morning jog. I remember recounting the basics of what had just happened and telling them to go the bridge to raise the alarm. Then I must have passed out, because the next thing I remember is waking up in the recovery position with the stench of my own vomit in my nostrils and a dull ache in my upper back which exploded into a searing pain if I moved. My head was resting on a rolled blanket. It took me a few seconds to orientate myself, but I quickly realised that I was still on deck, and that Polina was sat to my right.

'How are you feeling?' she said.

'Shitty,' I managed to croak back.

'I took out the knife. It was lodged in the muscle in your shoulder. Luckily, it didn't nick any arteries or anything. I've patched you up the best I can – stemmed the bleeding. You'll need some antibiotics and plenty of rest, but you should be okay.' I gritted my teeth and tried to push myself up into a sitting position, away from the contents of my stomach that splattered the deck and blanket. The explosion of pain made my head swim, but I managed to retain consciousness.

'What about Paresh...and Dmitriy?' I said quickly, suddenly recalling the sequence of events that had brought me here.

'I don't know. I came here to tend to you, the rest of them went down to the hold. I'm just as much in the dark as you are. What happened?'

'We found him in one of the containers. It was where he'd been hiding...well, more *living* than hiding.'

'What, did you just happen upon it?'

'Not quite. It's a long story...for later, maybe. Anyway, once we were inside, he jumped us. It was pitch black, so I don't know what happened to Dmitriy...there was some kind of fight, then he told me to get out...so he was alive when I left. I don't know about Paresh. I managed to lock the door so Paresh couldn't escape.'

'Or Dmitriy!'

'He told me to. I didn't want to, but what good would it have been if Paresh was able to get out and hide somewhere else? We might have never found him again, and all this would have been for nothing.' Polina nodded solemnly and looked out to the horizon.

'I guess we'll just have to wait,' she said matter-of-factly. She turned to her right and picked up something from the deck, before passing it to me. It was a three-inch penknife, with a faux bone-come-plastic handle. There was still blood...my blood...on the blade. 'This was what was in your shoulder, pretty much up to the hilt. He must have hit you pretty hard.' I held it in my hand, feeling the weight. Then I closed it and tried to put it in my pocket – the sudden pulse of pain forcing me to reconsider. Was this the same knife that, a few hours before, had been pressed up against my throat?

The sound of heavy boots colliding with hollow metal dragged our attention to the left, and the entrance to the hold. We watched as the back of Henning's head materialised goffer-like from the deck, followed gradually by the rest of his body as he stiffly negotiated the last few runs of the ladder. He seemed to compose himself for a second or two, before lumbering slowly in our direction. We expected the others to join him, but he was alone. It felt like an age before he finally reached us.

'Donal, it is good to see you...' he hesitated, obviously searching for the right word.

'Alive!' I suggested.

'Restored to consciousness,' he said. 'How are you feeling? I see that Polina has done a good job removing the knife.' His eyes dipped to the knife that still sat in my lap.

'I'm sore,' I said, '...but in one piece. How is Dmitriy?' I felt my blood run cold, and a new wave of nausea sweep over me as I anticipated Henning's response. It may have been my imagination, but Henning appeared to take an intake of breath – chilling me even more.

'He is fine. Bruised and battered, but he will be okay.' I felt a lump appear in my throat and the tell-tale sting in my eyes as I tried to fight back tears of relief.

'And Paresh?'

Henning, looked down at his shoes, shaking his head. 'When we found them, they were both laying on the floor in a pool of blood. Dmitriy was slumped against the wall, cradling Paresh. At first, we thought that they were both dead, Dmitriy had his eyes closed and he was so...still.' Henning paused, obviously replaying the scene in his head. 'Then he looked up. He said that Paresh had bled out from a wound to his lower back.' I remembered the loud crash in the darkness, the sound of an impact, the splintering of wood and breaking glass.

'So, Paresh is...dead?' asked Polina.

'He is,' said Henning. 'Despite all the things that he did, we didn't want this. He was a troubled young man.'

'What happens now?'

'Ton sent me up to let you know what had happened, and to check you were both okay. Now that I have, and you are, I am to go to the engine room to prepare the ship to set sail. We are going to make haste for Ascension. With fair weather, we should be there the day after tomorrow.'

#

The rest of that day was a haze. After Henning left us, Polina helped me to my cabin. She fed me antibiotics and pain killers and tried to do her best to make me comfortable. The pain in my shoulder was now a dull ache, but it spiked hideously if I tried to twist my body or raise my arm. As soon as I lay down on my bunk, I was consumed by an overarching weariness, a fatigue that practically pulsed behind my eyes. I couldn't bring myself to eat but managed to sip down a sweet tea. When she was satisfied that I was okay, Polina left me to sleep. I barely recall her leaving.

I remember the notion of dreaming, but not the dreams themselves. They were those intense, senseless dreams that you get sometimes – all colour, and noise but nothing tangible to grab onto upon waking. They were the type of dreams that thwarted the whole point of sleep, leaving you somehow more tired than before. I tried to sit up, the resulting flash of pain accompanied by a vision of that morning's events. After a few gulping breaths, I tried again – this time putting my weight onto my other elbow and swinging my feet around. My clock said it was 21:34; I must have been asleep for nearly twelve hours. Bracing myself again, I stood and walked to my bathroom and switched on the dull strobe light that fizzed noisily like an angry fly. I looked in the mirror. My face was grey, with a fuzz of stubble. My hair was lank and greasy. I tried to twist so that I could see the bandage that covered my shoulder, to see if I had bled as I slept. There was a dark, brown stain whose shape reminded me very much of Italy, with a Sicily-like blob at its base. It was not as large as I had feared; Polina had done a good job strapping me up. I spent several painful minutes trying to put on a shirt, leaving it unbuttoned, and eased myself into a fresh pair of trousers. Putting on socks was all kinds of agony, so I gave up and kicked on a pair of deck-shoes.

I left my cabin and made my way four doors down the corridor of E deck until I reached Dmitriy's. I knocked quietly and waited for a response. There were voices from inside and the sound of movement, then the door swung open. It was Polina.

'Hey, how are you feeling?' she said.

'To be honest, a combination of the worst hangover imaginable coupled with falling off an elephant.'

'Possibly the weirdest description I've ever heard!' She opened the door wide, and beckoned me in. Dmitriy was sitting, slouched on the bed with is head in his hands. I noted that there was a half-empty bottle of whiskey by his feet.

'How is he?' I asked Polina.

'Dmitriy is in room,' he said gruffly.

'Sorry, Dmitriy, how are you?'

'I am *working* on having worst hangover imaginable.' He looked up at me, his uncovered eye was bloodshot, and his whole face seemed to have sagged. There was a gash over his right eye, and a bruise that was already experimenting with a collage of blues and purples.

'What...what happened when I left?

'I think it was more what happened *before* you left!'

'I don't really remember. I know he must have lunged for

me. I saw a shape come at me, and I fell. Then I saw you and he locked together, some kind of fight – but only intermittently when the light allowed. Then it went dark, and I heard a crash.'

'I was behind you. I saw Paresh jump on you, and the flash of light on a blade. I saw you fall – I thought he'd killed you. Then he came for me. I was confused – I thought I'd seen him leave the knife in you, but he seemed to have another – a bigger one. I managed to grab his wrist – he was strong, much stronger than I could have imagined. He wriggled like an eel, trying to break my grip. I think that that is when he did this.' He pointed to the side of his face. 'I didn't have any choice: I had to try and get him away from me. So, I grabbed his throat with my other hand and...kind of threw him backwards. By this time, my light had gone off, so I couldn't see properly. There was a crash, of wood and broken glass, and I heard him exhale a big breath of air. Then nothing. That is when I found you – I could hear you breathing. That is when I told you to get out. I thought he was still there somewhere, in the darkness.' He paused to pick up the bottle and inhaled two-huge gulps.

'I'm sorry I left you Dmitriy. I shouldn't have done.'

'I told you to, of course you should. We needed help.'

'So, then what happened?' This from Polina, who had been hovering in the corner of the room, nursing her own glass of whiskey.

'There was another torch in the corner of the container – Donal's. It was right up against wall, so barely giving any light. I made my way to it, with my back against the side of container so that he couldn't take me from behind. I picked it up and looked around room. Paresh was lying on floor. He had hit little table with the glass top, which had shattered. There was pool of blood next to him.'

'He'd fallen on his knife!'

'No, it was the glass. It had broken into long shards. One had pierced his back, about here.' He turned and pointed at the fleshy area of his lower back, to the left of his spine. 'He was still alive. He looked up at me, his eyes wide. He was so frightened.' He stopped again, reaching for the bottle and the dampening solace within.

'I knelt, and he grabbed my hand. His breathing was very rapid, very shallow. He told me he was scared, that he was sorry, that he never wanted this to happen. I moved the debris from the table out of the way, and sat behind him, my legs either side of his body so that he could rest his head on my thigh. He said he wanted his mother, and he wept. I stroked his hair, his cheek. I said it would all be all right. His breathing came out in little puffs, then one, final rattling breath. Then nothing. I looked at his eyes; they were like glass. So, I switched off light and waited. It seemed right to give him the darkness.'

'I'm sorry,' I said, 'That you had to deal with that, alone.'

'It doesn't matter that I was alone. The fact is that I...I killed someone. I caused their death.'

'But you had no choice, you were trying to defend yourself!' said Polina.

'And even then, it was an accident Dmitriy. You couldn't see what you were doing. It wasn't deliberate, you were just doing what you had to do to save your own life,' I added.

'I know,' he said, taking another slug. 'I know all this, but that doesn't stop the ache deep in my heart. He was young man. He was sick, but still had whole life to live. Maybe it is a pain that all people who take another's life feel – the murderer, the soldier with gun, the reckless driver, the doctor that makes mistake. Maybe some are better at bearing it than others. Maybe it deadens with time.' We sat in the semi-darkness of Dmitriy's cabin, the chorus of background noise filling the conversational void - the creaking metal, the hum of distant engines, the heave of waves against the hull. There was nothing else to say.

36

Soul birds

How do you mark the passing of a killer? Is it right to pay them homage, to write and share a eulogy? Should you focus on their life before their crime, place the knowledge of their violence in a cold, dark recess – pretend it didn't happen? Should you offer excuses; they only did it because...? Should you mention their victims in the same breath, or does that add insult to injury, an affront to their memory? Nature's plans for his corpse meant that we had only a short time to reach our conclusion.

Paresh's lifeless body had been rolled up in the Persian rug that had covered the container's floor and left where it was. I imagine that it had slowly stiffened with the effects of rigour mortis, leaking viscous crimson into the carpet's woollen weave. Maybe someone had had the compassion to close his glassy eyes as the lights were extinguished and his body was left to the darkness. There he had lain for the last twenty-four hours: a pariah and persona non grata.

'What should we do with Paresh?' asked Rieko at breakfast

the next morning.

'I don't know,' said Ton. 'I guess we should bury his body at sea. I appreciate that there may be some of you who don't wish to mark his passing, on the merit of his actions. That is understandable.' Ton looked at me as he said this, perhaps thinking that as a victim of Paresh's violence, I was a prime candidate for such a withdrawal. It wasn't how I felt at all. In a way, Paresh was as much of a victim as the Captain, or Li or Banya. He had succumbed to an altogether more powerful adversary, the uncontrollable force of insanity. I looked around the room at the reaction of the others. There were furtive glances exchanged between members of the crew.

'I think I speak for others, as well as myself in saying that Paresh's body cannot be committed to the sea,' said Jerzy. Alon and Roy nodded their agreement.

'Why not?' asked Ton.

'Come on, Ton, you know why,' said Henning, leaning forward in his chair. It wasn't an aggressive intervention, more fatherly; a paternal reminder to a forgetful son. Henning held Ton's gaze for a second. I couldn't work out what was going on between them.

'Well, I don't!' I said. I thought that sea burials were more than just a tradition, I thought that they were a necessity. In the past, before refrigeration, those that died at sea were normally shrouded and buried in the waves. It made practical sense. There were, of course, exceptions; I seemed to remember that Nelson's body had been festooned in a barrel of brandy and returned to a grateful nation. I assumed that more recently bodies might have been preserved and repatriated, but we had effectively stepped back in time. Repatriation, for us, was an impossibility. Besides, the crew had buried both Li and Banya at sea. There had been a collective desire to do the same with the poor souls in the life raft. Why should it be different with the body of Paresh?

'It may not have escaped your attention, Donal, that mariners are quite superstitious folk,' said Henning patiently. 'We harbour ideas and beliefs that might seem...how shall I put it...out of step with the modern world. We attach ourselves to a long list of portents and omens to help us navigate the dangers of the sea. The origins of most are lost in the mists of time. For instance, we believe it to be bad luck to set sail on a Friday or to have redheads as passengers. We frown upon those that whistle onboard as it is seen as a challenge to the wind. We wear tattoos of anchors as we believe that this will stop us from floating away from the ship if we fall overboard. All silly things, you might say, in a world of atomic physics and chromosomal sequencing. Seamen also believe that the souls of those who die and are buried at sea are scooped up by sea birds to continue their voyage. In my own country, we believe that the spirits of those lost visit their loved ones disguised as cormorants. As such, the killing of a sea bird is deemed to be wickedness of the highest order.'

'Why should Paresh's soul be denied such a thing?' I asked. I liked the idea that one day, embodied as a gull or a tern, he might fly in the skies above his native India and, if they were still alive, look down upon his family once more.

'Paresh's soul is tainted,' said Alon. 'He has killed another. He has let malice into his heart. It would be wrong of us to release his spirit, to allow him to roam the skies and oceans.'

'And you all believe this?' I said incredulously, as I looked at one face to another.

'Some more that others,' said Ton stoically.

'So, what should we do instead?' I asked.

'We take him ashore at Ascension, as he desired, and we bury him in the earth there,' said Jerzy. 'We will be there very soon. In the meantime, we can place his body in one of the refrigerated holds.'

'But he didn't want to go to Ascension *because* it was Ascension, he wanted to go because he believed that his loved ones were there?' I countered.

'But his soul is still tainted,' argued Alon, as if it was an indelible truth that was beyond question.

'What do the rest of you think?' I asked the room. There was a pause. Shuffled feet. An exchange of glances from the tail of eyes.

'I see no reason why we shouldn't bury him at sea,' said Polina, 'all this talk of spirits and birds is superstitious nonsense. Even if it wasn't, what harm is a murderous sea gull going to do in the world? There's far worse out there than that.'

'Plus, we don't know what Ascension is going to throw at us. There might not be the opportunity for a leisurely burial,' added Rieko.

'It just doesn't sit well,' said Jerzy. 'It feels wrong.'

'Okay,' said Ton. 'I think it best if we put it to a vote. All those in favour of a sea burial?' Eleven hands went up, including my own. Ton abstained. Motion carried eleven to six.

'So, gentlemen...Polina...there is no time like the present. I suggest we convene on the foredeck in an hour's time. If you don't feel comfortable attending, then no-one will think ill of you: it is a free choice. Please can I have some volunteers to collect Paresh's body.' Dmitriy and Palvinder raised their hands, along with Henning. I raised mine as well, but Ton ignored it. 'Thank you, gentlemen, I'll meet you by the ladder down to the cargo bay in a few minutes. Could you get one of the stretchers please, and some rope: we're going to need it to get him up.' They nodded their agreement. With that, everyone melted away from the galley, focused on the daily rota and what lay ahead. As I awaited my turn to leave, Ton tapped me on the shoulder.

'Can I just see you for a minute?' he said. I nodded, hovering by the cutlery trays until everyone had left. When we were alone, Ton closed the door. 'I'm sorry about that. You must think them parochial idiots. Personally, the sooner we tip him over the side the better.'

'You're not a believer in bird souls then?'

'Of course not, it's a load of superstitious clap trap, but I didn't want to risk setting them against me again. Easier to go with it and put it to the vote.'

'I don't know,' I said. 'I quite like it. It's no more fanciful than pearly gates or a final journey towards a bright light. Sailors and sea birds have had an affinity since the beginning of time. The notion that there might be a symbiotic relationship in death has some kind of logic to it. If not logic, romance. Is that all you wanted, to apologise on behalf of some crew members? There really is no need.'

'No, I just wanted to see how you were doing.'

'I'm as good as could be expected. My shoulder still hurts.'

'You don't need to come to the burial, you know. Everyone would understand. The man held a knife to your throat, before trying to kill you.'

'I know, but he was ill. Before, I liked him. He was a good man, trying to do right by his family. He just couldn't cope with their loss, or the idea of it anyway. In fact, if I may, I'd like to do the eulogy.'

'Really! Are you sure?'

'Yes. Perhaps for it to mean anything, I'm the only one who can.' Ton put his arm around my shoulder and guided me towards the door.

'I'd better go and meet the others. They should have the equipment by now. Do you want some time by yourself, to collect your thoughts?'

'No, I think I'll come with you. I'd like to go back to the container, to see it again. Paresh had lived there for weeks. I'd like to see it properly: it may help me to better understand him, and where his mind was at the end.'

#

We met the others at the top of the stairwell leading into the cargo hold. As instructed, they had collected the medical stretcher and the ropes and pulley system needed to help winch Paresh's body up from the hold. We lowered the stretcher and followed it down. Henning had had the foresight to reconnect the electrics so that the space was now illuminated in bright white light that stung the eyes. The hold had lost its labyrinth-like allure, the impenetrable walls of black that shaped the maze from two nights before now exposed as the crimplene steel of a patchwork of multi-coloured containers. Navigation to Paresh's container, so perplexing in the shroud of darkness, was now startlingly perfunctory. We reached Bay 14, Row 4, Tier 1 in no more than a minute. The doors were wide open, a collection of crates and boxes that had formed the outer screen to Paresh's room were stacked haphazardly to the side. The light from the outer walls of the hold hadn't penetrated this far, and the inside of the container was still blanketed in shadow. Dmitriy and Henning switched on their flashlights. The first thing that struck me was how small it was. It had seemed cavernous before; now the bright light sucked in the walls, drawing the meagre pieces of furniture closer together: the small table and chairs, the armchair, the shattered glass and splintered wood of the coffee table. The back-wall of boxes that shielded the mattress felt claustrophobically close. The rolled-up carpet that cocooned Paresh's body lay diagonally across the floor, a dark purple stain the colour of blackberries spread across its base.

'Should we leave him as he is, or...unwrap him?' asked Dmitriy in a low voice. He looked pale, dark circles framing his eyes. It was only then that I considered Dmitriy's motivations for volunteering to return; I guess that he too wanted to gain perspective, to look on the scene again in a different light. Perhaps he felt an obligation, born from guilt, to guide Paresh on this, the final part of his journey.

'No,' said Ton. 'I think we should just take him as he is. This is as good a shroud as any.' There were no complaints; I don't think any of us really relished the idea of seeing his waxen features again. Palvinder and Henning placed the stretcher next to the body, and Dmitriy and I positioned ourselves at the head and tail of the rolled-up rug. On the count of three we lifted him across, the dead weight of Paresh's body sending lightning bolts of pain through my shoulder. Ton busied himself fastening and tightening the straps so that the rug and its contents were firmly secured in place. All this performed in solemn quietude, the only sounds the creaking and clicking of knee joints, the scuffling of shoes on the metal floor, the exhalations of heavy breath from our exertions. 'Are we ready,' said Ton, finally breaking the spell. His voice sounded hollow and reedy in the small space, strained an octave or two higher than his normal range; a peephole into the emotion that we all felt.

'If you don't mind,' I said, 'I'd just like to stay here for a while longer. To gather my thoughts.' Ton nodded his understanding, and Palvinder passed me one of the flashlights. The four men lifted the stretcher and shuffled backwards out of the container. I listened as the sound of their coordinated movement, their whispered instructions to each other, faded into the distance. I sat in the armchair and looked around me, my eyes resting on the montage of Paresh's family and Samira that covered the wall. The meticulous detail of his drawings; madness and artistic genius intertwined. The opened can of peaches still sat on the table, the spoon pointing skywards; somehow, it had survived the violence of a few nights before. There was a stale, sweet smell in the air; the sugary, syrupy odour of ripe fruit mixed with the dusty odour of old furniture – the kind of smell you get in stately homes or past-their-best guest houses.

As I cast my eyes around the room, I noticed that there was a book lying face down on the floor to the left of the chair, its spine arched towards the ceiling. It had a plain green cover which, when I stretched down to retrieve it, I realised was made of fine leather. It felt soft and cold in my hands. As I opened it, I could see that it was a sketch book, the thick, cream paper covered in small, intricate pencil drawings. I flicked to the front page: a picture of the *Thalassa* at ease in a calm ocean. The next: a series of quick sketches of a herring gull, a daub of red and yellow on its beak the only colour. Then caricatures of the crew, all identifiable yet moderately grotesque in the elaboration of certain features: the Captain's protuberant nose; Henning's lofty forehead; Dmitriy's bulk; Alon's squint. As I flicked through, there were detailed land and cityscapes, pictures of dogs and cats, clusters of people going about their everyday lives, unaware of the eyes and hands working in tandem to freeze them in time. All, I assumed, from time spent onshore. There were also drawings of other ships, of cranes and tugboats – the machinery of commerce. Then, abruptly, the same image replicated page after page – the family group, followed by drawings of Samira from every conceivable angle. Then, inexplicably, the drawings changed. Gone was the light touch, the breeze of graphite on paper, the joy of creation. The lines were now darker, impressed into the paper with a heavier hand. Figures lurked in black, cross-hatched backgrounds. There were a series of portraits, clearly representations of Li and Banya, torment and suffering etched onto their emaciated faces. Two pages depicting a figure floating in a dark abyss, monstrous fish circling in the shadows. Then, finally, across a double page, a cityscape of ruin and destruction, humanoid creatures crawling from the devastation; scenes to rival the very worst of Bosch's depictions of hell. I closed the book and then my eyes, the final image etched into my memory. He had been here, alone. Battling his demons, releasing them onto the purity of the page. Despite everything he had done, I felt a wave of sympathy envelope me. I switched off the flashlight and sat in the darkness.

#

When I reached the foredeck, I found the others waiting for me. There were nine in total: Jerzy, Alon and Roy, along with the others that had voted against the sea burial were unsurprisingly absent, as were Arjun and Crisanto – who hadn't. I could only assume that they had not objected to the burial but couldn't bring themselves to pay their respects to Paresh. The stretcher had been placed on the floor, transecting the small group. A light brine drizzle was falling from the marbled grey skies, leaving the deck slick and greasy. Ton, who had been leaning on the guardrail and looking out to sea, turned upon my approach.

'Are you ready?' he said.

'As I'll ever be,' I replied. The others shuffled around the stretcher, their backs now to the ocean, and looked at me expectantly. I cleared my throat, my mouth suddenly drained of all moisture; usually, I was fine with public speaking – I'd rattled off my fair share of best-man speeches, spoken at conferences, but this felt different. An image of the cold granite church in Ireland flashed through my mind, my father's porcelain flesh encased in green velvet.

'Take your time,' said Ton, perhaps sensing my discomfort.

'No, really I'm fine.' I took a deep breath. 'I hope he won't mind my saying, but Ton questioned whether I would want to be here, let alone sharing a eulogy. The fact is that it was never in question. I can't judge Paresh for what he did. Yes, his actions were reprehensible, but born from a sickness that we can only imagine. We have all descended into the darkness these past eighteen months, all wrestled with our own demons. I hope I speak for us all in saying that these have been short visitations, that we've all of us managed to kick for the light and with burning lungs break the surface. Paresh just sank deeper, drifting further and further from the light. So, its right that we remember him as he was before he was consumed by sorrow and despair; before his longings poisoned his mind and drove his actions.

Many of you knew Paresh longer than I did – in that respect, I feel a fraud standing here now. What right have I to lecture you? However, I remember a conversation I had with Paresh at the beginning, before the bombs. It was when I was still a passenger, a writer trying to populate my unwritten book with *your* stories. He opened up like few of you had. He told me about his childhood, his family, his brother, and the short, blissful period when he followed his dreams, attending university and studying engineering. But then everything changed. He father became sick, and they could no longer afford to pay the tuition fees. He was forced to leave and follow a new path. This one, a life transversing the oceans. He showed me a spreadsheet he had made. It detailed his projected career progression through the merchant navy – when he would achieve specific ranks, salary expectations at every point, when he might have to settle for a sideways move rather than continuous upward trajectory. I thought at first that this was born from ego, for his own personal sense of self-worth. But it wasn't. He told me that he was driven by a desire to ensure that his brother, Charun, could enjoy a future that he had been denied. This was the real Paresh: selfless, loyal, sacrificing. I can only imagine that the thought of none of this existing anymore was beyond him. It switched a switch deep within him.

So, as we commit his body to the waves, I would like us to remember *this* Paresh. The young man whose heart, despite where he was in the world, was always back in his native Mumbai, who dreamt of his brother's success, whose love and passion for his family brought him here, to the *Thalassa* at the end of the world.'

Polina edged closer to me, and I felt her hand rest reassuringly on my lower back, a gesture of solidarity. The others lowered their eyes to the deck, as Ton, Dmitriy, Palvinder and Tanmay lifted the stretcher, and placed the front-end on the guardrail. Ton unfastened the straps and gave the order to tip the rug and its contents into the ocean. We moved to the rail, watching as it hit the water, bobbing briefly on the surface before tipping and sinking like a miniature ship.

It was then that we saw it. It materialised from behind us, gliding past the bow of the ship like a phantom. It was so white against the slate-grey sea that it seemed to glow, a simmering purity that transcended nature. The tips of its huge wings skimmed the water, its eyes fixed on a destination that only it knew. An albatross. Paresh's final vessel.

37

Land

It appeared on the horizon at around noon the next day, the first land we had seen for nearly eighteen months. Angelo saw it first. With the exception of the engine room team, we had all gathered on the forecastle in anticipation of gaining our first sight of Ascension. Angelo had shouted, and then pointed south-south-east. I'd followed his finger but initially seen nothing but a vague nodule of cloud that broke the perfect line of symmetry between sky and sea. I'd looked around at the others sceptically, but they all seemed as excited as Angelo. Finally, taking pity on me, Roy had passed me a pair of binoculars. I trained it on the horizon, sweeping to my left and then, suddenly, there it was: a dark brown blob rising from the ocean, a halo of cloud encircling its highest point like a crown.

I joined the others with smiles and celebratory slaps on the back – but inside I was experiencing a smorgasbord of emotion. Yes, there was a feeling of elation that here, finally, was land – and all that that represented. There was the fear and trepidation of what we might find; that all our hopes might be dashed, that even this remotest of outposts might have been left barren and lifeless. But strangely, my abiding emotion was a profound sense of sorrow. It sat in the centre of my chest, a deep relentless ache. Ascension had become a symbol of our possible salvation, but it was also a manifest of all we had lost. The very thought of the island, and what it could offer, had sown the seeds of insanity that had grown like bindweed and strangled Paresh's grasp on reality. The fear of the unknown that Ascension represented, had led the Captain to dig in his heels, to ostracise, to divide. Arguments about the pros and cons of heading for the island had caused the crew's comradery to fracture, the seeping poison of a hundred years of western colonialism and corporate exploitation oozing between the cracks. Ascension, as a mere conception, was death, division, madness.

We sailed on, and the island's features began to sharpen. It was dominated by a single peak that, as we got closer, shone a vibrant emerald green against a burnt umber base. Ton had explained that it was a volcanic upstart that had blossomed from the boiling, bubbling rock of the mid-Atlantic ridge, a geological infant that was no more than a million years old. By all rights, it should have been a guano covered lump of basalt and pumice, but the seeds of life had drifted across the wide oceans aboard millennia of winds and currents. More recently, the very same winds had brought the ambition and vision of man to its shores.

It had been Henning that had told us about the horticultural wonders of Ascension. On his first visit to the island in 1836, Charles Darwin had reported the presence of a mere thirty species of plant, ten of these being endemic to Ascension and nowhere else. Six years later, his good friend, the botanist

Joseph Dalton Hooker, had drifted to the island mid-way through a voyage to the Antarctic. He had proposed a plan to plant the island with non-indigenous species with the aim of increasing the levels of rainfall and, in so doing, make the lives of the garrison stationed there more bearable. His vision was put into action and, with the help of two centrally located natural springs that provided irrigation, a forest slowly crept up the mountain. By the 1900s, mangoes and guava were growing naturally and although there was no evidence of greater rainfall, the increased vegetation had caused mist to cling to the mountain, creating a mosaic of new habitats. It was this invention, so long ago, that accounted for the Verdigris that now clung to the copper slopes of the aptly named 'Green Mountain' that dominated the island's skyline. The colours became more verdant as we clawed our way through the ocean, reeling in the island like a prized fish.

As we got closer, the sky became peppered with sea birds; an encyclopaedia of gulls and terns, low-skimming shearwaters and skuas, dive bombing gannets and the majestic symmetry of the frigatebird, with their deep vermillion throats. This was life and nature on a scale that we hadn't witnessed for so, so long. A lump appeared in my throat, and a tear streaked my cheek. Surely this meant that the island had been spared, that it remained untainted and unblemished.

We approached from the north, heading towards the island's only deep-water port. As we neared, we could see that there were two other cargo ships anchored in Georgetown's bay. Even from a distance, we could see that both were streaked with rust; either their crews had been far less fastidious in their ship's maintenance, or they had been abandoned long ago. Both vessels sat about a quarter of a mile from the coast, and the same distance from each other.

A mile from the shore, Ton gave the orders to cut the engine and maintain our position. The skies were darkening, not only with the onset of evening but also with the gathering of towering cumulous clouds to the south. The wind was also picking up, the smell of the rain to come thick and cloying. The crew, minus Henning and Arjun who were in the engine room, met on the bridge.

'We have a storm brewing,' said Ton, 'So we are going to seek the sanctuary of the bay. Ideally, I would have preferred to stay further out to sea until we had had the opportunity to observe both the ships and the shoreline, but with the weather turning, we have little choice. We'll head for the southern-most lip of the bay, as far away from the other two craft as possible. As you would have seen, one of them is a fellow Maersk vessel, *The Edith*. The other is a bulk carrier, *The Santos Eagle*. Rieko and Roy, who have been with me on the bridge, have been keeping a close eye on each as we've got closer, and neither have reported any attempt at communication or movement onboard. When we're safely at anchor and it's a bit darker, we'll try signalling them ourselves – we'll go old-school and use a flashlight. It could be that the crew are on the island, so that way, they'll see us from the town as well. Depending on what happens with this, we'll see out the storm then sit here and watch for a day or so. I'll put an observation rota in place. I'll need you to note everything you see – any sign of life at all – so we can try and build up a picture of what's going on. I'll also need a team to man the pilot ladder and keep an eye out for any approaching small boats: we don't want anyone trying to board us. Dmitriy, can you set up the pressure hoses and anything else you think necessary to enable us to ward off any unwanted company?'

'Sure, I will get rolling pin from galley,' he said, flashing a smirk in my direction. My choice of weaponry was now legendry, and a bottomless pit of gentle ribbing.

'So, folks, lets prepare to set anchor and weather the storm. Donal, Polina – could you take the first observation shift please. You'll be relieved in three hours, at which time you can debrief me on anything you've seen.'

Everyone scattered to prepare the ship for anchor. A mere two weeks before, Ton's dictatorial tone would have created division and rancour. Now, after Paresh's uncloaking and the focus on Ascension, his orders were carried out without question. In retrospect, it was difficult to imagine that the crew had nearly fractured so completely, and that Ton's leadership had been so bisecting.

Polina and I took a pair of binoculars each and headed for the port deck; the weather was still fair, and we both hankered for the fresh sea air. Having the wind in our faces somehow made Ascension feel more real, as if viewing through glass gave it a film-like quality that detached it from reality. We were now close enough to see the dark larval rocks that guarded the coast, punctured occasionally by a sweep of golden sand that was so incongruous to the blackened basalt that it appeared man-made. In the centre of the bay sat Georgetown itself, a cluster of low-level buildings that divided the shoreline and the coarsely vegetated hill behind it; Green Mountain reached for the sky beyond, pulling in the clouds to mask its nakedness. A single, white spire broke the horizontal line of dwellings and out-buildings, a call to the island's congregation of gulls and gannets. Importantly, the town seemed to be intact. There was no sign of destruction, no bomb scorched skeletal remains of civic buildings or wind flattened streets. As we drew closer,

Polina voiced what I was thinking.

'You see any movement at all?'

'Nothing!'

'Shouldn't we? I mean, if things were all okay!'

'I guess. Maybe they're keeping their heads down. They must have seen us by now, so perhaps they're just being as cautious as we are.'

'What about the ships?' I'd been constantly sweeping these too for sign of life. They were like rotting carcases succumbing to the salty onslaught of the sea, leaking putrefying rust and other tell-tale signs of corrosion. They were dead things, like the whale corpses that we still all too frequently encountered.

'Nope, nothing. It looks like they've been abandoned, but you'd expect that wouldn't you? The crew would be onshore.'

'Okay, but where?' Polina was right. The initial elation of finding the island unsullied, the ships anchored offshore and Georgetown seemingly unscathed was gradually being replaced with a sense of unease. For a settlement with a reputed population of over eight hundred, and the crew of at least two ships to boot, it was bizarrely lifeless. I couldn't help thinking of the *Mary Celeste*, crewed by shadows and the spectre of mystery.

38

Ghost town

By the time we laid anchor, the storm had finally broken. Thankfully, we were protected from the worst of it by the island itself, which acted as a buttress to the battering wind. Even so, we were buffeted by waves that crashed into the leeward side of the ship, threatening to push us further towards the shore. The rain lashed down, trapping us inside.

As nighttime came, and despite the storm, Ton flashed his message towards the beleaguered ships and the ominously still shoreline. It declared our status as disease free, and that we wished no harm. It asked for permission to come ashore, and that we were open to trade. There was no reply, from either of the ships or from Georgetown itself. The other blinding omission, as the blanket of night descended, was the lack of any illumination from the town. It remained bathed in darkness – not a single light piercing the black curtain.

We had gathered in the Officer's Mess after dinner to discuss our next move. Everyone over the course of the previous hours had watched Georgetown descend into complete darkness, and had heard both my and Polina's, and Roy and Rieko's, reports: none of us had seen any movement or evidence of human habitation in over six hours of meticulous observation.

'Maybe there are no lights because they haven't got any electricity?' suggested Tanmay.

'So, what, no candles, no lanterns, no fires? No solar power at all?' countered Jerzy.

'It's not just that,' added Rieko, 'even before it got dark, there was nothing, nothing at all. Surely, you'd expect to see some movement. Not even a dog!'

'So, what do we think? I must admit, of all the possible scenarios I'd played out in my head, a ghost town wasn't one of them,' said Polina.

'Maybe it was evacuated before the bombs?'

'Or the disease got here first?'

'Or there are people here, but they don't want to be found,' I suggested. 'Maybe they had a bad experience with the other ships.'

'Perhaps the ships brought the disease?' There was a brief pause as everyone digested the different possibilities, and what they might mean.

'We'll continue to make our observation during the night, and through the morning until noon tomorrow. Assuming nothing has changed, I think we should send a party of four to check things out. Who's up for it?' Everyone raised their hand. 'Okay then, I guess the fairest thing to do is call lots.' He stood and went to a cupboard and pulled out a wad of post-it-notes and some pens. 'Write your names on these, fold them up and put them in this jug.'

Once he'd collected all of the tightly folded squares, he leant on the table, placed his hand over the top of the jug and shook the contents vigorously. 'Right, let's see who the lucky ones are!' He tipped his head upwards and focused on the ceiling as his he rummaged around blindly for the first piece of paper, before drawing it and out and unfolding it far too slowly. 'Jerzy,' he said.

'You'd better come back, we won't survive on Crisanto's cooking,' quipped Rieko.

Ton pulled out the second, again taking his time for dramatic affect. 'Alon.' Alon smiled nervously, as Roy gave him a congratulatory slap on the back.

'Next...Polina.' There was silence.

'What?' said Polina incredulously, 'Is it because I'm a woman?' I think it was all our first thought. We didn't know what we would be walking into, and the possible dangers for a woman seemed to be so more multi-layered. 'Look, I can more than look after myself, and if you are worrying about what I think you're worrying about, can I point out that there is such a thing as male-on-male rape! Just look at pretty boy Alon, he's far more at risk than me.' We laughed, but it was a nervous laughter born from a misplaced and outdated sense of chivalry. It wasn't so much Polina's pugnacious defence of her own credentials to join the landing party that surprised me, but her eagerness to volunteer in the first place. As a stalwart defender of the Captain's strategy to stay at sea, and my knowledge of her reasons behind it, I would have expected her to have politely declined the opportunity.

When there was a semblance of hush, Ton rummaged around in the jug one final time and pulled out the fourth name. 'Dmitriy,' he announced.

'That is good,' said Dmitriy, 'but I would like to give my place to someone else.' Again, the room went quiet. 'This could be historic event, so I think someone who is able to record it properly, with words, should go. I would like Donal to take my place.'

'Don't be silly, Dmitriy. You were picked out, you go!' I said. I seemed to be the only one in the room who harboured serious misgivings about the whole venture, so I more than half meant it. 'Besides, if I was one of the other three, I'd want you there as my bodyguard.' Casting a half-glance at Jerzy and Alon, I got the impression that they thought the same; this wasn't one of those circumstances where the pen was going to be anywhere close to being mightier than the sword.

'No, my mind is made up. You must go in my place.' And that was that.

#

We continued to monitor both the town and the ships throughout the night, and into the morning. Still, there was no sign of life. On the bright side, the storm had blown itself out and a new tranquillity had descended on the island. The sky was again awash with a dazzling array of birds, and the angry cumulus clouds had given way to streaks of high cirrus that criss-crossed the sky like the skin of a mackerel. Dawn brought with it the usual post-apocalyptic kaleidoscopic explosion of reds, oranges and yellows that crept over the mountain from the east, lighting up the horizon in a collage of flame. The early morning shadows somehow made Georgetown look emptier, even more abandoned.

At noon, we congregated at the top of the pilot ladder. Palvinder and Roy prepared the inflatable, which was winched down to the waterline. Alon, Jerzy, Polina and I were each equipped with backpacks containing provisions and water, as well as a kitchen knife – our only means of defence – and a single flare. Our mission was simple: to determine if there was anyone on-shore, and to scope out the fuel depot. Ton wanted us back by sundown; we had just over six hours.

39

Watchers

We bounced over the waves as Alon steered us ever closer to the beach at Catherine Point, a stretch of sand about a mile southwest of the centre of Georgetown. We'd decided to explore the fuel depot first, and then make our way into town from there. It felt safer somehow, entering through the back door.

The water, as we neared the beach, was crystal clear and it was easy to see the jagged veins of dark volcanic rock that split the sand into pools of golden luminosity. I trailed my fingers in the cool water, enjoying the sensation that sent shivers up my arms. Then, suddenly, Alon cut the motor and, following Jerzy's lead, I leapt out of the boat and dragged the inflatable through the final few metres of shallow water and onto the dry land. My feet were swallowed by the soft sand, gobbled up in a frenzy of denied greed; this was the first time my feet had touched terra firma for eighteen long months, and it was as if the land wanted to reclaim me as its own. We were all breathless as we pulled the craft further up the beach – with both the effort and the enormity of the moment.

'They say that you can feel land-sick,' said Jerzy, 'if you spend too much time at sea. Your body has got so used to the motion, that it can't cope with the solidity of dry land.' I stood up tall and closed my eyes. It did feel weird, as if my brain was still swilling from side-to-side in my skull. Whether land sickness was a real thing, or it was pure psychosomatic suggestion on Jerzy's part, I had to open my eyes to stop myself from collapsing to a heap on the ground.

We gathered our bags and made our way to the lip of the beach. We could see the low-level domes of the fuel depot, and the fence that surrounded it a mere hundred metres ahead. Four or five cars languished on the far side of the facility. As we neared them, we could see that each was covered in a thick layer of pockmarked dust, so welded on that even the recent storm had been unable to wash it away.

'I don't think these have been anywhere in a while,' said Polina, as she pulled her sleeve down over her hand and wiped a peephole into the side window of a battered blue Toyota. She peered in, gave a small whoop of elation, and then tried the door. It opened with a metallic clunk. Reaching inside to the passenger seat, she re-emerged triumphantly clutching a packet of cigarettes. 'Anyone?'

I was never a real smoker – more of a social smoker following the fifth of sixth glass of Guinness, but at that moment I would have sold my soul to have just one drag on those wonderful little cancer sticks. Polina distributed them with shaking hands, and we all put them between our trembling lips, expectantly.

'Lighter?' asked Jerzy, the cigarette hanging precariously

off his bottom lip. Polina swore, then dived back into the car's cabin, rummaging in the side pockets and glove compartment. In desperation, she pulled down the sun guard above the steering wheel, and miraculously a set of keys fell into her lap.

'Wow!' said Alon. 'I thought that only ever happened in movies.' Polina thrust them into the ignition and turned. The starter motor coughed and spluttered, whining its reluctance to wake from its slumber, but incredibly the engine roared into action after only the third go.

'Hey, there's more than a half tank of gas!' exclaimed Polina, 'At least we're not going to have to explore this place on foot.' She went to switch off the engine, but Jerzy stopped her.

'Keep it running for a bit, we can use the electric lighter.' We all got into the car, listening to the idling engine. Sitting in the passenger seat, I re-opened the glove compartment and sifted through the jumble of sweet wrappers and maintenance manuals. Hiding at the bottom, I found a dog-eared map of the island.

'This will be useful too, it's quite detailed.'

'Okay, let's smoke these, check out the fuel depot and then head on up to the town. In that order – I've waited nineteen months for a smoke, I'm not waiting any longer,' said Polina as she pulled out the now glowing coils of the lighter.

We sat and smoked. Never could a tightly bound collection of leaves and chemicals have given so much pleasure. The cabin filled with smoke, but we breathed it in wantonly. After a while, it became so dense that we were forced to open the doors. Sated, we left our bags in the back of the vehicle and made our way to the mesh gates of the depot. An unlocked chain hung uselessly between them. We swung them open and walked in, down the dusty track. To our right, were two huge storage tanks. To the left, was a small, concrete office.

'So, what are we looking for?' I asked.

'There should be a control panel somewhere, which will tell us how much fuel is still stored here. This place would have supplied the island, as well as the airport and the naval operations, so there will be both aviation fuel and oil for shipping.'

'Try the office first then?' I suggested. Polina and I walked up to the peeling green door, whilst Alon and Jerzy went to check the storage tanks. I tried the door. It swung open, again unlocked. Inside, it was dark and cloying. I tried the light switch, but nothing happened. The blinds were pulled down over the windows on the far side, so I strode over and opened them. The sun streamed in, illuminating a panel with a myriad of buttons and dials. It too was covered in a blanket of dust. I tried pushing and turning anything that looked remotely like an 'on' switch, but it remained as lifeless as the island itself. Meanwhile, Polina had been leafing through a logbook that lay open on a table by the control panel. She picked it up and blew, launching a billowing cloud of dust that sparkled like tiny, floating diamonds in the sun beams. She put it down again and flicked through the pages.

'If this is to be believed, there are still five thousand metric tons of fuel here. It had only been refilled two-months before the bombs. There is a list of drawings taken out of the facility over that time...but that only amounts to about eight-hundred metric tons.'

'If anyone has come in the last nineteen months for a withdrawal, they're not going to have filled in the log sheet, are they?'

'True, but you'd be hard pushed to draw off five-thousand tons of the stuff. Even a fraction of that would get us around the world and back.'

'So, you've saying our fuel issues are solved?'

'It appears so.' Just then, Alon and Jerzy entered.

'We've found the fuel tank gages,' said Alon. The one holding the aviation fuel is about three-quarters full. The two holding the oil are about the same, maybe a bit more.'

'Well, that confirms what we've found here,' said Polina, gesturing to the book.

'Stage one of mission, complete' said Jerzy, in a terrible, Hollywoodesque, American accent.

'Please, Jerzy,' said Polina, fixing him with a stern stare, 'Never do that again!'

#

We jumped back into the Corolla, Polina taking the driver's seat as if it was her birthright, and me in the passenger seat. Alon and Jerzy sat in the back. Polina turned the ignition again and in a homage to the wonders of Japanese engineering, the little car sprung into life first time.

'So, where to?'

'We'll head up here,' I said, tracing a route on the map with my finger, 'on this road and into the centre of Georgetown. We'll go past Government House, here, and then take this road past St. Mary's Church, and on to Port Napoleon.'

'Great, let's go. Keep your eyes peeled, guys.'

The car rolled forward, and we bumped along the rough, tarmacked road away from the beach. Within a few minutes, we rumbled past a few single-story houses on our right. Polina slowed to a crawl. A swing sat in the front garden of one, the rusted chains rigid in the tepid air. The whitewashed walls of the houses, all made from prefabricated steel, had yellowed and paint peeled from the window frames like wood shavings. The buildings looked dejected, abandoned to the hostility of sun and rain.

'Is it worth going inside?' asked Alon.

'Let's get nearer to the centre, then we'll stop and have a proper look around.' We carried on, passing two, large warehouse buildings to our left and more slumbering houses to the right. As we neared the centre, we saw a smattering of dust-covered cars crouching in the lee of buildings or gathered quietly in small packs by the side of the road. Government House appeared to our left, and Polina rolled the car into the kerb and switched off the engine. The building was unusual in that it was double storied. Although by no means ornate, it had a certain grandeur that set it apart from its neighbours. It too was whitewashed, with salmon pink paint daubed around the edges of the building and the thick-set windows. This, coupled with the angular roof, gave it the appearance of a jaded wedding cake. A central arch, flanked by two other arches on each side, led to a covered veranda and a set of stained, heavy wooden doors. A ragged Union Jack flag hung limply on a flagpole and a sun-leached plastic bin sat pride of place on the front path. We took in the scene from the safety of the car.

'Shall we check it out?'

'We'll go,' said Jerzy. He and Alon opened the doors and eased themselves out of the back seats. We watched as they walked up the path and onto the veranda. Jerzy tried the door, but it appeared to be locked. They both leaned into the windows, shielding their eyes from the light with their hands.

Alon broke away and walked along the side of the building, disappearing around the back. He reappeared a few moments later, and joined Jerzy as he walked back towards the car.

'Nothing,' said Alon as they got back in. 'It's all locked up. Everything looks perfectly normal inside, as if people have just stepped out. There's a reception table at the front with loads of leaflets spread out. Its like everyone went home one evening, went to bed and then were beamed up!'

We carried on, past the Court House, a bar, shops and St. Mary's Church, whose white walls seemed to have resisted the yellowing effect of the sun, shining pure and resplendent in spite of the elements that had so dishevelled the rest of the town. Polina pulled over again, bringing the car to a gradual halt opposite a small supermarket; the type you get in those terrible British enclaves of Spanish holiday resorts. We could clearly see an 'open' sign on the door. 'Well, let's check it out guys,' she said. 'It's time for some retail therapy.'

We all got out of the car. A sign, fixed onto a bracket on the wall, advertised Coca-Cola in the old-fashioned bottles. It swung from side-to-side in the breeze, squeaking on rusty hinges. I walked over to the entrance. On the inside of the glass, a collection of hand-written adverts had been stuck on with tiny daubs of Blu Tack on each corner: a child's bike, nearly new; a blue Toyota for sale (I wondered if it was the car we were driving); baby-sitting services offered; a lost tabby cat, missing for a week. The cards were yellowed. I pushed the door, and it opened with little resistance, a high-pitched chime announcing our arrival. I went in, followed closely by the others.

It was clear from the onset that the shop had been cleared of practically everything. In the gloom, we could see that most of the shelves were empty, covered in a thick layer of dust. There was an old-fashioned till on a counter to our right, fashioned in grey plastic with a yellowing clear Perspex moulded sheet covering the keys. In sharp contrast to the barren shelving in the rest of the shop, the shelves behind the counter were well stocked with dusty bottles of whiskey, gin, tequila and vodka. There were some bottles of sherry, port and a small collection of red and white wines. All proudly boasted their price on tiny, sticky labels. Other 'behind the counter' merchandise remained; boxes of condoms, cigarettes, cigars, pouches of tobacco – even some boxed pregnancy tests. There were gaps too – things that should have been there, but weren't: lighters, matches, paracetamols, aspirin. 'Why don't we pan out and have a look around. There might be something useful?' said Polina.

'We've already found the useful stuff,' replied Jerzy, gesturing towards the bottles of liquor and cigarettes.'

The shop was small, consisting of four aisles. The one directly in front of us, and the most illuminated by the weak sunlight that struggled through the grimy windows, must have been reserved for fresh fruit and vegetables: it was laden with green plastic trays and a stash of brown paper bags that sat on a hook above them. The trays themselves were bare. Further along the aisle were the occasional cardboard tray of grocery goods, but these were few and far between. A whole case of preserved lemons sat on one shelf, along with an assortment of green and black olives in jars. There was a box of stock-cubes, and a whole shelf of herbs and spices in little bottles. We spread out, reaching for the far corners of the shop that were shrouded in shadow. It was nothing like those apocalypse films I'd seen where the survivors wandered at leisure around fully stocked, brightly illuminated superstores, filling their trolleys to the brim; it was still, and dark and empty.

I made my way to the back of the shop to what must have been the dry goods aisle. Bottles of fabric softener, dishwasher salts and shoe polish stood, hunched at the edge of shelves. Between them were inexplicable gaps where things like washing powder, bleach and washing-up liquid should have been. Further down, household products made way for human hygiene; skin moisturisers, hair mouse, bath salts, razors, shaving foam. Once again, most of the shelving was empty; where was the soap, the toothpaste, the shampoo? I reached the end of the aisle and practically tripped over Alon.

'Found much?' I asked.

'Not a lot. It's weird. There are like, little clusters of some things, then loads of empty space with nothing. Why would you strip a shop of some things, but not touch others? Down there, there is a stack of different teas and coffees...loads of the stuff. Why wouldn't you take tea and coffee? But there's no sugar, or hot chocolate.' We made our way back to the front of the shop. Polina was looking whimsically out of the window whilst Jerzy was in the process of helping himself to a handful of cigarette packets. Polina turned and glared at him disapprovingly.

'What?' he said. 'It's not as if anyone else wants them. We might as well take some booze whilst we're at it.' He reached across the counter and plucked a bottle of vodka from the shelf. He blew the worst of the dust off, then rubbed it with the sleeve of his sweater.

'We don't know if anyone wants it yet?' she said sternly. 'We should leave it for the time being, until we have a better idea of what's going on.'

'What if we don't get another chance?' said Jerzy, who was steadfastly clinging on to the vodka bottle.

'If we don't get a chance to come back, it will be for a pretty good reason, and the fact that we've passed up on a few cans of prunes will be the least of our worries.' Jerzy looked back at her petulantly but didn't argue any further.

We left the shop and made our way back to the car. Jerzy hungrily opened a packet of Marlborough Lights and offered them around. The street remained deserted. A plastic bag bounced tumbleweed-like along the kerb, carried by the strengthening breeze. We clambered back into the Toyota and waited in silence as the engine thrummed and the lighter warmed. Jerzy deftly removed the screwcap from the vodka and took a heavy swig before passing it around. In a smoky haze, with fire at the back of our throats, Polina eased off the hand-break and we rolled forward again, making our way down the road towards Port Napoleon, the main boarding point to the island. We stopped in a parking bay next to the shoreline. To call it a 'port' was a grandiose gesture – it was more of a small quay. Another warehouse sat to our right, a sweep of golden sand to our left. We could see the *Thalassa* floating sullenly in the bay, the *Edith* and *Santos Eagle* eyeing her suspiciously from either side. We got out of the car and walked to the seafront, feeling the breeze against our faces, the brine alive on our dry lips.

I watched the progress of a small group of gannets as they flew across the skyline, their yellow throats bright against the slate grey of the sea and sky. Then, as if by order, they plunged, missile-like into the frothy waves. Out of the corner of my eye, I saw something that caught my attention. On a small plateau that sat between us and the beach was a long strip of raised earth. It seemed incongruous, alien somehow.

I walked towards it. As I got closer, I noticed that the earth became blackened, as if it had been scorched or burnt. The mound itself was covered in an irregular blanket of weeds and grasses, but where it poked through, the earth was lighter in colour. It was wider than I had first envisaged, perhaps five or more metres across. It must have run for ten metres in either direction from where I stood. A giant's grave.

I walked back over to the car and retrieved the map from the side pocket.

'It's like the place is a museum. Where did they all go?' said Jerzy, who, along with Polina, had also made his way back.

'Well, there's certainly not anyone here...in Georgetown. Could they be somewhere else?' I opened the map fully and plastered it against the bonnet of the car.

'Georgetown is by far the largest settlement, but there are some smaller ones here and here.' I prodded the map with my index finger. 'Cat Hill and the RAF Base are both down to the south, Two Boats and RAF Travellers Hill are both inland and near the centre of the island. We can try those, but if there *were* people here, why would they abandon their main town?'

Whilst Polina, Jerzy and I had been focused on the map, Alon had picked up the binoculars and was slowly making a broad sweep of the island behind us. 'Hey!' he said suddenly, 'What's that?' We all looked up.

'What's what?' said Jerzy.

'I thought I just saw something, up there at the top of that hill. There are some buildings. It looked like a light, or maybe the sun reflecting off something.' I reached into my backpack and pulled out my own binoculars. I trained it on the place that Alon was indicating, struggling to both focus and find the exact spot. Then I saw it, a brief flash of bright light.

'I just saw it too,' I said. 'It's something reflecting the sun.' Then, I saw a movement – a shape that briefly moved the shadows, skittering between two buildings. I passed the binoculars to Polina and studied the map. 'That's Two Boats, the nearest settlement to Green Mountain. If I'm not mistaken, we're being watched.'

40

Operation

We made our way steadily up the road towards Two Boats, gaining altitude as we went. On the outskirts of Georgetown, the landscape became increasingly Martian, with a small, cone-like hill to the left seemingly made from red dust. The plain to our right looked like burnt terracotta, scattered with low-lying green shrubs that, from a distance, had the appearance of sprouting mould. It reminded me of pictures I'd seen of the Australian Outback.

'This would be a great place to dump people if you were preparing them to live on Mars,' said Jerzy, as if he was reading my mind. 'I mean, it *looks* like Mars, and it's in the middle of nowhere.'

'Well, the European Space Agency did have a base here,' I said. 'It's not that far-fetched.'

We drove on, past what looked like abandoned agricultural buildings and then into Two Boats itself. It was, like Georgetown, characterized by single-story houses with neat, parched front yards which were pitched together in small double plots.On the outskirts, there was a row of much larger shed-like structures that must have been for storage or some other light-commercial use. As was the case with its larger sister, the village appeared lifeless.

Polina brought the car to a standstill in what was the closest we were going to get to a high-street. She switched the engine off, and we sat in the subsequent silence, taking in the scene around us.

'It looks pretty dead,' said Alon. 'Maybe it was just the sun reflecting off a window, or a piece of metal?'

'Maybe, but it wouldn't have kept appearing and disappearing like that,' I said. 'Plus, I'm sure I saw something move.'

'Might have been a dog!'

'Or a Martian!' added Jerzy.

'Well, we might as well get out and have look around. What shall we do, split into pairs or stick together?' said Polina.

'Safety in numbers, I'd say. Let's stick together, it's not exactly going to take us long to search this place.'

We all got out of the car, taking care to close the doors as quietly as possible: the sightings from the port in Georgetown had put us all on edge. Whether or not I was just scaring myself, I had the distinct feeling that we were being watched. The hairs on the back of my neck rose to attention.

'I've got a weird feeling that we're not alone,' whispered Polina, mirroring my own thoughts.

'Let's carry on up the hill,' I said. 'I think there's a school up there somewhere.'

'Why's that significant?' hissed Jerzy.

'It isn't, I guess. It's just...' I stopped mid-sentence as I thought I saw movement through the window of a house to our left. It lasted a nano-second, like the twitching of a curtain. 'Did any of you guys see that?'

'See what?'

'I thought I saw something inside that house...a shadow of movement behind the window.' I opened the gate and walked down the unkempt garden path towards the front door, and then veered off to the window. I cupped my hands around my head and peered in. I was in time to see something disappear into the farthest room. Then we heard the unmistakable sound of a door slamming at the back of the house. We looked at each other, then simultaneously sprang into action – Polina and I running one way around the house, and Alon and Jerzy the other. This time, as we reached the back yard, we all saw the same thing; a child had just cleared the back fence and had vanished around the side of another house. Alon made to give chase, but Jerzy put a hand on his shoulder.

'You all saw that, right?' said Alon.

'Yep, a boy. Maybe ten years old.'

'Then why did you stop me from chasing him?'

'For starters, you wouldn't have caught him. Secondly, you might have been running into a trap.'

'Well, he can't be here alone. If there's a ten-year-old boy, there must be others!'

'Exactly,' said Jerzy as he ambled over to the fence, peering in the direction the boy had run. 'We need to stick together, no heroics.'

'Let's check out the house,' said Polina. We turned and tentatively made our way to the back door, which stood slightly ajar. Reaching it first, I put my ear to the thick Perspex panel that sat above waist height and listened. Hearing nothing, I slowly pushed it open with the tips of my fingers, my heart beating like a drum in my chest. Inside, was a galley kitchen. An opened can of baked beans sat on the kitchen surface, a spoon sticking out of the top. Next to it, was a half-drunk glass of orange squash. The kitchen was clean, but lived in. There was dirty cutlery and plates in the sink. A fridge hummed in the corner. I opened it, the sudden light infiltrating the gloom of the room.

'Hey! There's power here?' I said, pointing out the obvious. Polina, who was closest to it, turned and switched on the main light, causing us all to squint as the fluorescent bulb above us exploded into life with a stuttering buzz. She quickly switched it off again, the brightness feeling like an affront.

We moved through the kitchen and into a large reception room, a dining table and set of four chairs at its epicentre. A pile of paper and a chaos of coloured pencils were strewn across it, a half-finished drawing of a boat, that looked uncannily like the *Thalassa,* sat at the top of the pile. A myriad of little 'm's' filled the sky, some with tiny yellow beaks.

We continued through the house. A small corridor led off from the dining room, housing three open doors. The first was a bathroom. There were three toothbrushes sitting brush-up in a mug on the sink. Splashes of toothpaste clung to the sides of the bowl. A hairbrush, deeply woven with long, dark hairs, sat on the edge of an avocado-coloured bath. There was a faint smell of lavender soap and bleach.

The other two doors, we discovered, led to bedrooms – one with a large double bed, the other with bunk beds. All had been recently slept in, the crumpled duvets pulled back, the imprint of sleepy heads still visible on the pillows. The floor of the bunk bed room was covered in plastic action figures; a battle was raging between the cast of Marvel and Star Wars, stuck in freeze-frame. Crumpled socks and a pair of stiff-looking underpants provided cover for a cluster of storm troopers.

The carpet of the main bedroom was also strewn with discarded clothes, which also found themselves draped on every available flat surface. Cups and mugs huddled together in small groups, harbouring rings of mould at various stages of petrification. A tower of books sat by the bedside, a copy of 'To Kill a Mockingbird' at its apex. An array of posters looked down on the bed from the wall opposite, an odd mixture of film titles, cutesy animals, and Indie bands. It was strange. This should have been the private space of adults, but the ambiance was very much 'teenage grunge'.

We made our way back through the dining room and into the front room. It was shrouded in darkness, with heavy curtains blocking out the sunlight. An open game of Operation sat on a rug in the middle of the floor, a scattering of fake banknotes covering the floor like leaf litter. A saggy settee crouched in the corner. Polina walked over to the curtains and pulled them open, allowing a knife of sunlight to bisect the room.

'Er, guys. You better see this,' she said, looking out. We made our way to the window and followed her gaze. Outside of the picket fence at the front of the property stood a group of about forty people. They stood in silence, looking at us. They were armed, with an array of makeshift weaponry: baseball bats, hammers, spades...a few tennis rackets. They were all children. At their head, standing by the opened gate, were two girls – perhaps fourteen or fifteen years old. They appeared to be the eldest of the group. They both wore military fatigues, seemingly a few sizes too big so that they had had to roll up the sleeves and trouser legs. It might have been funny, if they hadn't also been holding rifles.

41

Hope

'What do we do? said Alon.

'We need to go speak to them,' replied Polina, who was already making her way to the front door.

'But they've got guns!' I ventured.

'If they'd wanted to shoot us, they would have done it by now,' she said. We followed her as she opened the door and made her way onto the front path. The group stood in an eery silence, observing us. Some of the smaller children at the back fidgeted with their weapons or hopped from foot to foot.

'What do you want?' said the taller, blonde girl at the front. Her hair was scrapped back into an untidy ponytail, her expression rigid. She had the poise of someone much older, much more experienced, but her puppy-fat cheeks and freckles alluded to the tenderness of her years.

'We're from a ship in the bay,' said Polina, who had automatically taken on the role of our spokesman.

'Well, der! Obviously!' said the smaller, brunet girl. She

was more sinewy than her companion, with sharp features and piercing eyes like a rodent. 'We didn't ask where you were from, we asked what you wanted?'

'We've been at sea for eighteen months...since the bombs. We'd decided it was time to find land...to find people. Ascension seemed like a good starting point.'

'So, what? You're lonely?' said the blonde one.

'Something like that,' said Polina. 'We felt it was time to see if our future held anything more than just floating in the middle of an ocean. Plus, we need fuel. We knew you had a fuel depot here.'

'How many of you are there?'

'Eighteen,'

'Are there more women?'

'No, I'm the only one.'

'Are you the Captain?'

'No, I'm the Chief Steward. I look after everyone on board.' The blonde one cocked her head thoughtfully.

'How did you survive the disease?' said the brunet bluntly.

'We've managed to avoid it,' said Polina. 'No-one on board has had it.'

'You wouldn't be here if you had,' said the brunet. Her tone was brisk and accusatory, which I felt was perhaps masking a deeper emotion – fear perhaps. The blonde seemed more confident, more in control of her feelings.

'Look, my name's Polina, and this is Donal, Alon and Jerzy. Perhaps we could continue this inside? We don't want to hurt you. Besides, you're the ones with the guns.'

'No, not inside,' said the blonde one. 'Outside. There are some benches in the school playground, up there.' She pointed in the direction of the hill with the gun.

'Now we've introduced ourselves, what are your names?' asked Polina. The two girls looked at each other, obviously wondering if such a divulsion of personal information was a step too far.

'My name is Savannah,' said the blonde one, '...and this is Hope.'

'Can we meet your parents, Savannah?' Again, there was the eye contact between the two girls, a flicker of panic.

'They're not here, they're working on the other side of the island, they all are,' said Hope, a little too quickly. It was the first time I'd picked up on her American accent; from the South somewhere, I thought. I was watching Savannah as she said it, watched an emotion I couldn't place wash over her features. She looked down at the ground briefly, as if coming to a decision.

'There's no point, Hope,' she said. 'They'll find out eventually. Hope shot her a look of pure disdain but didn't say anything. 'Come with us up to the school...,' she said to us, '...and we'll tell you everything.'

She turned to the crowd of children behind her, some of whom were obviously getting restless. 'Arron, Karl, Alice, Thomas...come with us, the rest of you can go and play.' Four of the bigger, older children stepped forward – I was shocked to see that two of them held hand pistols – probably only airguns, but guns all the same. The younger children melted away, leaving a small group of twelve or thirteen-year-old girls who lingered behind us as we made our way up the street towards the school.

'How old are you, Savannah?' asked Polina as we walked.

'I'm fifteen, nearly sixteen.'

'And where are you from? Is that a British accent?'

'Yes, my dad was a RAF engineer. We'd been on the island for two years, before...' She broke off mid-sentence.'

'So, you were what, just fourteen when it happened?' Savannah nodded.

'And Hope...?

'I'm from Florida. My parent's worked for a telco. I'm fifteen,' Hope said, her rapid-fire answers tinged with a note of annoyance, as if she resented having to engage in any conversation. I felt that she still felt chastened by Savannah's decision to override her story about the missing adults.

'I had a daughter about your age,' Polina said to Hope specifically, 'she looked a lot like you.' I caught Jerzy and Alon exchanging a side-glance.

We carried on up the road, past at least ten houses that were perfect carbon copies of each other. Within a few minutes, we reached a set of green metal gates. Beyond it was a white-washed, single-story building that was dominated by a tall clock tower that stood at its entrance. The courtyard before it was painted bright green and pink. Savannah opened the gates and led us into a corner of the play area where there were a set of three benches. She beckoned for the other children to sit at one and gestured for us to sit at another. She and Hope sat on one side – Polina, me and Alon on the other. There was no room for Jerzy, who sat cross-legged on the floor.

'You understand why we don't want to meet you in a confined space, indoors?' she said.

'You're worried about the disease?' I said.

'I know that you say that you have avoided it, but we've been told that before.'

'The ships in the bay?'

'Yes...' She trailed off, obviously deciding where best to start.

'I'll tell you our story, and then we can best decide how to help each other.' She possessed the quiet confidence of a diplomat, or the CEO of a multinational. 'In the week leading up to the event...the bombs...there was talk of evacuation. There were 806 people on the island, including 84 children. Two days before, there was one flight in, and one flight out. Families had been given the choice of whether to go or stay, as no one was sure if the island might be vulnerable to attack if events escalated. Around 120 had decided to go, mostly those with really young children. The plane brought in a team of high-level RAF and US military guys from Brize Norton. The island is strategically important, so they were sent here to...well, I don't know what exactly. When it all kicked off two-days later, the whole of the island's population went into the bunker on the RAF base. It's big, but it was never designed to accommodate nearly seven hundred people. We were packed in like sardines for two days and nights. We monitored the annihilation of the world's communications systems, and waited until we felt there was no-one left to bomb us. The whole point of a nuclear bunker, obviously, is to shut you off from the outside world – so we were all breathing in the same air, trapped in a hermetically sealed box. Nobody thought about the disease.

Within the first twenty-four hours, one of the outsiders – the men that had come in with the evacuation flight – came down with flu-like symptoms. But nobody knew, because he had locked himself in his room in the bunker. Before that, he'd been helping to settle everyone in, reassuring the families – touching people, breathing on them. He'd had contact with practically everyone. If he hadn't spread it with personal contact, the air conditioning system did the rest. He was found dead the next day. Then the other outsiders came down with it. Within three days, all twenty-six of them – the people who had been sent to help us, to protect the strategic status of the island, to secure us a means of rebuilding communication if any conflict was to happen – where dead. On the next day, thirty-four islanders died. The day after that, eighty-three. Then two-hundred and ten. By the end of the first week, five-hundred-and-eighty-one had died. All adults.' She recounted it so matter-of-factly, so devoid of emotion. It was difficult to comprehend that these numbers included the children's parents, their teachers, friends. She continued. 'Anyone under fifteen, or who hadn't hit full adolescence seemed to get milder symptoms and recovered in a few days. Some of the older kids at school died, those who were fifteen or sixteen at the time. There were thirteen in total. That left 71 children: 26 boys and 45 girls aged between five and fourteen. Hope and I were...are the eldest.'

'So, you were left totally alone – no adults at all?' said Polina, tears welling up in her eyes.

'No, initially there were some. Sixteen adults survived the first outbreak, five of them were so ill that they were practically bed ridden. Three of those died a week later. In the days and weeks afterwards, the older children helped the healthy adults to collect the bodies. They said we needed to cremate them, to get rid of the pestilence and to stop other diseases breaking out. We took them down to the old cemetery by the port, and we laid them to rest in a mass grave. You can still see the scorched soil. That's one reason we abandoned Georgetown: it was too full of memories, terrible memories.'

Polina reached out across the table, placing her hand on Savannah's. It was an instinctive reaction to the horror of what we were hearing, but I felt it was more than that. I'd never thought of Polina as a tactile person, usually she hung in her own personal space, avoiding all human contact. I felt that something was happening here, some reckoning with her own past, that perhaps this was the time to stop running from it. Savannah momentarily flinched but accepted the gesture. She took a deep breath and continued.

'The adults that were left – they couldn't understand why they had survived when so many others had died. They were a mix of ages, genders and ethnicities. Some had health issues, others didn't. In the subsequent weeks, they worked hard to teach the older children what we would need to survive, as if they somehow knew that they were on borrowed time. They showed us how the desalinisation plant worked, how to fuel the generators, how to grow crops in the hydroponics barn – all the essential stuff so that we'd be okay if we were left alone.

Then, in the sixth week, the first ship arrived. At the time, it felt like salvation. We all went down to Port Napoleon to welcome them ashore. They were good people. They gave us food and all sorts of other things in exchange for fuel. They talked about joining us, staying on the island. Then, one of them fell ill. It was only then that they told us that they had just come from the west coast of Africa. They had docked in Dakar – but had fled when they had realised the extent of the lawlessness, and the spread of the disease. They had sailed for five days, straight to us, incubating a new strain – a new strain that swept through them, then the adults who were left. On the 15th of November, the last one died. His name was David, one of the little-one's dad. He was 28-year-old telecoms engineer from Iowa. He was kind. He had played the guitar to the younger children and sang them songs. Then it was just us.' She took in another deep intake of breath before letting out a heavy sigh, self-consciously flicking a loose cascade of hair behind her ear.

'Since then, we've done our best – Hope and I and the older kids - to look after the younger ones. We all work together to make sure that everyone is fed and watered, that we have power. We've even opened the school so that we can teach them: maths, reading and writing, life skills, what things were like before...stuff like that.'

'What about the other ship?' Alon asked.

'That turned up much later, maybe six of seven months after. We'd learnt from the first ship that we should keep away, but we watched them closely. Eight of them came ashore - to escape disease on the ship. They didn't last long. We buried them in the cemetery too. Since then, there have been other ships. We've hidden if they have come ashore. Some just took some fuel and went, others snooped around for a while, took what they wanted and left. You are the first outsiders that we have spoken to in over a year.'

'Why did you show yourselves to us?' asked Polina. 'You could have kept away, avoided us if you wanted to?'

'Because of you,' said Savannah, fixing Polina with her pale blue eyes. 'You've a woman. The rest have all been men.'

It was difficult to comprehend what these children had endured. To bury their loved ones, to take on the mantle of providers and guardians to the younger ones, to wrestle with their own demons and find a semblance of normality on this tiny island in the middle of nowhere. It was truly Herculean.

#

We were all lost in our own thoughts as we rumbled down the

road back to Catherine Point and the inflatable. We had told the girls something of our own journey, missing out those elements that might have caused them concern, such as our own brush with the disease. We talked about the things that we had on board that might be useful to them, how we might be able to help. We didn't discuss the future; what we might mean to them, and them to us. It was too early for such things. They invited us to bring the others ashore.

As she drove, Polina seemed particularly lost in thought. She'd been quiet ever since we had left Savannah and the others.

'A penny for them?' I said.

'A penny for what?'

'For your thoughts.' It was funny how some common sayings failed to cross both geographical and language barriers.

'You know what this means, don't you, Donal?'

'It means that we can come ashore, that we have a purpose.'

'Yes, but it means much, much more than that. These kids survived the disease. Twice. Children must have an immunity. And if they have immunity here, they must have immunity everywhere. Donal, it means hope!'

42

Epilogue

Dmitriy's huge bulk blocked out the sun. He'd stopped again, turning to flash me a scornful look. The back of his T-shirt was dark with sweat, and a fug of moisture radiated from his body.

'Why you bring me up here?' he wheezed. 'What have I ever done to you?'

'The kids told me about it. Trust me, it'll be worth it.'

We had been climbing Green Mountain for over an hour. The views of the island had been spectacular, the full palate of reds, browns, greens, and the pale gold of the sand laden beaches combining to create our very own Eden. The ocean stretched to an unblemished horizon in every direction. As we ascended, we had stepped through a layered cake of biomes: the dense succulents of the arid lower slopes; the small oaks strewn with Spanish moss, like green candyfloss; the strip of giant bamboo that closed in on the narrow-stepped pathway that had been cut through them like the walls of a maze. We were approaching the final stage of our journey as we launched ourselves towards the topmost layer of the biosphere.

'It better be good, to warrant such torture,' said Dmitriy, sweeping his forehead with the back of his hand. Beads of sweat dripped from his thick set brows, splashing onto the dark soil below.

We climbed another thirty or forty metres, reaching the final wooden step and a small plateau. The wall of bamboo had stopped abruptly, surrendering to a cornucopia of trees and shrubs surrounding a pond of glutinous water that heaved with luminous green algae. Dmitriy bent over double, his hands on his knees, and gulped oxygen into his lungs.

'Tell me...,' he said, after recovering enough to speak, '... that whatever you have dragged me up here to see, is *here*, somewhere. I go no further!'

'Well, as a matter of fact, it is, somewhere.' I led the way around the pond, trying to remember exactly what Savannah had told me the night before. 'I think it's just at the back of the pond, behind those trees.' I pushed my way through the undergrowth, Dmitriy following limply behind. Then, suddenly, we hit another small clearing...and there it was.

'*Fagus sylvatica purpurea*,' I said. 'A Copper Beech.' It wasn't a big specimen by any means, perhaps only twenty feet tall and a little spindly, but its deep purple leaves were unmistakable. 'No-one knows how it got here. It's not indigenous and it wasn't deliberately planted. The seed must have drifted on the winds.'

'A little like us,' said Dmitriy. He stood, staring at the miracle tree before us, an expression of wonderment on his weather-brushed face.

About the Author

Simon Dieppe lives near Worcester in the UK. He has been a lawyer, worked in the international conference industry and was a director in a UK PLC, but has now settled down as an English and History teacher - a career that he loves. Simon started writing in the first lockdown, and hasn't stopped. In the Doldrums is his third novel, but the first that he has published. He is currently re-working the first two books with the aim of publishing them later this year. He has an eclectic taste in literature, but has always been drawn towards dystopian fiction. He lives with his wife, two children and dog, Bernie.

You can connect with me on:

- https://www.simon-dieppe.com